When I Was a Child

When I Was a Child

VILHELM MOBERG

Translated by

GUSTAF LANNESTOCK

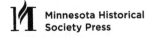

Minnesota Historical
Society Press

Original edition published in three volumes as *Soldat Med Brutet Gevär*,
©1946, 1947 by Albert Bonniers Forlag, Stockholm.

Translated and adapted into a single volume by Gustav Lannestock,
© Alfred A. Knopf, 1956
New material © Minnesota Historical Society, 2014

For information, write to the Minnesota Historical Society Press,
345 Kellogg Blvd. W., St. Paul, MN 55102-1906.

www.mhspress.org

The Minnesota Historical Society Press is a member of the
Association of American University Presses.
Manufactured in the United States of America
10 9 8 7 6 5 4 3 2 1

♾ The paper used in this publication meets the minimum
requirements of the American National Standard for Information
Sciences—Permanence for Printed Library Materials,
ANSI Z39.48–1984.

International Standard Book Number
ISBN: 978-0-87351-925-0 (paper)
ISBN: 978-0-87351-931-1 (e-book)

Library of Congress Cataloging-in-Publication Data

Moberg, Vilhelm, 1898–1973.
[Soldat med brutet geviir. English]
When I was a child / Vilhelm Moberg ;
Translated by Gustaf Lannestock.
pages cm.
"Adapted by the translator from the original edition,
published in Sweden . . . as Soldat med brutet geviir . . . 1947"
"Translated and adapted into a single volume by
Gustav Lannestock, Alfred A. Knopf, 1956."
ISBN 978-0-87351-925-0 (pbk. : alk. paper) —
ISBN 978-0-87351-931-1 (ebook)
I. Lannestock, Gustaf, translator. II. Title.
PT9875.M5S5613 2014
839.73'72—dc23
2013039322

This and other Minnesota Historical Society Press books are
available from popular e-book vendors.

When I was a child, I spake as a child, I understood as a child, I thought as a child: but when I became a man, I put away childish things.

—I Corinthians XIII, 11

To my American friend

LUCILE LANNESTOCK,

wife of the translator of this book, who has so
ably aided him in rendering it into English.

When I Was a Child

CHAPTER I

O n March 14, 1885, Nils Gottfried Thor, representing district 128 Strängshult, entered the Uppvidinge Company of the Kalmar Regiment as a recruit. He was the son of August Thor, who had served in the same capacity for Korpahult in Madesjö parish. As a soldier he was given the name Sträng for the district he represented. At the regimental muster in 1887, recruit 128 Sträng is listed as the tallest soldier of his company, being six feet four and a half inches in height.

At the age of twenty Sträng had married Hulda Jacobsdotter; her father had been a cotter at a place called Trångadal, near Strängshult; he had died young, but Hulda's mother was still living in the cottage.

Sträng and his wife begot seven children, six sons and one daughter. Their youngest child was born in 1897, a son named Karl Artur Valter.

128 Sträng had a poor memory for years and dates, but concerning his youngest son's birth he had one sure point to rely on: Valter was born the year he received his new gun. One day in October he had returned from maneuvers at Hultsfred with a new gun, which

he had hung on the wall above the sofa-bed of his soldier-cottage. In that bed was born a few days later his youngest son.

Valter Sträng was born under a gun, a Swedish Army gun, 6.5 millimeter, model 1896.

It is known about his birth that it took place on a weekday morning, during the potato-picking, while the father was away. The labor was so trying for the mother that Balk-Emma, who was called in to help, sent for Grandmother Mathilda at Trångadal; she in turn thought that perhaps they had better send for the midwife this time. But the soldier's wife replied that if she had managed without a midwife six times before, she might as well do so the seventh time. Thus it was decided. But she fared so ill that she was unable to leave her bed until the third day after the birth.

The widow Balk predicted that Hulda Sträng after this would be spared further childbeds, and her prediction proved to be right.

Balk-Emma tied the child in a woolen shawl, which she hung on the steelyard to weigh the new life; thus it was discovered that he entered the world fully developed—he weighed eleven pounds and a few ounces. The neighbor-village soldier, Oskar Banda, and his wife were asked as godparents, and on All Saints' Day they carried him to the minister for christening. While Banda's wife held him at the baptism he reached for the minister's book as if he wished himself to perform the ritual. This made the godmother predict that the boy would become a minister. During the drive home from church he cried so loudly and persistently that the godfather predicted he would become choirmaster.

Valter was not denied the child's first and natural right in this world: from the very first day he could still his hunger at a mother's breast that gave milk in sufficiency.

Grandmother Mathilda was of the opinion that children who did not receive enough milk from the breast went through life dissatisfied; such children grew into difficult people, penurious and evil in character. A child satisfied at his mother's breast, on the other hand, became a good-natured, kind, and generous person. The grandmother consequently did not worry about Valter's character or disposition.

Much of his first years was spent outside in the fields and woodlands. When his mother went haying or harvesting, she would carry the boy in a bundle, in order to suckle him when need be. Thus, he often slept under some bush in the meadows, moors, or clearing-edges. In the bundle with him were the wool shears and a knife as protection against trolls, changelings, and other evil beings. But the steel did not protect him against the pismires that crept into the bundle and bit him until he was red all over like a fox pup.

Years passed him by in memoriless darkness. Only an occasional unusual happening, connected with intense pain or joy, etched itself into his soul and became a memory: he upset a kettle of boiling water, was put to bed with blisters on his legs, and was given an egg to eat. The cow had calved and he was given sweet milk, and butter on his bread. He threw a knife at his sister, Dagmar, which made her forehead bleed; he was spanked until his behind hurt and he cried until he lost his breath.

He would lie in bed and reach for the objects around him. He saw a big blue flower on the wall; he picked the flower, yet it remained; he could pick the wallpaper flower whenever he wanted to, yet it always remained in its place. One of the first objects he reached for in this world was the yellow gun belt over his head. But he could not reach it, and so the belt remained in its place. When he grew old enough so that his arms could reach it, he was not allowed to touch the yellow belt: it belonged to the Crown. The gun on the wall was Crown property. Anything belonging to the

Crown he was forbidden to touch. Valter sat on his father's knee and he wet the knee of his father, he wet the yellow-striped pants that belonged to the Crown. It was forbidden to pee on anything that belonged to the Crown.

He also sat on his father's knee in the evenings when his father had come home from work in the forest. Then his father's leather breeches were shiny and worn and smelled of pitch and perspiration. These were Father's own pants and did not belong to the Crown, and it mattered not even if he peed on them. Father had a prickly beard, hard hands, and a hard knee. Father called Valter his "big helper."

He sat on the knee of Grandmother Mathilda, who moved close to the fireplace and put both her feet on the hearth. She was cold. She had a big nose and watery eyes. Other people's eyes were watery when they cried, but Grandmother's eyes were watery all the time, even though she said she was not crying. In her nostrils hung black specks with a strong smell; she used snuff. Grandmother's skirt was coarse and gray and hard, her knee was sharp and rough. She called Valter her "poor little one."

He sat on the knee of his godfather, soldier Banda. He was a shoemaker and smelled of leather and cobbler's wax. The godfather rocked him frightfully, pressed him against his big, soft stomach, and tickled him in the armpits until he was forced to laugh even though it hurt so much that he would have liked to cry instead. Soldier Banda called him "my little godson."

He sat on the knee of his sister, Dagmar, but her knee was small and uncomfortable and he did not like to sit there. It sloped so much that he skidded down to the floor. Dagmar grabbed him under the arms and pulled him up again brusquely, but again he slid down. She blamed him—he was unable to sit quietly. She called him "the brat."

He sat on his mother's knee in front of the fire. On a soft, checkered apron with a fragrance of sweet milk. Mother's knee was soft, her hands were soft, everything about her was soft and sweet and smelled of fresh milk and breast. Mother would sing a ditty while rocking him. When a spark from the fire flew in his face, she would blow on the smarting skin. Mother called Valter her "sweet friend." Her knee was the best of all.

The beginning of Valter Sträng's existence was in a hundred-year-old soldier-cottage, deep in a forest glade. A few acres of the village woodlands had once upon a time been set aside for the man chosen to serve in the Army. The timbered walls were covered with a beautiful green moss, in the yard lay great rocks, wonderful to climb, and between the rocks grew flowers. Valter no longer reached for the wallpaper flowers; now he picked them in the yard—dandelions, buttercups, bluebells. In the yard grew also a crabapple tree with a wide-spreading crown, a pear tree whose fruit became sweet preserved pears in the fall, and a few gooseberry bushes. From the cottage a road led through the forest out into the World.

In this out-of-the-way place Valter's soul emerged and awakened to its own consciousness. He began to call objects by name and repeat words. One of the first words his tongue pronounced was a short one of three letters: God. It was the first word of a prayer which his mother had taught him to repeat:

God Who loves the children all,
Look to me who am so small.
Wherever in the world my way I wend,
My earthly field lies in God's hand.

His tongue pronounced the words clearly, but their meaning was dim to him. He listened to those around him, questioned, pondered. God was the one who lived up there, high above the roof and above the crown of the crabapple tree. He was the one who had made everything and was in charge of everything. "Me who am so small"— that was he himself, Valter. He was the smallest one in the cottage and hereabouts. The world—that was everything, both outside and inside: the apple tree, the pear tree, the big stone at the stoop, the cellarhouse, the well, the barn. But what did "field" mean? God and the world and himself he understood. But what could the field be?

"I shall sow the rye in the field," his father said.

"I'll pick the potatoes in the field," his mother said.

"I saw someone walking across the field," Dagmar said.

Thus it was made clear to Valter that the field was the narrow strip of tilled earth at the edge of the woodland.

He grew, his horizon widened, and when summer came and he was allowed to go barefoot he wandered a bit out into the world. But a short distance away, at the edge of the property that his soldier-father occupied, there was a heavy gate across the road which he could not open. Here the world came to an end for any-one as little as he. The grown-ups could open the gate and walk still farther into the world and then turn about. But he could only stand there and peer between the slats. He craned his neck, he turned his head, he wanted so to look into the world. The road continued into the forest and disappeared at a bend. And on the other side of the gate, behind another fence, lay the field.

Wherever in the world my way I wend,
My earthly field lies in God's hand.

Out there lay his field, in God's hand. Great green plants grew there, and Mother hoed under the plants and found potatoes, which she boiled, a full pot of them, so that all of them could eat their sufficiency. "It's from the field we get the food," Father would say as the peelings grew into a tall pile at his plate. But the field was supposed to lie in God's hand. Where was God's hand? Standing at the gate, he looked about. God's hand could grab the field and lift it into heaven, but he did not see the hand. How could this be? Wherever he turned, his field was supposed to be in God's hand.

He asked his mother: "Our field—is it mine?"

"Yours? No—it belongs to the village, of course."

"Where's my field?"

"You have no field, my little friend."

"I mean the one in God's hand."

"Nonsense, little child. Those things you don't understand."

The field in the evening prayer was not a piece of ground. He must learn to understand what he read.

"But where is my field? The one in God's hand?"

"It means your fate. Your success in life."

"What is success?"

"It means good luck. You'll have good luck in everything you do."

Valter thought deeply and sucked the knuckle of his right index finger. This he always did when he thought deeply about something. The knuckle was rather bruised.

Good luck. That was his, then.

"Where is my luck?"

"Your luck, little one? Don't bite your knuckle."

His mother was sitting in the yard cleaning lingonberries that she had poured in a heap on one of her largest aprons, spread on the ground. She was weary of his many questions.

"What did you say, my little one?"

"Where is my luck that I shall have?"

"Your luck? It comes and goes. As it does for everyone."

"Can I see it when it comes?"

"No! Luck is not a person."

"Can't I see anything when it comes?"

"No, of course not. It isn't visible."

"How does one know when it comes, then?"

"One feels it."

"How does one know when luck leaves?"

"One soon gets to know." His mother sighed deeply as she picked leaves and twigs and rubbish from her hand that was heaped full of lingonberries: Bad luck and misfortune existed also. One got to know these, too. "Now you know. But you don't understand as yet."

So now Valter knew that the field in the prayer was his success in life; it was the same as the luck that followed him. Luck was not a person, it was something that no one could see; but you were sure to feel it as it came and went.

He put his knuckle in his mouth and thought: Luck would have been easier to understand if it had been their little field near the road.

He began to ask his mother again, but she would no longer answer his questions. She had other things to think of, she said.

"Don't bite your knuckles!" she scolded him.

As he stood there, pondering deeply, the thought came to him: Perhaps Mother herself wasn't quite sure what luck was; she had so many other things to think about.

Valter Sträng began to wander about in the world and look for himself. He had already picked flowers in the yard; now he walked to the woodlands and picked lingon twigs and tore moss from under the junipers. Wherever he turned, luck was in his hands.

His soul groped for the light of knowledge as the shoots from seed force their way through the crust of earth toward daylight. He recognized himself as a being, apart from the others. He called himself "I." The others, they were Father and Mother. The others, they were all his brothers and his sister: Albin, Ivar, Dagmar, Fredrik, Anton, and Gunnar. And the others were also the people who lived in neighboring places: Grandmother Mathilda, Balk-Emma, Carpenter-Elof, Shoemaker-Janne, and his godfather Banda, and Banda's Valfrid who was almost as tall as Albin, and Banda's Edvin who was as little as he himself. The others, they were also the soldiers from neighboring villages: Hellström and Flink and Nero and Bäck and Tilly. Those were the others. He was Karl Artur Valter. He had been given three names; there were names enough in the Almanac, said Father. He could not be confused with anyone else, because no one else was called Karl Artur Valter Sträng. Yet he called himself "I." He said: I am hungry. It was inside, in his stomach, that the hunger was. No one else could feel it. Valter was I. And he was the smallest and weakest of the human race in this place.

Father was the strongest and biggest person in the world. He had to stoop when he stepped through the door of their cottage. He was so big he could travel as far out into the world as he wished. When he left he would be dressed in his uniform with its shining brass buttons, and the cap with the plate; and sometimes he had the plume in the plate—it was like the tail of some animal, a tail of horsehair. Father was a soldier. This made them different from the people in the other cottages—they were called *the soldier's*. Mother was called Soldier's Hulda. And his brothers and sisters were Soldier's Albin, and Soldier's Ivar, and so on to the youngest one: he was Soldier's Valter.

Albin and Ivar were so tall that they almost reached their father's shoulder. They were away in service with farmers, and when they came home on Sundays they would measure their length and pull out their pocket knives and mark the doorpost. They carved the marks higher and higher toward the ceiling. Valter stood and looked on while his brothers grew. He himself did not yet reach to the door handle; he must ask Gunnar to help him open the door. Gunnar was next to the smallest, yet half a head taller than he. Gunnar had already cut a mark in the doorpost.

In the road Valter would stand and look through the slats in the gate, out into the world. He had heard his father speak of the Big Field, which lay beyond the bend of the road, in the woodlands. And on the first spring day, when the earth was warm and he could walk barefoot, he was allowed to go there with his father.

Father carried a sack of oats on his back and held his son by the hand. Valter reached only to the knees of his father, but he walked proudly and with straight back at Father's side, out into the world. They walked all the way to the Big Field, where Father would sow the oats. The world had many fields, big ones and little ones. But the field that meant luck he knew little about as yet. Valter asked his father, Soldier 128 Sträng, what luck was.

Luck, that meant good health, said the father. It meant being able to walk, move about, see, hear, and work. It meant being strong and not having to ask others for help in lifting a log or rolling away a stone. To manage one's own, that was luck. To have food and clothes and not have to go begging. To eat one's sufficiency when hungry. To lie down and rest when tired. To arise in the morning rested. That was luck, the field in God's hand, said Father.

And Valter understood as he walked at the side of his tall, strong father and held on to his hand: If he didn't get food, it hurt in his stomach so much that he had to cry. Then he would go to Mother and ask for a slice of bread, which she would cut for him. As he ate, the hurt in his stomach disappeared. If he got food, he need not suffer hurt in his stomach, and that was luck. And luck for

Soldier-Sträng's family was that they had enough herring and potatoes and rye porridge and lingon sauce so that they could sit down and eat their sufficiency. It was bad luck and a misfortune to be hungry.

Father was so strong that he could lift the heaviest log in the forest. He knew what luck meant. And it was safe to walk with Father out into the world, all the way to the Big Field. Father held him by the hand and took short steps to allow his son to keep up with him. Valter hurried along and moved his short leg-sticks as quickly as he could, but Father had to shorten his own steps for his son's sake. They walked through the woodland among bursting birches and heard the play of birds in the thickets. The oats in Father's sack smelled pungently, like the earth.

He felt secure, walking like this. Valter knew that Father never would leave him.

Then there were also many people whom Valter had not seen in real life but only heard of. But he saw pictures of them. They were the relatives in America. They stood on the bureau, in frames of shells—red, white, and blue. They were called the America-pictures. They were the finest objects in the room, and it was with them as it was with the Crown gun and other Crown property: they must not be touched. No hands except Father's and Mother's must hold the America-portraits. Those who lived in America were better dressed than others, and there must be no thumb marks on them. Valter could stand below the bureau and look up at his relatives in America: Uncle Jacob, Uncle Algot, Uncle Frank, Aunt Lotten, Aunt Anna, and many more.

Valter liked best Uncle Frank, whose name had been Frans while in Sweden. He wore suspenders and a broad-brimmed hat and had a pipe in his mouth. Uncle Frank dug gold in a mine and he would come home when he had dug up enough. Uncle Jacob was in his Sunday best, with slicked-down hair, a white collar, and a large tie. He would come home next summer. Aunt Lotten and Aunt Anna had lace collars and long watch chains of gold hanging down on their breasts. In one large shell frame were four children holding one another's hands. They were Aldos, Mildred, Kennet, and Mary. They had finer clothes than children hereabouts, the boys with ties and the girls with brooches. Those were his cousins. Cousins were better-dressed children who lived in America only.

Valter was proud to have cousins. Not all had them. How many cousins in America were his? Mother counted on her fingers and added: Uncle Jacob had six children and Aunt Anna three, Uncle Frank none, Aunt Lotten four and Uncle Axel two. She was not sure about Uncle Henrik and Uncle Aron, but she thought they must have four or five each. She supposed there were about thirty cousins that were his.

Why were there cousins in America only? Mother replied: Because all the brothers and sisters of Father and Mother were in America. She and Father alone of that generation in their families had stayed at home.

Why weren't Father and Mother also in America? To that question Valter did not receive a clear answer. Perhaps they were destined to remain at home, she said. But Valter thought that Father and Mother would not fit in with their brothers and sisters in America: they did not have such fine clothes. Nor did he fit in with his cousins; he did not have clothes like them.

America had existed in the soldier-cottage long before Valter was born. It occupied the foremost place in the room: on top of the bureau. Here stood all the shell frames in their bright colors. America, too, was a land in this world, said Mother, but it was so far away that it was almost as if it had been in another world. It was a long way to church, but the way to America was more than a thousand times longer.

From America came newspapers in big bundles. Indeed, the only newspapers they received in the cottage. From America came letters in long white envelopes. They were the only letters that came. The word *America* was used every day in the house. It was their whole family; one could look at them but not touch them. When visitors came, Father and Mother were anxious to show the pictures on the bureau: This is my brother Jacob, who has a store in Michigan, and this is my sister Lotten, who married an American in Seattle Wash. And the visitors were permitted to hold the frames and thumb them.

The soldier Sträng and his family revered America. The word itself sounded big and imposing, and Valter pondered it and wished to know its meaning: A-me-ri-ka. Amer-ika. A-merika. That was it! *Mer rika!* More rich! Now he knew—those who lived there were richer than others.

And in that country were all the brothers and sisters of Father and Mother and all of his thirty cousins. He could already count to thirty on his fingers.

But he lived in another land, their cottage here in the clearing lay in another country, and as yet he did not know the name of that country. He asked his father.

"It is called *Sverige*, Sweden," replied Father.

Soldier-Sträng pronounced the word so that every letter could be distinguished; it sounded almost formidable. Valter spelled the word to himself and found it more difficult to pronounce than America.

"The land of your forebears," said Father.

Why was it called Sweden? His father did not know for sure, but thought it had something to do with "Svea." One time at a parade his colonel had spoken of "the Svea of ancient days." Valter knew

that the word *sved* meant to smart, so he supposed the name came
from something in ancient history that still smarted and hurt and
made people remember. Yes, Svea and *sved*, hurt, were much alike;
the soldiers must have been badly hurt in some war.

And so Valter knew why it was called America, and why it was
called Sweden. In the America-letters that their father read aloud,
the question was often asked: How were things in *poor old* Sweden?
And as he added what he had heard, he understood: In America
lived the rich, in Sweden lived the poor.

Soldier-Valter's nature was such that he must know the truth
about all things.

One spring evening as he played in the yard, poking sticks into
the earth, he stopped still and looked out in deep thought over
the world around him, where he was the smallest of all humans. In
front of him lay the gray cottage with its sway-back ridge like
a huge, hairy animal, pressed to the ground by its hundred years'
weight. Round it lurked the forest, thick and black. High above the
yard rose heaven, vaulted above everything like an immense kettle
of shiny bluing. In this heaven-kettle, light glittered through in a
few places.

And just then, in the falling twilight, a bird came flying over the
roof, black as coal against heaven's blue. It made a harsh, unearthly
sound and flew like an arrow shot from a bow; at once it was lost
behind the forest's edge. It could not have been a real bird that flew
like that. Next evening it returned and disappeared equally fast,
a pair of vibrating wings against the sky. Whence came the bird?
And whither did it fly? A touch of fear passed through him, and
curiosity about the mysteriousness that surrounded him when the
forest blackness caught the clearing in the evenings: Where am I?
I—Soldier-Valter—who am I? Where am I now? A demand for
clearness possessed his soul, always and ever. He stood still and

thought deeply, sucking his right index knuckle while he pondered; that knuckle was badly bitten.

Soldier-Valter opened the gate by himself and wandered out into the world. He walked by the Little Field and the Big Field. His father led him by the hand, and he walked with his father all the way to the village.

His world expanded. He walked all the way to the neighbor village, to Soldier-Banda's, where he played with Banda's Edvin. They stood back to back and measured their height; they were equally tall. They made friends and got along well, he and Edvin. They quarreled, and called each other brat and pig. They fought and fell on the ground. They made friends again and got along well. Then they bragged to each other about all their worldly possessions. Valter named the most important he owned—his thirty cousins in America. Edvin said he had three cousins here in Sweden, in Hermanstorp. Valter insisted that this was a lie since cousins existed in America only. Then he bragged about his tall father who was taller than anyone else's father. Edvin counteracted this undeniable truth by saying that his father was fatter than any other father. But he was not quite sure that this was enough, and so blurted out what must give him final superiority:

"We have a privy. You have no privy!"

This was a murderous blow to Valter. He felt deeply humiliated. It was true, at Banda's one could sit on a bench in a small house when one needed to. But at home one had to go to a ditch behind the cottage to squat. This was called the dungditch. Edvin would announce proudly: I'm going to the privy! Valter could not say the same, as they had only a dungditch. I'm going to the dungditch. It didn't sound good at all. And during the winter when the wind swept around the corner it was cold to go out there. During the summers one sat hidden in tall grass, almost as if in a small grove, and bluebells and dandelions and wild chervil grew all about, protected by the cottage wall, which had no window on that side.

Valter's humiliation lasted only a few seconds; then he found himself.

"Your privy is nothing. You should see the one my uncle has in America!"

"Have you been there to see it?"

"No, but Uncle Jacob has sent us a picture. His privy is much larger than yours!"

In fact, Valter knew suddenly that Uncle Jacob's privy in Michigan was much bigger than the whole Banda cottage. It had several rooms, and a kitchen, and a veranda. Twenty people could use it at one time.

"Really?" Edvin was suspicious. "You lie!"

"I tell you it's the truth! We have a picture of it."

"Let me see it!"

Valter said that his mother had locked the picture in the bureau drawer. She was afraid someone might put finger marks on it.

Edvin could not keep on denying the existence of a house in America. He had to try something else. He went inside and came out with a rabbit skin; his father had shot the rabbit.

Valter found himself quickly. "Only a small rabbit," he said. "My father shot a wolf!"

"You lie! There are no wolves around here."

"My father shot a wolf! I'm telling you the truth, as truly as I live!"

Such words were only used to confirm something important which the listener might doubt: As truly as I live! There could be nothing more true. And now Valter suddenly remembered that the wolf had come to their house early one morning and tried to get into the barn to tear the cow to pieces. Then his father had taken the Crown gun from the wall and shot the beast through the window. The bullet had hit the wolf in the throat. The beast fell at the barn door and kicked with his legs, and the blood streamed from his throat. Mother had helped skin the wolf.

"Do you have the skin at home?" asked Edvin.

No, they had sold the wolf's skin for one hundred crowns.

"You lie!"

"As truly as I live!"

Edvin went inside to his father at the cobbler's bench and was assured that no wolves lived in the forests near them. It had been more than fifty years since the last one was shot. And Banda laughed until his fat stomach jumped up and down under the cobbler apron:

"Valter lies like a trooper! Next time I guess his father will shoot a bear!"

Edvin returned to Valter with the final confirmation:

"You lie! Everything you've said is a lie!"

And he told this to other children, and they in turn repeated it: Soldier-Valter was a liar!

Valter thought it over and wondered: Had he really lied? He knew what Uncle Jacob's privy was like, and how could he know if he hadn't seen it somewhere? They did not have a picture of it, but he had seen it nevertheless. And he had seen the wolf outside the barn, kicking with all four of its legs while the blood streamed from a wound in its throat. His father had not shot the wolf, but he, Valter, had seen it lying there. How could he otherwise have told it to Edvin? Consequently, he had not told a lie.

His father and mother learned what he had said.

"What is this story you're spreading that I shoot wolves with the Crown gun!" said Father.

"How can such a little one invent such lies!" said Mother.

Valter's cheeks burned red. To his parents he could not insist: As truly as I live! Nothing helped him now.

But his father only laughed and pinched his ear tip, not very seriously. Perhaps he understood the whole thing: Valter had to keep up his end of the bragging with Banda-Edvin. And Valter was convinced that what he had said was true at the moment he said it. But he must not say those things to others, for they only made fun of him. He heard and saw and experienced much that he must keep to himself.

His brother Gunnar, however, kept the secrets given to him. He listened in silence and understood that he must not betray Valter. He never said that Valter lied. Nor did he say he spoke the truth. Gunnar said nothing when his brother told stories, and that was how it should be.

Gunnar had started school and could read and write like a grown person. Valter was not yet old enough to begin school, but he already had learned to read and write, mostly by himself, with a little help from Gunnar. The first letters he recognized were those used in the name of a paper, *Svenska-Amerikanaren* (*The Swedish-American Weekly*). Soon he could read passably in the American papers and found the names of the towns where his relatives on the bureau lived: Chicago, Iron River, Duluth, Denver, St. Paul, and Seattle Wash. He saw pictures of tall houses: if all the cottages here at home were piled one on top of another, they would not be as tall as one single house in America. He saw a picture of the world's richest man, Rockefeller. His mouth was full of gold teeth, and he ate scrambled eggs from a silver plate and slept in silk nightshirts, it said. In America even the poor chewed with gold teeth. Here in Sweden they did not even have the old common bone-teeth to chew with. Mother had recently lost her last tooth, and this pleased her, as she hoped to be rid of the toothache from now on. The sooner one got rid of one's teeth, the better—they only caused pain and misery. And only upper-class people could afford to buy new ones.

Valter learned to write by copying the printed letters of the America-papers. He picked up pieces of charcoal from the ashes in the stove and printed the letters on board stumps he found in the yard. He had no paper to write on; as soon as a piece of wrapping-paper found its way to the cottage, his mother would fold it and put it away. But the boards could be used over and over; as soon as one piece was covered with letters, he would take a knife and scrape it clean. His hands turned black from the charcoal, even though he industriously tried to rub them clean on his face while writing.

One day in spring, shortly after barefoot-time had begun, his big brother Albin came home to the cottage. He had been to the parsonage for his papers, and now he went the rounds of the cottages and said good-by. An America-ticket had arrived from Uncle Jacob: Albin was going to America.

His brother Ivar, too, was free from his service and had come home. All of Soldier-Sträng's family were now gathered together, and at mealtime Valter could only find standing-room at one corner of the table. This was exactly like "free week" in the fall when the big brothers came home for visits. Albin and Ivar would then sleep on the attic floor, as there was no place for them in the one-room cottage, even though every wall had its pull-out bed; the kitchen was too narrow to hold a bed. There were nine of them in Soldier-Sträng's family. Albin and Ivar would return to their respective services after their "free week"; this time, however, Albin would travel far away.

Albin had become the central person in the family. All thoughts and words concerned his America-journey. He had become different, he was more important than before. His brothers and sister looked at him with a new respect, and Father and Mother treated him differently and spoke to him in a different way. Albin was emigrating to America.

He was broad of shoulder and tall, almost as tall as Father. He, too, must stoop when entering the cottage. To Valter the oldest brother was almost a stranger. As far back as he could remember, Albin had only come and gone. Now he was a new, strange being: he had an America-ticket, and he carried his papers in his pocket. He no longer belonged in this cottage, he belonged in another world. In a sense, Albin already was one of those in the frames on the bureau.

All listened when Albin spoke; he commanded almost the same respect as Father.

"I shall go on the White Star Liner," said Albin.

If anyone was making noise, at these words he would grow silent.

"I shall go to Alaska and dig for gold," continued Albin.

Now the silence was profound in the cottage where Soldier-Sträng's family were gathered.

Albin had brought home a copy of *Smålands-Posten*, from which he read about "Our Countrymen Out There." One Smålander from a neighboring village had made such a rich strike in Alaska that every spadeful was worth two thousand dollars.

The silence could not grow deeper around Albin. Valter sat oblivious of the fact that his tongue was hanging out.

"Almost eight thousand crowns in one spadeful," said Albin.

Father pondered this. Eight thousand was Riches. If he were the owner of this place he would be rich, he used to say. The soldier-cottage with its ground was perhaps worth a thousand crowns. But in America one could push the spade into the ground and lift it up again with eight homesteads on one spade.

"I'll send a ticket for Ivar next year," said Albin.

The eyes of the family moved to the second-oldest among the children. He had been sitting quietly and solemnly; after his brother's words he grew impressive. He, too, began to take on stature in the eyes of the others. Part of Albin's glory reflected on him: I'll send a ticket for Ivar.

Albin walked from cottage to cottage and said good-by. He carried his "papers" in his pocket.

Valter had spelled through the advertisement in the paper:

THE WHITE STAR LINE
The Favorite Line of the Swedes!
The World's Largest and Fastest Steamers!

He crawled up into the sofa corner and closed his eyes. He wanted to be alone with himself for a while as he traveled to America. He, too, took the White Star Line, because it was the fastest. At once he was on the ship that sped across the watery sea. It was like the picture ship on their wall, where Jesus calmed the storm. Huge, bearded men sat at the oars and rowed. They were bareheaded and resembled Christ's disciples in the picture. The storm thundered, the water splashed in furious waves around the ship. Valter was a passenger and need not row. He had his ticket, and in his pocket he carried his papers—a piece of wallpaper he had scraped off and on which he had written his name: America-farer Valter Sträng. All he need do was to sit quietly in the boat until he arrived. During the nights he could sleep in the bottom of the boat while it stormed. He never feared that the ship would turn over in the water. After all, he traveled on the White Star Line, the favorite line of the Swedes.

One morning he awakened and the ship lay still. He had arrived at the shores of America. There grew fig trees and palms and lilies, exactly as on the shores of Lake Genesaret. And on the shore Uncle Frank stood and waved to him, with his big hat, and his pipe in his mouth. And Valter stepped ashore in America and went with his uncle to the mine where he would dig so much gold that he could put teeth of gold in Mother's mouth; then it wouldn't take her so long to chew the hard bread crusts. And he would dig a few spadefuls for Father, enabling him to buy their home and all the farms in the village.

Then, suddenly, he was forced to cut short his America-journey: Mother called that he must help Gunnar carry in wood.

And one morning when Valter woke up, his oldest brother was gone. He asked for him and was told that he had left by horse from the village; Aldo Samuel had driven him on his wagon; they had left before daylight in order to catch the train.

Valter was chagrined and disappointed. He was long to remember the morning when Albin left for America while he lay in bed and slept; he never said good-by to his oldest brother.

Albin had grown up and was gone. Here, in Sweden, one was born and grew up. One went to America after one was grown.

CHAPTER II

Valter's world widened. He opened more gates and walked farther out into the world. He walked all the way to the village. Father no longer led him by the hand—he could walk about by himself and observe.

The farmers in Strängshult Village had bigger houses than the soldier-cottage. They had more than one cow in their barns, more than one pig in the pen, and they had a horse or two in the stables. The Alderman, Aldo Samuel, had two horses, one black and one red. The Alderman's house was finer than the soldier's.

Round about in the forest lay the cotters' places. They were smaller than the soldier-cottage, and the smallest of them all was Trångadal, where Grandmother lived, and where Mother had grown up, and her brothers and sisters before they went to America. To that place led a narrow, little-used path that wound its way like a snake across the woodlands. Grandmother's room was barely half as large as the room in the soldier-cottage. Round and about, in glades and openings in the forest, lived people who owned neither barn nor cow, neither pig nor sheep. There lived widowers and widows, crippled people and hunchbacks. There lived Välling-Lena, who was harelipped, and Tailor-Jan, who was deaf. People whose sight was poor or who didn't hear well, people who walked with canes, who were a little off, and people who lay in bed ready to die. These were the cotter people, and they were poorer than the soldier's.

The Christmas pig was slaughtered, and Valter was sent with lard and bacon to Balk-Emma, who had aided Mother at seven births and had helped him also into life. He knocked lightly on her door, and behind the smudgy window he could see a brown, wrinkled face peer out cautiously. Emma was afraid of stray men folk. At her door now stood a man, but he was so little that he barely reached the keyhole.

"Is it the little one from the soldier's?"

Balk-Emma dared open. But it took a few minutes to remove all the boards and bolts securing the door. She took Valter's basket and began to lift out all the food—a piece of pork, a chunk of lard, some bacon.

"She's too generous, your mother. I can't accept all this."

She looked once more in the basket to make sure she had found everything, then said:

"It's too much—I refuse it."

Then she put the food in a cupboard near the hearth and pushed the basket toward Valter. He picked up the empty basket and made ready to leave, but the old woman motioned to him to stay; she began to poke among the quilts and sheepskin covers of her bed. She was looking for something. She dug herself deeper and deeper into the pile of bedclothes. Valter knew what she was looking for. And he trembled at the thought of what he must go through.

He must have coffee. And nothing else he had ever taken into his mouth tasted as evil as Balk-Emma's coffee. She had her coffee container bedded down among the quilts, and her coffee tasted bitter and noxious; it was neither warm nor cold, but somewhat tepid. It was "bed-warm." And thick as dungwater. When one swallowed the coffee, it wanted to come up again; it did not wish to be closed in the stomach. He had drunk it last year and the year before when he brought Christmas food, so he knew.

At last Balk-Emma found her coffeepot deep down in the bed. It kept warm between the pelts so she need not put it on the fire each time a visitor came. Thus, she had always coffee ready for a caller. The pot was well tied up in a black-and-white checkered woolen shawl.

Valter made an attempt to escape: he must get home before dark. But Emma grabbed him by the shoulder as if he were still the newborn brat of eleven pounds whom she once had hung on the steelyard. She pulled him up to the table: no caller had yet left her house without coffee; as long as she lived, no caller would leave her cottage without coffee. It was a matter of honor.

He could not escape. The cup, the sugar bowl, the cream pitcher were already on the table. And on the table sat also the coffeepot in its shawl with the corners tied like the ears of a crouching, vicious owl. There was no getting away this year either.

The coffee clucked in the throat of the shawl-owl as Emma poured it into the cup. Its color was the same as Emma's face, dark brown like dried spruce bark. She must have drunk so much coffee that it had oozed through her leathery skin. With trembling hands Valter lifted the cup toward his lips. Last year he had managed not to vomit until he was outside; he hoped to do as well this year.

The old woman stood beside him and watched while he drank: her generosity and honor would be kept as long as she lived, she assured him. No one should be able to say over her dead bones that he had left her house without a treat.

Valter emptied the cup in deep swallows. He tortured himself valiantly for Emma's honor and generosity. And in front of him sat the black-white shawl-owl, threatening a refill from its throat. But because he was so very little he escaped with one cup. Then the owl with its thick black coffee flew back to its warm nest in the bed, there to rest until the next guest arrived at Balk-Emma's cottage.

Valter got out with the coffee still inside him. He stopped outside to vomit. But this year he was unable to. The coffee did not want to remain inside him, nor would it come up. During the whole way home he carried both his coffee and his feeling of nausea.

Dusk was already falling over the wide forest. Only in some openings between the fir-tops did light from the sky break through. He stumbled on a slippery root, tumbled over, and lost his wooden shoes. His father would say that it mattered little if such a short being fell—he was so close to the ground. He looked for his shoes and found them, but could feel from the pressure over the instep that the left one had broken in the fall.

Now he had reached Janne-Shoemaker's cottage. Janne came once a year to their home. He would stand at the barn gable and dig into a pile of alder logs until he had made two pairs of shoes for each one of them. When he left, sixteen pairs of wooden shoes would stand in a row in the attic at Soldier-Sträng's to dry. Valter had an extra pair up in the attic and he had been promised the use of them after Christmas. He might therefore just as well break both his old shoes; they would be thrown away anyway; there was no sense in having one broken shoe and one unbroken.

He stopped and took off the unbroken right shoe and hit it against a stone. It didn't break. He banged it against the stone once more, this time much harder. Now it broke completely, in two pieces.

Darn it! He almost swore. Darn it was as near as one could come to swearing without actually doing so. He hadn't intended his shoe to break so badly that it was unusable; he had only meant to crack it, like the left one. Now he had no shoe to put on his foot for his walk home, and he still had a great distance left. He put the two halves in the empty basket and walked on wearing only a stocking on his right foot.

There was no snow, but the ground was cold and muddy. The stocking had a hole in it, which left his heel exposed. Wooden shoes were always hungry at the heel and gnawed through the stockings. Now the stocking got wet and his whole foot felt cold. He had a wooden shoe on one foot but only the stocking on the other, and he limped along like a cripple. Darn! Damn! Now he swore outright. He would have to begin using the extra pair even before Christmas. But Janne made poor shoes that cracked easily; this he must tell Father.

He hopped along on the shod left foot to avoid putting the shoeless right one down on the ground.

In America wooden shoes were not used. All his thirty cousins might not have a single pair among them. Only here, in "poor Sweden" did people go about in wooden shoes. The ancient inhabitants of the cottages hereabouts must have worn out whole forests, having lived so long on this earth. Wooden-shoe people inhabited this land.

Now it was as coal-dark as it could get. Valter started to run. Not because he was afraid, but he would get home sooner if he ran. He was just passing the Stallion Moor where will-o'-the-wisps and trolls were supposed to run about with their lights after dark. He didn't look in that direction, he didn't need any light. At the edge of the moor lay Stallion-Daniel's cottage, now long deserted. When Daniel died and was buried, he had taken all his money with him in the coffin; he kept his money in a bag that he had tied around his chest. His relatives missed the money and dug up the coffin in the churchyard. They found a huge snake coiled on the chest of the corpse, and the coffin was lowered again without anyone daring to touch the snake or the moneybag. Daniel still lay in the churchyard with the snake and the bag on his chest, and here stood his empty cabin, which Valter must pass.

The snake on Stallion-Daniel's chest was said to be as thick as a man's thigh; Valter ran a little faster.

Then rose a shriek between the trees, from the right side of the road, from Stallion-Daniel's desolate cabin. It sounded like a human cry, like a person being slowly choked to death. It could come from someone being choked by a thick, enormous snake. Valter had heard the same cry before when passing this cottage; he took longer jumps in his single wooden shoe.

The shriek at Stallion-Daniel's old house was well known. Once, when he heard it in daytime, Valter had gone closer to see what it might be. He found two young firs, grown so closely together that when the wind moved them back and forth, an eerie, complaining sound was caused by the friction of their trunks. He wasn't afraid of a tree that cried. There was a wind tonight and the firs were crying, of course. It might be something else, but he wasn't going to investigate tonight. Moreover, it was too dark to find the trees.

Now he must be near Potter-Isak's place. Part of the chimney and a pile of stones with nettles were all that was left. Potter-Isak had practiced witchery with human bones, and one of his feet had been a horse's foot. Isak had worn an iron horseshoe on that foot. Potter-Isak had been dead a long time when Valter was born; he wished he could have seen the man with a horse's foot. Potter-Isak must have been the only one who didn't wear wooden shoes on both his feet. But, then, he had been a witch man.

Now Valter had reached the road that led to the soldier-cottage in Hellasjö. Mr. Hellström lived there; he was a corporal and bailiff, and had a long black beard. Little Bäck from Bäckhult was the shortest soldier. All the soldiers came to Father's Christmas party: Godfather Banda, the fat Nero from Bökevara, Flink from Sutaremåla—he got drunk and sang songs—Lönn from Hermanstorp, the tallest soldier except for Father, Tilly from Grimmanäs. They were Father's buddies from the other villages. Mother prepared a feast for them, Father bought a can of anchovies, and *brännvin* was poured from a keg and drunk. The soldiers ate and drank and made much noise, and Valter would sit hidden behind one of them to listen. He didn't understand all they said, and he heard that he was not supposed to understand. The soldiers were foul-mouthed, Mother used to say. But Valter liked to know the truth in all matters. He would not go to bed as long as the soldiers remained, but sat hidden and listened and learned. At last he would go to sleep in a corner with his clothes on.

From the soldiers he learned each Christmas a few more swear words, which he practiced while alone. He could practice also while Gunnar listened, for Gunnar did not tell on him. But Gunnar didn't know nearly so many swear words as Valter, even though he was older and the best in his class according to the teacher's report to Mother.

Valter wanted to become a soldier, too. If he didn't go to America, he would be a soldier.

But soldiering would be abolished, Father had said. No more young men were accepted. Valter was deeply disappointed.

"But you can be a volunteer," said Father. "You can volunteer for three years."

Volunteer—that sounded almost better than soldier.

"Can I have my own gun?"

Of course he could have his own gun if he volunteered, said Father. The volunteers had the same kind of guns as the soldiers, model '96, the same gun which hung on the wall and which Valter was not allowed to touch. Exactly the same, with a yellow sling.

He would be a soldier, with his own gun to fight with, but his name would be Volunteer Valter Sträng. This was something to think about for a long time.

Now his right stocking was dripping-wet and his foot felt terribly cold. Valter had reached Carpenter-Elof's cottage, and he slowed down—he had run so fast he had a pain in his chest; he panted and his stomach jumped out and in. Carpenter-Elof's cottage was not deserted and empty. Elof was a religious man, respected by all. He was sent for when someone was to die and needed comfort. Carpenter-Elof helped people die, because this was very difficult.

D-i-e. Valter tried the word. It could be pulled out as much as one wished, into eternity. But: *Dea-th. Death*—that word could not be pulled out. It ended inexorably on the last letter. One hit a wall, and then it became silent and over and done with: *Dea-th.* Strange how that last letter stopped and one couldn't do a thing with it. One's tongue seemed to be locked in the mouth after the word *Death.*

Carpenter-Elof was a God-fearing man who could help one get by death.

Valter walked by his cottage slowly. Elof never swore. And no one swore in his presence. Valter decided not to swear any more while walking homeward.

He made a jump backward, a yell froze in his throat. In the dim light he saw a wild beast rise from the edge of the road, its long limbs and claws flailing the air. Our Father Who art in Heaven! This was like dying, as he thought dying must be like . . . Then he remembered the fallen tree with its roots stretching skyward. He started running again.

Now there was only Miller-Kalle's cottage left before he reached home. The miller was the laziest man in the parish. He wouldn't do anything except make children, people said. He had seven in school, one in each class. Altogether, he had eleven. That's what happened when the father was lazy. And the miller's family had lice. Laziness was punished with vermin, Mother said. The greatest shame there was, to have lice. The only thing one got in life without effort. Father and Mother were not anxious to visit at Kalle's. The children in that cottage would scratch and twist their bodies from itching. They were skinny and miserable and coughed, and two had died from consumption. But their lice were fat and could make bigger and redder bites than any other lice hereabouts. If Father had some errand at Kalle's, he would take off his shirt on the stoop when returning and examine it carefully before he came inside. No vermin was allowed at the soldier's. No matter how poor, one could afford to keep free of vermin, Father said.

The biggest lice had the ace of spades on their backs. Valter had not seen them, but he had seen how big the ace of spades was. Banda's Edvin had an old deck of cards which his brother Valfrid had given him, and Flink's Ossian at Sutaremåla also had a deck. Valter would like to learn to play cards. Then he could play when he became a volunteer and had his own Crown gun to fight with.

Father served and defended King Oscar and the Crown. The King and the Crown belonged together and owned everything between them. The crown that sat on top of King Oscar's head owned practically all of Sweden. But the King didn't use the crown every day—Father had seen the King at a maneuver and then he wore a cap. He had left his crown at home, perhaps he was afraid of losing it. The great gold crown that Oscar wore at home when he sat on the silver throne, that crown owned the gun on their wall, as well as Father's rucksack, his coat, his pants, everything. The crown was richer than anyone else, Father said.

It was so dark in the forest that Valter really should have been afraid. And the closer he got to home, the more afraid he grew; on one foot he had a cracked wooden shoe, on the other his stocking; it was Janne-Shoemaker's fault, he made such poor shoes that they cracked for almost no reason at all.

Now he saw the light between the pines, the yellow light from a coal-oil lamp in a little cottage in the forest. It was a small tin lamp, but it spread a warm and friendly light. No longer did Valter's wet foot feel cold. Home.

He walked slowly and confidently this last piece of the way— this way that he would tramp at all hours of the day, at all seasons of the year, through all the years of his childhood. It led through the wide, desolate woodlands where lived the people of the small cottages, the people he belonged with. Here lived *his* people, among whom he was born, the wooden-shoe people—the rugged, proud, silent, paucity-people.

CHAPTER III

The Russo-Japanese War broke out during the winter. The Japanese had made an unexpected attack on the Russian fleet in Port Arthur harbor. Now frequent visits were made to cottages with newspapers. The name of the Russian fortress became *Potatur,* which was easier to pronounce. Valter was on the side of the Japanese; he had heard that they were yellow, and he thought yellow a beautiful color; he liked the color of the gun belt and the stripes on Father's Crown pants.

Toward spring two faces vanished from his world. Grandmother in Trångadal no longer came to warm her feet against the stove rail. Her eyes no longer ran—he had seen her in the coffin with her eyes closed. As a memento he kept the funeral candy with its black paper and silvery letters: WORLDLY WORRIES FLEE.

A few weeks later his brother Ivar went to America. Albin had kept his promise and sent the ticket. Ivar left in the company of Miller-Kalle's Albert and Ture, the son of the railroad section boss. They pooled their savings and bought a deck of cards so they could play blackjack during the voyage.

Those were the emigration years, and many people went to America, from Strängshult as well as from other places. It was a real America-spring. The youths still too young to emigrate sang songs about America's attractions: hundred-dollar bills grew on trees, and one sat in the shade and let the bills drop into one's lap.

Valter never got to know his older brothers. He was too small while they still remained at home, and as he grew up they left on the White Star Liners, the fastest in the world.

A few days after the outbreak of the Russo-Japanese War he began school, and many new faces came into his world.

He began to understand now, said Mother. Miss Tyra, the teacher, gave him many proverbs from the schoolbook which he must learn by heart: "Early liar, old thief." "Slow wind will also bring a ship to harbor." "Too wise is unwise." "Better poor with honor than rich with dishonor." "Teach youth, honor age!" These proverbs were supposed to give him much pleasure and comfort later in life. He learned to spell, and read the Catechism and the Biblical History, and began with the four rules of arithmetic. He managed well in everything except arithmetic. To add or subtract was easy enough, but to divide or multiply was an ordeal; he would concentrate until his head ached. Nor could he write the figure eight to please the teacher. One circle he might manage, but never both. Miss Tyra said his eights looked like deformed mice. Once he was told to stand at the blackboard for a whole hour—to write an endless number of eights.

From his comrades in school he learned a great deal: to understand the cards in a deck, which enabled him to play auction, knock, and five-cards. He also learned to fight—the neck hold and the waist hold were new to him. And of course the names of the sexual organs; he had heard the soldiers use these same words at the Christmas parties, but then he had not known their meaning.

Some of the boys already worked in the Ljungdala Glass Factory. They spoke disdainfully about the Catechism and the Biblical

History and said that these books were full of lies. Of the young glass workers, few believed in God; Valter was shy among these boys.

Gunnar was said to be the best student, and Valter was proud of his brother. Gunnar could solve the arithmetic problems in his head, and as Valter turned the leaves in his book he knew it would be two or three years before he could do the same. Gunnar wrote so neatly that he could be a bookkeeper, said Miss Tyra. At home he was already writing America-letters since Dagmar had gone away to serve as farm maid; she was now thirteen and would be confirmed next year. Pen and inkstand were locked in the bureau drawer, which was opened only when it was time to write a letter to America. Then Gunnar was allowed to sit with his elbows on the table like a grown-up. Father and Mother stood beside him and dictated what he should write: That they had their health, which was God's greatest gift on earth, and that they wished the same for those in America. And they hoped someone would soon come home, with affectionate greetings.

Soldier-Hulda could not write or read written text. She had gone to school only three weeks, and after school she had never had any time for further learning. Soldier-Sträng had learned to write in the recruit school, but he wrote badly—grotesque, straggly words, sometimes below the blue line, sometimes high above it. His fingers were so stiff and callous-cracked that he always asked someone else to write for him.

Valter no longer wrote with coal; he had climbed the first step on the writing-ladder and was now on the second: he wrote with slate pencil on a slate. But he was still climbing; he was aiming for pencil and paper. The thought came to him that the Crown which was so rich might help him with this.

"How rich is the Crown, Father?"

"Richer than all others."

"Richer than Rockefeller?"

"I imagine so."

Then he asked for the address of the Crown, but Father said it was only officials who got the letters, learned people, like governors and sheriffs. One could, of course, write to King Oscar personally, but probably some lackey would take the letter and read it.

Valter decided that he would not write to the King and ask for paper and pencil; some lackey might take his letter and use it in the royal palace privy.

Instead, he wrote to Rockefeller. He found half of a wheat-flour sack; it was smooth and white and made excellent stationery. He wrote that he was seven years old, that he lived in a soldier-cottage in Sweden. He had only a slate and a slate pencil, and he begged Rockefeller to send him kindly a dollar for paper and pencils. His mother gave him an envelope and he wrote the address: "Herr Mister Rockefeller, New York America." He gave the letter to his mother, who promised to mail it for him and pay the postage until the dollar came, when she would get back her money.

Rockefeller was the richest man in the world, but a proverb said "the richer, the meaner." Johannes at Kvarn, the richest farmer in the village, was so penurious that he couldn't afford to eat; nor could he sleep—he must stay up nights and guard his house against thieves. Rockefeller was said to have a million dollars locked in his safe. He need only open the door to the safe and take out one dollar. He wouldn't miss one single dollar.

Valter would buy a notebook with part of the Rockefeller money. He had seen notebooks with a pencil fastened to the back. That would look elegant.

He waited some time, but nothing was heard. Had the money perhaps gone astray? But he had printed his address clearly: Soldier-cottage, Strängshult, Uppvidinge County, Province of Småland,

Sweden. Or perhaps Rockefeller was busy momentarily. Perhaps he had other payments to meet first. There could be so many things to delay the money. At least Rockefeller had not written that he refused to send the dollar.

Valter waited, but no dollar came. Then he began to have bad thoughts about Rockefeller in America. He must be a thousand times richer than Johannes at Kvarn, and perhaps he was even meaner. "The richer, the meaner." He wouldn't take out a single dollar from his safe and give it away. Valter intended to write a second letter to Mr. Rockefeller and tell him the truth. Misers should be told the truth.

Then one day he saw a piece of paper in the dungditch. It was the flour sack with his letter to "Herr Mister Rockefeller, New York America." Someone had done with his letter what he had feared the lackeys at the royal palace would do if he wrote to the King.

The letter had been lying here in the dungditch all the time. It was not Rockefeller's fault that no dollar had come.

He reproached his mother for having deceived him.

"You mustn't be a beggar!" she replied. "Begging is disgraceful! Everyone must take care of himself! That you must learn!"

It was for his own good that his mother had thrown away the letter to the richest man on earth.

Thus Valter learned that each one in this world must take care of himself. He must do the same.

The autumn evenings were bleak and lonely while Father was away for the yearly maneuvers. Mother was afraid of hobos who asked for shelter. She never opened the door to a stranger after dark. She always had Father's jacket or pants on the line outside to give the impression that there was manfolk in the house. But while Father was away, thirteen-year-old Fredrik was the oldest manfolk in the cottage.

It was at the height of the lingonberry season. One afternoon Mother had gone into the woodlands with Fredrik, and to make sure the smaller children would not open for some stranger, she had locked the door and taken the key with her. Mother said she and Fredrik would pick only a gallon each at a certain moor and would be back before dark.

The three locked-in children—Anton, Gunnar, and Valter— huddled close together at the window looking down the road. It was already growing dark outside. The children pressed their noses against the windowpanes, waiting for Mother's return. So they had been sitting many afternoons during these gray, monotonous autumn days. As twilight fell, Mother would return. Inside, it was almost dark already, for they were forbidden to light the lamp; they were not allowed to touch matches. Nor were they permitted fire in the stove while alone—Mother was that afraid of fire.

Valter pressed his lips against the cool, hard pane; his breath warmed it. They had nothing to do but sit and look out. Valter and Gunnar had occupied themselves for a while in counting the freckles on each other's noses, but now they were through with this. Valter was quite freckly, but they had now found out that Gunnar had forty-three more than his brother on his nose alone. Anton, to the envy of the others, had no freckles at all.

Valter sat at the window and observed the blue mantle of night draw closer, the forest's black wall creep nearer the cottage. Wasn't someone approaching? Was it Mother and Fredrik? Someone was calling, anyway, loudly and persistently—now plaintively, now shrilly. Anton said it must be a crane on the moor. Valter's eyes peered through the window, but he could see no one near the moor.

Everything changed with twilight. The gate seemed to flow together with the barn. The gooseberry bushes crouched until you hardly saw them, the top of the pear tree bent its head. And someone was moving in the road; a figure took shape and stepped cautiously through the darkening dusk.

It was a man. Valter saw him first, a huge man, almost as tall as Father. He wore a fur cap, and he stopped at the gate, apparently headed for the cottage. Or would he walk by? Then he opened the gate, and Valter could see that he pulled a cart behind him; with bent body and slow steps he pulled the cart toward the stoop.

"There's a man coming!" Valter warned his brothers.

Anton and Gunnar took one look through the window, but quickly turned away in fright. How fortunate that the door was locked and that no one except Mother could unlock it, they comforted each other.

But Valter remained at his lookout post. His eyes could not leave the figure in the yard. The man was dressed in a long, black coat that hung all the way to the knees, and his face was all covered with beard, the part Valter could see below the fur cap. On the cart lay a big sack; it must be very heavy, the way the man stooped as he dragged the cart behind him. What might he have in the sack? Now he had reached the pear tree; he stopped and straightened his back and looked toward the cottage. However scared Valter was, he could not leave the window; it was not only fear that he felt; he caught himself wishing that the man would come in.

Anton and Gunnar dared not look out, but Valter told them what he saw.

The stranger struggled on with his heavy cart; it must be an awfully heavy sack, and Valter wondered about it. Now the man had reached the stoop. He looked toward the window with a horrible bearded grin; he leaned the cart handles against the stoop and began to unload the sack.

"He's coming up on the stoop!"

Anton and Gunnar held on to each other back in the corner, but Valter followed every movement of the man. Particularly the sack—what could he have in the sack? The man put it down on the stoop, panting noisily. Valter could now observe him more closely—a red beard, a crooked nose, lardy eyes. He was looking toward the window, where he had discovered Valter. He made ready to knock.

Valter kept his brothers informed about the man's smallest activity; they felt far from secure even though the door was locked. Gunnar suggested that one of them should go to the door and tell the man that no one was home, but Anton thought this silly, as it wouldn't help if the man were dangerous.

Valter was concerned with the stranger's sack—what could he have in the sack?

He remained at the window, following every move the man made. Now the man was knocking lightly on the door. Gunnar and Anton listened, but could not hear back in the corner.

"He's opening the sack!"

The man was fumbling with the sack's long strings, and now they were loose and the sack was open. Valter craned his neck; he must know what was in the sack.

The man stooped and put his hand in the sack. He pulled out something which he held up for Valter to see as he nodded and grinned. And Valter had already guessed what it was—a child's head!

He yelled to his brothers: "The man took a child's head from the sack! Just cut off!"

Anton yelled at the top of his voice and scampered to the darkest corner behind the stove. Gunnar crawled under the bed, so afraid he dared not let out a sound. But Valter remained in the window, watching the man with the child's head in his hand. It was the head of a small girl, with long flaxen braids and wide-open eyes. Valter thought it strange that the eyes should be open. He tried to look into the sack's mouth—it must be full of children's heads. But he was glued to the window, he must follow everything that took place outside, the man, the sack, the cart.

Now the man was knocking again; perhaps he was trying to break down the door.

And someone was indeed coming in. But Valter sat quite calmly on his bench at the window and waited for the caller. He was not in the least afraid as they heard steps in the entrance hall. A moment passed, then the door opened. But the man with the sack never came in; instead, Mother and Fredrik entered, their baskets full of lingon from the moor.

Two of the little boys crept forth from their respective hiding-places, crying, trembling with fear. But the third and youngest one remained calmly on his bench at the window, without the slightest sign of concern.

What had happened here at home? Had someone tried to break in while the children were alone? What had frightened the two boys out of their senses?

Anton and Gunnar told the mother between sobs: A horrible man had come with a cart and a sack, and the sack was full of children's heads that had just been cut off.

But the mother would not believe them. She questioned each of the boys in turn: Who had seen the man with the cart? Not Anton. Nor Gunnar. Only Valter had seen him. He had been sitting at the window the whole time and had told the brothers about the man. Anton and Gunnar had been too afraid to look out of the window. Now they were ashamed of having been so scared.

"Why didn't you look for yourselves?" asked the mother. "Must you big ones rely on the little one?"

"We didn't think he was fooling us," sobbed Anton.

"I did not fool you!" said Valter, hurt. "As truly as I live!"

"You've lied and scared your brothers!" said the mother.

"I have not lied!"

"You invented the whole thing!"

"No! I saw the man—as truly as I live!"

"You persist, little one?"

"Yes, I saw him the whole time."

"You have told a lie. And now you deny having told it. This calls for more than words!"

This time it didn't help to say "As sure as I live!" Soldier-Hulda went to the fireplace to fetch her rod from behind the damper handle—a bunch of birch twigs. She let down Valter's pants and switched his behind. It was a thorough beating he received that time. Afterward he felt as though he had been sitting with his bare behind in a stand of nettles. Mother seemed regretful and kind after the punishment: Why must he lie and invent stories so that she was forced to beat him? Think if Father had been home and heard this! He was only seven, yet already an inveterate liar. Didn't he remember the proverb: "Young liar, old thief"? Did he want to become a thief and spend his days in prison when he grew up?

Valter had not thought that the proverb about the thief might apply to him. Another proverb said: "Begin with a pin, end up with a silver bowl." So that was how one became a thief: first by lying and inventing stories, then stealing pins, at last by taking silver bowls.

But Valter had not lied. And Mother could not beat him enough to make him admit he had lied. He had seen the man with the cart and the sack. He knew how the man was dressed and what his face looked like. This he could not have known if no man had been there. And his brothers had been scared—Anton had crawled under the carpet. Anton and Gunnar could not have been scared if no man had been there.

But he, Valter, had not been scared. Because he knew that the man was not dangerous. When he no longer wanted to see him, then he was there no longer. He had just walked off as Fredrik and Mother came home. Anton and Gunnar could never have seen the man—no one could have seen him except Valter, because *it was his man.* He had been sitting there at the window in the twilight, and *wished* the man from the shadows in the yard. And the man had come. He had enjoyed telling his brothers about him, but it was not his fault that they were frightened.

How foolish that he hadn't kept the man and his cart to himself! And why had Anton and Gunnar feared the man? He had never said that he was dangerous.

And so Valter learned something that evening: He must keep things like this to himself. He must never tell others, it did not concern them. And he could no longer trust anyone, not even Gunnar. He must forever keep to himself what belonged to him only.

The man with the cart and the sack stayed with Valter for a long time. He wondered about the secrets in the sack. Because it contained more things than children's heads. It might contain almost anything. He wished to share his discoveries in the sack with someone, but there was no one he could trust.

And then Father returned from the maneuver and brought him a notebook with yellow covers and a pencil in a holder at the back. It was exactly the kind of book he had wanted. And it came at the right moment: in the yellow book he wrote down a story about a man who walked through the world, pulling a cart with a big sack. All people wondered what the sack contained, but the man never opened it, and no one knew. No one except Valter knew, and he wrote a story in his book to tell the secret.

Now he had found the solution—he could confide, yet keep it to himself.

He wrote and told those things that were his own. This writing was not a pretense; it was not for fun; to him it was deeply serious, perhaps the most serious thing that was. There were moments when he felt something must happen; he wished it might happen—and his wish was fulfilled in this way. It was not a surprise to him, nor to anyone else—now that he kept it to himself.

Thus Soldier-Valter had found an outlet for the experiences of his imagination.

CHAPTER IV

Valter went with his father to the forest to peel fence posts. Now he was big enough to do useful work. And being seven years of age, he was supposed to earn his food. During the spring his schoolwork prevented him from helping Father, but during the fall he attended school only on Fridays and could help in the forest other weekdays.

It was a nuisance that school took so much of the children's work time. And Valter preferred the forest. He used a debarking-knife almost as long as himself. Father piled the posts on sawhorses and Valter peeled off the bark until they lay there like skinned calves on a slaughter bench. The posts were used for the railroad fence; between the beautiful posts that his hands had peeled the trains would rush. The travelers on their soft seats would perhaps look out through the windows and see his posts. "They're peeled well," they might say. "Wonder who did it."

When Valter came home evenings he now smelled like Father. He smelled of pitch, pine needles, wood, and sap, a manfolk smell that made him proud. Now all would recognize his smell and know that he performed a man's work and earned his food. One must earn one's food before eating it to enjoy its blessing. If he spent the day in school and made no use of himself, he would not relish his food in the evening. Then he would sit and swallow his unearned bites with the knowledge of denied blessing.

He was growing up. He was his father's working-comrade. On the way to or from the forest he would trudge a little behind Father, but this was not because his legs were so short, but rather because Father's were so long. But Father never left him behind entirely; he would stop at intervals to let Valter catch up; then he would walk slower. Returning home in the evenings, it might sometimes happen that Soldier-Sträng would pick up his son and carry him on his shoulder. Valter held on to Father's neck; Father could carry a whole tree on his shoulder as easily as a hazel branch; he could splinter a thick log with a single ax-cut.

They walked together along the timber-drivers' road in the winter, following the white sled marks in the snow with its glittering frost stars. The timber road was two bright lines through the forest, like the White Star Line that crossed the sea to America. And tall forest crowns soughed softly, protecting the workers below busy peeling posts.

Valter and his father were comrades. "Confidence, friendship, assistance must exist between comrades," read a paragraph in the *Instruction for the Infantry*. This was the soldiers' catechism, and Valter had read it from cover to cover many times. It gave advice as to those things a soldier must guard against: dishonesty, debt, drunkenness, debauchery, swearing. Yet Valter had heard his father as well as his father's soldier-comrades use swear words, like the devil and hell. If the Crown had heard this, they might have been discharged. And the soldiers drank *brännvin*—Flink in Sutaremåla used to vomit on the stoop at the Christmas parties. If the Crown had known this, he might have been discharged. What did Father think of this?

"Flink would not have been discharged," said Father. "It didn't happen in the service. He vomited in civvies."

However, Flink had recently been given a year's probation.

Well, perhaps the soldiers could swear and carry on when not in the service. But there were other things that were forbidden in the *Instruction*. Valter knew whole paragraphs by heart: "Insubordinate speech and intercourse with base and lewd people disgrace the soldier and might lead to bad reputation, punishment, and finally dishonorable discharge." Who were those people called base and lewd?

"It means they must stay away from bad women while on the maneuvers," said Soldier-Sträng.

"Those women at the maneuvers—are they bad?"

"Some of them are. Some are even dangerous. Don't have anything to do with them when you grow up! They might make you sick."

"Those women, are they sick?"

"Well, some are sick. They're not bedridden, exactly, but they are dangerous."

Now Father had warned Valter against sick women who were not exactly bedridden. They were base and lewd. Hereabouts were no such women, said Father, but they looked so much like decent, fine women that one could easily make a mistake.

The soldier and his youngest son talked like comrades—"in confidence, friendship, assistance"—and Valter was proud of being a comrade to his father. He really wasn't old enough for that yet. But as soon as his legs grew a little more he would be able to keep up with Father. Meanwhile, when he lagged behind, his father slowed down his pace until his son caught up with him. Father would wait, however great his hurry.

So it should be between comrades. Valter knew Father would never leave him behind.

Soldier-Sträng usually returned from the maneuvers the second week in October, but in the fall of 1905 he failed to return when expected. There was talk of war with Norway, and he was ordered to remain. Those troublesome Norwegians, they always wanted things their way. They were a different people from the Swedes. Colloquially they were called the Norwegian "rams," and Valter thought of them as having one horn in the middle of the forehead; this wasn't true, of course, but they butted in and annoyed the patient and good-natured Swedes.

A Norwegian ram. Well, they had had a ram at Soldier-Sträng's last summer, and he was a most stubborn and impossible animal. However much Valter had pushed and pulled him, the ram had refused to budge. He had remained in the place he himself had chosen. Valter had beaten him with a stick, but the ram had only retaliated with his stone-hard forehead. It had not gone any better for Valter's mother or brothers. If they annoyed the ram too much, he would take after them with his horns.

Norwegians were like that ram. If they decided to jump on the Swedes, there would be a war. And what would happen to Father in a war? Father who must defend the King and the Crown?

Mother said that God and King Oscar had Father's welfare in their hands, but if all of them helped in the work, particularly at the potato-picking, then this, too, would aid.

And late one evening Samuel's wagon drove up at the cottage with the returning soldier. The children were already in bed, but they quickly woke up and jumped to the floor. Father had brought home a mysterious parcel, a large, pyramid-shaped object in thick gray paper with heavy strings. It was nothing less—nothing less indeed—than a whole ten-pound sugarloaf! In his joy at getting home, the soldier had bought a sugarloaf at Hultsfred. He himself liked sugar, and now for once all of them were allowed to stuff themselves with sugar.

Father took the hand ax and cut the loaf in six more or less equal pieces—one for Mother, one for himself, and one for each of the children. The pieces were as large as two fisted hands. The sugar-eating began, and for a long while all you could hear was the crunching of sugar. Mother was toothless and had trouble with the chewing; she saved most of her piece to use for sweetening in cooking. And Father carried part of his piece in his pocket for several days.

The peace with Norway was celebrated in the soldier-cottage with this sugarloaf.

It was King Oscar who had averted war, said Father. King Oscar had said he would not shed one drop of Swedish blood while he held the scepter and reigned. He would rather lose Norway. King Oscar would lose half his salary now that one of his kingdoms was lost, but he cared not a bit about that. He would rather reign for half pay than sacrifice his soldiers' blood. It had been said at Hultsfred that Crown Prince Gustaf was much bolder, because he was worrying about his inheritance, but he couldn't do a thing about his father. It was evil of the Norwegian rams, though, to shove out King Oscar in his old age, said Father.

So ended that year, and a new almanac was bought. In the year 1906 the following events took place in the world: King Christian of Denmark died and was buried, the robber Aberg was sentenced to death for murder, there was an earthquake in San Francisco, and a revolution in Russia because they had lost the war with Japan. At the Strängshult soldier-cottage, at long last a privy was built. The family had long complained about the dungditch, particularly this last cold and windy winter. Soldier-Sträng had spoken to the villagers, but when all papers and contracts and regulations had been looked into, it was discovered that the village was not obliged to furnish a privy for its soldier. That miser Johannes in Kvarn, who was Alderman that year, had said that if their soldier wanted such a house then he must foot the bill.

And Nils Sträng did build the privy. He bought a load of one-inch boards and nailed together a house among the alder bushes below the yard. Suddenly there stood a building for two people, with a door and hasp, and the old dungditch went into disuse. He also built a new stoop, and his wife Hulda papered the kitchen and nailed cardboard to the ceiling in the big room to hide the ugly old beams. Things improved; when their cow bore a heifer calf, they decided to keep it; in a few years they would have two cows, and if they could manage rightly with the bull so that one calved in the spring and one in the fall, they would have milk and butter the year round.

Yes, things improved for Soldier-Sträng, and tongues began wagging from envy in the neighbor cottages: they had an easy life. There were no longer so many brats in the family. Fredrik, now the eldest one at home, would be confirmed next winter. Dagmar—in service with Aldo Samuel in the village—was seventeen. She was well developed and capable of heavy work, and Aldo bragged about her and said he had never had such a good maid before; she could load her end of the dung-wagon as quickly as he filled his, and this was quite remarkable in a girl of her age. But this last year he had also paid her a grown woman's wages—eight crowns a month.

Then, in April, Dagmar left her service and came home. She began to sew new clothes for herself—the America-ticket from Ivar was expected any day now. It was her turn to emigrate. Albin and Ivar had already sent their pictures, which were now part of the collection on the bureau; Albin and Ivar had become America-relatives.

Yes, it was Dagmar's turn. She had bought a hat, a handbag of shiny oilcloth, a muff for her hands, and a brooch for her neck like Aunt Anna in the picture. And she bought hair in big wads, which she pushed under her own hair until it stood up in the air and looked real fine and upper-class. Her mother asked if the way she bought and decked herself without shame or decency meant that she was trying to ape upper-class people. Soldier-Hulda was afraid that her only daughter might grow vain if she carried on like this.

"I've earned the money myself," said Dagmar.

Indeed, she had served for three years, and saved and gone without.

To Valter, Dagmar had never meant anything special when she had come home before, but now he eyed his sister in admiration: she had a hat, and a shiny handbag, and much hair. She was his only sister, and he approved of her being like better-people.

She was kind to her young brothers now while waiting for the America-ticket. When Valter was a little tyke and she took care of him she used to call him a brat and box his ears and spank his behind. At that time he had decided bitterly and definitely that he would repay her in like manner when he grew up. Now he was a manfolk and worked in the forest and felt that he could have repaid her. But nobler feelings made him refrain from vengeance. Dagmar seemed to regret her earlier bad behavior and was kind to him. Furthermore, no man could be such a coward as to take revenge on a woman.

He was thinking about the fact that his only sister was going to America, and the more he pondered over it, the sadder he grew. Mother, too, looked serious as she helped Dagmar with the sewing of her traveling-clothes. At last her thoughts came out: Dagmar was their only girl—she ought to stay at home.

"You have enough of brats without me," said Dagmar.

It was true, there would still be four children at home after she had left.

"You're so young, only seventeen," said Soldier-Hulda.

"Ivar wasn't older when he left."

"It's different with boys."

"What is the difference?"

"They can take better care of themselves than girls."

"I have taken care of myself here at home, slaving for the farmers. I can take care of myself in America," said Dagmar with confidence.

Seventeen-year-old Dagmar stood there proudly, displaying her work-developed, round arms, her breasts bulging under the blouse. Health shone in her blossoming cheeks. She was tested in hard service, she was strong. She could lift almost as much as a man; Valter thought his sister was beautiful.

There was a well-known song that warned beautiful girls against going to America:

. . . but the rose might wither on your cheek—
In A-me-ri-ca!

was the refrain. The rosy-cheeked Dagmar only laughed at this ditty.

"You might have waited another year," said Mother.

"I'm tired of slaving for the farmers," replied Dagmar.

"You might get a job with better-people."

"I don't want to work for anyone. Life has other things to offer."

Valter understood and guessed that his sister wanted to become upper-class herself, and he did not understand why Mother was against it. Three things were degrading: to beg, to be lazy, to have vermin. But what was there against being upper-class? He asked his mother about this.

"Each to his own," said Soldier-Hulda. "Upper-class is upper-class. The others should never mix with them."

"In this country, yes," said Dagmar. "But in America all are equal."

That was the reason so many went to America: to be considered as equals.

One evening Aldo Samuel came to call to persuade Dagmar to forget the America-journey and return to his service. He had not been able to find another maid, and a better one than Dagmar he would never find. The farmer praised and lauded her beyond reason. Then he promised to raise her wages: he would pay her ten crowns a month if she stayed one more year.

"Ten crowns a month!" repeated Hulda and took a step backward.

It was indeed high pay for a seventeen-year-old girl. Hulda had in her youth served a whole year for twelve crowns and a shift.

Dagmar did not answer, and Aldo Samuel increased his offer with one crown after another. Besides, he would be willing to give her two whole days free so she could attend the fair.

"No!" said Dagmar.

"Your conceit has grown beyond rhyme and reason," said the farmer.

"I'm tired of spreading manure for you, Aldo Samuel."

At this the peasant turned angry and began to argue so loudly that Valter got scared. Aldo Samuel swore at youth in general. Nowadays they had grown so uppity that they couldn't even stand the smell of dung. Dagmar and her ilk had never learned respect and decency. And before he left he cursed America, which had turned the heads of servants. America was taking the best manpower from the land; what a pity that country in its entirety hadn't sunk below with the city of San Francisco!

Afterward Father reproached Dagmar for having aroused Aldo Samuel; he was the most decent of the villagers; his bite wasn't so bad as his bark.

Dagmar left on a spring evening when the crabapple tree had begun to shed its blooms. Gunnar and Valter each had picked a bouquet of flowers for their sister—buttercups, bluebells, fragrant lilies of the valley. Dagmar said she would keep them as a remembrance of her home, if they didn't wither away on the Atlantic Ocean.

Aldo Samuel had not refused his wagon to Dagmar, and his hired hand drove the red mare that had pulled the wagon when Ivar and Albin left for America. Father and Mother stood at the wagon and looked solemn. His sister hugged Valter so hard that he almost felt ashamed of her farewell. Then Dagmar's little America-chest was lifted up behind, while the restless mare pushed and pulled the wagon back and forth.

"Don't let any menfolk fool you," admonished Soldier-Sträng.

"I'll take care of myself! I'm strong enough!"

But her voice was not quite so sure or so light as usual. She stepped up and sat down beside the driver. Mother turned for a moment toward the gooseberry bushes as the wheels began to roll.

And the wagon with Valter's only sister moved slowly down the road and disappeared at the bend near the Little Field.

Soldier-Valter now wrote with pen and ink as he related his life's experiences. He read the installment stories in the American papers and relived their happenings all alone. Then he himself wrote several novels. When he ran short of paper, he would pull off a piece of the wallpaper; he confined himself to spots behind the beds where it wouldn't be noticed. He was writing a big novel entitled *The Million-Dollar Inheritance*. It was along the lines of the installment story he had read in *The Swedish-American Weekly*, about Count Eberhard in the Castle Waldhof, whose inheritance had been stolen by a swindler and who now must live in a forester's poor cottage. *The Million-Dollar Inheritance, Original Swedish Novel by Valter Sträng*, was also about a count who had been swindled out of his inheritance and now lived in a cottage, hunting and fishing.

He hid his work well, against the roof bark in the attic. No outsider must see it. But there was a leak in the sod roof, water dripped through the bark exactly in the place where he had hidden his papers, and after a persistent rain he discovered that *The Million-Dollar Inheritance* had rained to pieces. No outsider ever saw his original novel.

Soldier-Valter demanded true answers to all questions and wanted to know the truth about all things. He wanted to know the truth about himself. He thought about this at times: he was Valter, the soldier's son, one of seven children in this family. But this knowledge was not enough, now that he had grown. Mustn't he be something more than Soldier-Valter?

God had created him, with the aid of Father and Mother; the circumstances that brought a child into the world he had discovered by himself. But why had God created him? Why had Father and Mother brought him into the world? He had asked them about this, but had not received a satisfactory answer; his parents only looked embarrassed. Perhaps they themselves did not know. They had only meant that he should live, that he should become Soldier-Valter.

And he would live and grow old and die. It was not as he wished. Was he nothing beyond Soldier-Valter?

He thought and thought to discover himself. He must be someone in himself, not only someone else's, not only the soldier's. He wanted to be someone or something that no one else was. And he wanted to do something in this world that no one else had done.

Carpenter-Elof came to mend the roof that the wind and the rain had torn, and Valter helped him by handing up the sod. The religious Elof spoke to him about something no one else had spoken of before: man's soul.

Carpenter-Elof said that Valter had a soul, and a soul was something that never died, that lived for all eternity. The most precious and most valuable human possession was the soul.

And this—the most precious and most valuable—he carried inside himself. Soldier-Valter was visible, but his soul was invisible. Soldier-Valter could die, but not his soul. Because he carried it invisibly within himself, he was something more.

Carpenter-Elof said that Valter had a white and innocent child-soul which could be compared with a newly washed and ironed shirt that had been given him by God and that God would some-day take back. As he grew up, his shirt would become spotted and soiled with sins and vices. But God demanded that his soul must be pure and white when He took it back, as pure and unsoiled as when He had given it to Valter. Therefore the spots must first be removed with Christ's blood. His soul must be washed in the Lamb's blood and ironed with blueing of Grace, exactly as one washed a dirty shirt in lye soap and then put it on Sunday morning, starched and ironed.

Valter asked: How did it feel when the soul began to get dirty?

Old Carpenter-Elof pulled his red timberman's-pencil from his mouth. "One feels it. It aches in one's conscience."

Thus Valter learned that it was his conscience that hurt him in his breast when he had done something wrong. It pained and ached as it did when one coughed with a bad cold. One's conscience sat in there some place like a sensitive wound, a place that hurt. The greater a person's sins, the greater the sensitive place. In cruel murderers, like the Atorp murderer he had read about in the papers, the whole inside of the breast was one great big wound, one sensitive conscience. That was why Atorp had been unable to endure living but had hanged himself in his cell, said Elof. It was because of his conscience.

Valter had a soul, but it was not his, for God owned it. His body that he walked about in was his own. His body he himself could make decisions for. It was divided—in his schoolbook—into head, body, and limbs, and it was in the head, body, or limbs that it hurt or felt good; it was the head, the body, and the limbs that worked and earned the food; it was they that became soldiers, or farmers, or shoemakers, or upper-class people, or traveled to America. This was the human body. But the human body died and turned to earth again, because, explained Carpenter-Elof: The body belonged to this earth.

Now Valter wondered what remained to himself. His soul belonged to the Creator, his body to the earth. Neither soul nor body was his own. And there was nothing more. Nothing that he owned himself. Himself was nothing, nobody. Everything that he had to live with here on this earth belonged to somebody else, to God or the earth.

But he was not satisfied with this explanation. *He wanted to be someone himself, someone or something.* He wanted to, he wanted to. He could not stop wanting to. He was not satisfied with a soul that God would take back, and a body that belonged to the earth.

CHAPTER V

O n a drizzly day in December when Soldier-Sträng and
Gunnar and Valter were out in the forest cutting posts, a
timber-driver passed by with his load and told them King Oscar
had died. A message had arrived by telegraph to the minister that
he must toll the churchbells.

Nils Sträng put aside his ax and sat down on a stump. "The King
is dead. We take a five-minute rest."

Gunnar and Valter were eager to rest; they stretched out full
length on top of the fresh, fragrant spruce bows. Father pulled out
his handkerchief and dried the sweat from his forehead; Father
always perspired on his forehead. He also dried his eyes, perhaps
because of the perspiration, perhaps not.

During one of the maneuvers the King had happened to ride
close by Father.

"Oscar made peace with Norway," said Sträng.

Valter recalled the autumn two years ago when he had waited
for Father to come home and had picked potatoes industriously in
order to avert the war. It was King Oscar who had sent the soldiers
home safely; if Oscar had not been, he would not now have Father.

Soldier-Sträng was glad to give his sons five minutes' rest from post-cutting in memory of Oscar II. The spruce bows around them smelled like a funeral. Corpses and spruce bows belonged together. Now a royal funeral was impending, with smell from all the firs in the forest. When a cotter died, only two small firs were cut; when a farmer died, one dozen. When a king died, perhaps the whole forest would be cut down, because the whole country mourned.

Soldier 128 Sträng sat these minutes on the stump and said good-by to Oscar II, whom he had served for twenty-three years. He had got a new boss this misty December day. When again he picked up his ax to fell trees, the reign of Gustaf V would have begun.

King Oscar had died from hardening of the blood vessels in his heart and his brain. Now royal tolling or the churchbells would take place for half an hour every day, between twelve and half past. The tolling of the clear bells could be heard all the way to the forest where the soldier and his sons would sit at their box lunch about that time. It had said in the paper that the old King had been religious. "Thank you, Jesus" had been his last words.

Valter's father was now serving a new King, yet the Crown was the same as before. It had only been moved from the old King to the new; it was now sitting on Gustaf's head. But the new King refused the expense of a coronation.

"He's thrifty, is Gustaf," said Father. "He won't spend foolishly."

For Valter's father no change in the service took place with the reign of Gustaf V. Everything remained the same in the cottage. But this winter the soldier himself was not as he had been earlier. He was tired in the evenings, which he hadn't been before. He walked slower on the way home, so slowly that Valter could keep up with him without having to run. And this not because Valter was walking faster, but because his father was walking with slow, heavy steps. Father had never before said that he felt tired; now it might happen that he would sit down on a stone at the edge of the road.

"Go on home, Valter. I want to rest a minute."

But Valter would sit down and wait. He wouldn't leave his father on the road. Father had waited for him when he was little and didn't manage to keep up; now he in turn must wait for Father, who was tired and had to rest. So it must be with menfolk and comrades, and Father and he were comrades. In that way they were in some sense more than relatives.

Soldier-Sträng was always thirsty nowadays. He would drink in the forest, throw himself headlong to slake his thirst from water in stump-holes. At home he drank water, home-made beer, butter-milk, or anything Mother would hand him. He drank, but he was immediately thirsty again.

"You ruin yourself with all this drinking," said Soldier-Hulda as she handed him the half-gallon stoup.

"But I'm so utterly thirsty."

"You never used to drink like that."

"I guess I sweat more now."

So much perspiration ran from his body while he worked in the forest that he needed to replenish the fluid. He was the tallest man in Uppvidinge Parish, and the bigger body a person had, the more fluids and bodily juices were required. That was why he was so thirsty.

"You'll drink some ailment into your body," said Hulda.

"I'm not sick! Don't worry about me!"

Nils Sträng brushed a few white buttermilk drops from his long blond mustache, and his blue eyes were filled with assurance: No one need worry. He perspired, and drank much, and that was as it should be. And his fatigue in the evenings, forcing him to rest on the way home—that, too, was natural. After all his tramping on the maneuvers and all the many years of labor here at home, it might happen that a soldier, too, would feel a little tired.

⟨ ⟩

When school ended in spring the forest work also came to an end. As there was nothing else to do, Valter got employment as a carrier at the Ljungdala Glass Factory. He now had his own job.

The parish lay in the center of the Småland glass-factory region, and there were six glassworks in the neighborhood. The small factories lay close together here, and only twelve miles away was the biggest of them all, the Kosta Glassworks. In this forest region there was plenty of fuel for the furnaces; it was an advantage for the farmers to sell their wood so close to home. And the factories were an advantage for the cottage people, who could send their children to work while still very young. When school didn't interfere, the children worked in the factories. All the little ones in Kalle-Miller's family worked at Ljungdala—Viktor, Ernst, and Teodor. And the soldiers Banda and Flink had two boys each at the factory. The children began working when about six or seven as form-holders or carriers. The little boys need not be paid much. Nor did the factory-managers wish to refuse the parents when they asked for work for their children. Mr. Lundevall at Ljungdala, however, liked the boys to be eight before he employed them. He was considered a friend of children.

Ljungdala Glassworks lay about two miles from Soldier-Sträng's cottage. The work began at five in the morning, and Valter had to get up at four. But now it was summer, with light mornings; it would be harder in winter. The boys were supposed to put everything in order around the five furnaces, lay out the tools, fetch water, before work began. Valter was assigned to Master Sjölin's furnace. Master Sjölin was a fat man with reddish face and bald head, so bald that it shone red in the light from the furnace. On the first day he said that the carrier would get a box on the ear for each glass he broke. Valter had heard about boys whose eardrums were split in the factory. And some of the boys were so scared that they dared not even ask the master to go out when they needed to, but did everything in their pants. So scared he would never be, thought Valter the very first day.

Ljungdala Glassworks manufactured wineglasses, cognac glasses, beer glasses, *brännvin* glasses, lamp chimneys, and coffee bottles. It was a drinking-glass factory. Master Sjölin blew beer glasses. Valter's job consisted in carrying the finished glasses on their forks and piling them on the cooling-trays. At this one furnace were blown six or seven full trays of glasses in a single day, from five in the morning to five in the afternoon, with two hours' lunch rest. It surprised him that so many glasses were needed in the world. How many barrels of beer these glasses would hold! And how many people would drink themselves full from the glasses he carried in only one day! He soon learned the right way to carry by observing the other boys, but he broke a few in the beginning. Sometimes Master Sjölin would give him the promised box on the ear, sometimes he forgot. But his hands were not as hard as Valter at first had feared.

In the factory Valter earned his first money in life. He was paid five öre an hour, fifty öre a day after ten full hours. Every fortnight he received his wages—six crowns, which he gave to Mother. Each time she gave him back fifty öre; he had money of his own and was independent.

He had his own job. Now he could say: "Today when I went to my job," "Yesterday when I left my job." So spoke the grown-ups, and it was not bad to be able to say the same. Then he felt he was becoming his own.

It was fortunate for the cotter children that there were factories. Where could they otherwise have found work, little boys of eight, nine, or ten? Brats that were of no use at home? It was lucky for them, and for the parents, that they had the glass factories.

But Valter would rather work in the forest and be a comrade with Father. With Father he was equal; here in the factory he was not equal with his co-workers. He was the youngest, and all were above him, all could order him about: the blower's helper, the blower, the stem-maker, and the master. Even the stoker's helper, Ossian Flink, wanted to boss him, though they were the same age. Ossian had been with the factory a whole year and let the new-comer know it. One noon rest Valter had taken off his wooden shoes, and Ossian nailed them to the floor of the glass-storage shed. Valter fell on his face and hurt his forehead when he put his feet in his shoes. This entertained everyone in the factory; a new-comer must be taught manners—it was done in this way. "Honor the old, teach the young." If Valter held the form and happened to bend down, someone was always ready to pour a scoop of water down his back. The lesson was even greater should someone manage to pour it into his pants. A small boy must be taught whenever the opportunity offered itself. Also, some fun must be had during the working-hours, and the fun brought this advantage with it: the boys learned manners.

Everything was done for the boys' own good: a kick in the pants in all friendliness, a pinch on the neck, or a box on the ear when someone passed by. There was teaching of a sort in all this. To force snuff between a boy's teeth was, however, the most useful and the funniest of all. Nothing surpassed it, nothing was more instructive.

Soldier-Valter had no manners when he first came to Ljungdala Glass Factory, but he learned them little by little. What luck for children that there was a factory in the neighborhood!

In Ljungdala Factory drinking-glasses were blown by the thousands and the ten thousands. But it was a drinking-factory in another sense also: the workers drank. The blowers became thirsty in the sultry air near the furnaces, perspiration ran from their bodies, ever exposed to the heat. A blower must drink whatever was handy; the boys were told to fetch the drinks. The first days after payday a beer called *lousbeer* was in demand, bought at Hedda Larson's Bakery & Café, half an hour away. Valter carried beer for everyone who worked at his furnace. It was the poorest beer obtainable and required thirty bottles to make a man drunk—that is to say, if all thirty bottles were emptied within the hour. Which meant a bottle every second minute. Some of the men had learned the trick: throw the head back and push the bottle down the throat, where it remained until empty—one long swallow. Then a rest of one minute for belching. In this way one could get drunk in an hour.

A few days later everyone drank pure water, which was fetched in buckets. Only Master Sjölin drank beer constantly; he earned at least five crowns a day.

There were also a few workers who always drank water and never asked to have beer brought to them. One of these was the blower's assistant. During his very first days in the factory Valter realized that Elmer Sandin, a tall, skinny youth of about eighteen or nineteen, was different. He never poured water down Valter's neck. He never even kicked his behind. There was something strange about Sandin; Valter had no confidence in him and thought he was thinking of something worse than scoops of water or kicks in the pants.

Sandin changed clothes every day after work; he put on a big black bow tie; he was an odd glassworker. There were a number of the younger workers who wore black ties. One day Valter learned what this meant. Master Sjölin called to the blower's assistant:

"Get me a bucket of water, you 'sossy' there!"

Everyone laughed except Sandin, who grew red to his ear tips.

He was a *sossy*, a Young Socialist. All the ones who wore black ties were sossies, and all were members of the Liberty Club, the local organization of Young Socialists.

Valter wanted to learn about all things, and Sandin had noticed this. He took the boy aside at the lunch hour, spoke to him as an elder and friend, and soon Valter had confidence in him; Sandin was not contemplating anything evil against him.

"You are too young to know that we have an upper-class and an under-class," said Sandin. "But you are old enough to become class-conscious."

He lent Valter a paper, *The People's Will*, in which the boy could read the same thing: "Comrade! Be class-conscious! Join the class fight!" When Valter had read a few issues of *The People's Will*, he understood what a sossy was and his thinking began to clear.

Already in school he had compared his own lot with the lots of others. He had discovered great differences in the lunch boxes his comrades had brought. Some had whole baskets full of food, others had only a few breadcrusts, without butter or meat, wrapped in paper. His own lunch he carried in a blue-checkered handkerchief; when things were low in the cottage it consisted of only bread. Now dawned on him the difference between rich and poor: the rich had many kinds of meat with their bread, the poor had none at all. Earlier the words *rich* and *poor* had meant as much to him as *fair* and *dark*; a person was one thing or the other, but which was unimportant. He himself had happened to be poor, but he had thought as little about it as the fact that he was blond. He had been born among cottage people, all poor, and he did not miss the things he did not know existed.

His vague curiosity concerning his school chums' different lunches took on a clearer meaning when he worked in the factory and read

Elmer Sandin's paper: The people in the world were divided into two classes—upper-class and under-class. The first was parasitical, the second sustaining. The first was useless, the second essential. The upper-class owned the sawmills and the factories, and the under-class sustained the upper-class by working in the mills and the glass factories. He was a carrier at Ljungdala at five öre per hour; it was easy for Soldier-Valter to figure out which class he belonged to.

Now he was sharing great truths, and he made many discoveries in a short time.

"You must see through the humbug in society!" said Sandin. "That is the most important in the class fight."

Valter realized that he had as yet seen through nothing. He had read only the books the ruling upper-class had supplied him. Now Sandin brought him the right kind of reading. He must begin from the very beginning in order to understand the socialist doctrine. He wanted to learn, he couldn't help it, and to recognize humbug was to learn. One must penetrate lies to discover truths, said Sandin.

One evening Sandin took him to the factory polishing-attic, where he lived in a small garret. He took out a black cloth that he had hidden under a pile of old newspapers. On the cloth was painted in tall, red-flaming letters: DOWN WITH THE THRONE, THE SWORD, THE ALTAR, AND THE PURSE! This was the worker's standard, forbidden everywhere by the police. Sandin had carried it at Kosta in the May Day parade and had managed to escape with it when the sheriff came.

Valter's hands cautiously touched the forbidden banner. He felt solemn in its presence. Sandin pointed to the eleven red words, one after another, and explained their meaning: Society was built on four kinds of humbug, which he must learn to see through.

First was the Throne, the humbug about the King. The King was the monarch of the big robbers and thieves, and he protected them so they could keep what they had stolen. The Throne was inherited from father to son, and it might well happen that it would be inherited by an idiot heir. Nowhere in the Swedish constitution was it forbidden for a King to be an idiot. Indeed, Sweden had had several monarchs who had been feeble-minded. The old decayed Swedish Throne must be overthrown.

Then there was the Sword, the military humbug. With its armed power, militarism defended all the other humbugs. It was the upper-class's protection against the under-class. The military humbug was called the nation's defense, but it defended only the possessions of the rich and the injustice of society. Therefore, one must refuse to do military service. No worker must ever be induced to serve. The Sword must be broken.

The third humbug was the Altar, the religious humbug and the nonsense about heaven. The minister at the altar was the hired hand of the upper-class. He preached the old superstition that a God existed who had created the capitalistic world order for eternity. The under-class must live in patience and be satisfied here on earth, to gain heaven after death. The rich kept the earth's glory for themselves and generously relinquished heaven's bliss to the poor. The priest-trick about God and heaven was meant to deny justice in this world to the poor. Therefore, the Altar must be erased.

On the fourth humbug, the Purse, rested the other three. On the Purse rested the King's Throne, the officers' Sword, and the priests' Altar. The King, the Officer, the Priest, all three were hired to defend and protect the robber-barons' Purse, which the workers filled for them with their sweat. The Purse was the capitalistic society's foundation, and the greatest oppressor of all. Therefore, the workers must pierce the Purse.

All this Valter must now learn to see through, and it was a great deal at one time. He read eagerly the pamphlets Sandin lent him and he asked questions when he didn't understand. He was beginning to understand.

"You have a good head!" said Sandin. "You'll soon grow class-conscious! You must join the Club!"

Sandin did not treat him as a small boy, but as a grown comrade. And Soldier-Valter joined the Young Socialist club at Ljungdala Factory; at eleven he was one of the youngest members in all Sweden.

CHAPTER VI

O n Sundays Valter and Gunnar roamed the forest wastelands, searching for groundhog nests, throwing stones at squirrels, fishing in the lakes. They came upon hidden glades deep in the forest and stopped in surprise; here grew planted gooseberry bushes, covered with red, ripe berries. No one picked these gooseberries any more; these bushes were forgotten.

Here had once been a human habitation, but the cottage had been torn down so long ago that only very old people remembered the names of those who had lived here; the last generation of children to grow up in this house were in America. The ones who had planted the gooseberry bushes were forgotten, hidden in the churchyard. Now the berries ripened in the warmth of the glade, but no hand picked them. Gunnar and Valter came to the place and picked and ate until sated.

There were many deserted places in the wastelands. Stones placed in a square indicated where a cottage had stood, and how big it had been. The floor had been of earth, and in some cases the whole hut had been dug into the ground. The boys would always find a waterhole close by, once the cottage well. But all paths leading to the place were long overgrown. The treetops around soughed sadly, almost nostalgically: Desolate! Deserted! Never more!

Valter's forebears had lived in such earth huts; here he found the imprints of the cottage people from whom he had sprung.

They roamed all the way to Fågeltuva moor, a wide region with neither tree nor bush in sight. The heather covered a waste with nothing for the eye to rest on. The emptiness over the moor was forbidding; it was endless, it frightened, like the thought of eternity which had no end. The treeless ground created a loneliness that choked one's throat. The boys found skulls and whitened bones from animals that had got stuck in the mud pools. Flying life, however, was visible—the woodcocks, those twilight birds that shot across the yard, had their nests at the edge of the moor and flew up from the grass. The heath-piper made its nests on the tussocks far and wide. Many birds lived on the moor, and here they lived in undisturbed peace.

Thus, of a Sunday, Gunnar and Valter would roam as far away as the Fågeltuva moor, where eternity began.

Gunnar wanted to be a hunter and go out every day with a gun. It must be a breechloader, with two barrels. He was now working at the sawmill as lath-cutter, but in this job he would never earn enough to buy a gun.

Fredrik was now Valter's big brother. He was only half a head shorter than Father and had a job as millhand in Hermanstorp. He could walk on his hands, turn somersaults, swim dog-fashion, and chin himself on the bar. He was the brother Valter bragged about in school—he could do more than the brother of anyone else.

But soon Fredrik would go to the minister and fetch his papers. It was his turn now. Albin and Ivar had been younger than he when they left. If he waited too long, he would not get his papers; then he would have to stay home and do his military training.

Valter had begun to see America in a different light. On the bureau stood the pictures of Albin and Ivar and Dagmar and all the other relatives, and they were all alive and healthy. They were as much alive as the people here at home in the cottage. But they were gone and would never return, and no one would see them hereabouts again. They were not dead, nor did they live in this world. So America, to Valter, became a world outside the world, where his brothers and sister lived; yet they were gone, as if having left life forever.

Soldier-Sträng did not think Fredrik should go to America if he did not want to and had no other reason than to escape military training. He said the service was nothing to flee from; no healthy person suffered from this training.

One evening, after the lamp was blown out, Valter heard his father and mother in bed across the room talking about Fredrik's America-journey.

Father said: "We can't stop him from going."

"But America is like eternity," said Mother. "We'll never see the boy again."

"Maybe not, and then again—maybe."

"My mother never saw her own again. She used to say she followed them to the grave when they left."

"But Albin keeps writing that he will come home some summer," comforted Father.

"My brother Frans has written for twenty-three years that he'll come 'next' summer. He won't come."

"You could be right."

"If Fredrik had a way of earning his living—"

"He could volunteer and be a soldier like me."

"It's too confining."

"He doesn't have to sign up for eternity—he could try for three years."

"Well, at least we wouldn't lose him."

"Banda's Valfrid has signed up. A volunteer is well paid. And he can become a policeman afterward."

"Yes, it isn't bad. And it isn't forever. Three years will come to an end."

"I'll talk to him," said Father. "He might stay and sign up for three years."

"I wish he would."

"I must try to persuade him. He might listen to me. Oh, Fredrik!"

Valter lay awake a long while afterward and thought about Father's words. This was dangerous, he must warn Fredrik. His brother must not remain and become a soldier. Father didn't understand, he was easily swayed when the military lured with hopes of a good future. But a young man who was enticed to volunteer failed his class-comrades. Banda's Valfrid had signed up last summer, persuaded by his father, who now bragged about the forty crowns he had received in advance pay. Banda had sold his son to the Sword for forty crowns. After this outrage Valter could only hate his godfather; he refused to shake his hand when they met; he went outside as soon as Banda came to visit them. The Sword condemned the workers to death on the battlefield where they were defending the upper-class. At the induction centers only the healthy boys were considered worthy of slaughter. Banda had sold his son to be slaughtered for forty wretched crowns. He was nothing but a murderer, and Valter was ashamed that this man had carried him to baptism.

Father must not do what Banda had done, he must not sell Fredrik to the Sword. Valter must warn his brother so that he wouldn't fall into the trap. His big brother must not be hired to slaughter people and himself be slaughtered—not Fredrik, who was so strong and healthy and capable that he could turn somersaults and walk on his hands and do a number of other things that no one else could top. This must not happen, he must talk to his brother. Fredrik did not read papers and books and was not class-conscious as yet; he, Valter, must awaken him. If Fredrik signed up, he would be forced to fire on striking workers; he might receive an order to aim his gun at childhood comrades—at his own brothers, even. For Valter himself would undoubtedly be among the strikers sooner or later. But in such a case Fredrik would refuse to shoot. And Father, too, for that matter; he felt sure his father would refuse to fire on a friend.

It was not nice to have Fredrik leave for the New World. Now half of Valter's brothers were in America and half were in Sweden. They ought all to be in one country. And if they had had a decent homeland, they would all have lived here. It was because of poverty that they were forced to emigrate. It was like playing hide-and-seek—half in, half out. Now half were in—here—and half were out—over there. After Fredrik was gone, more than half would be out.

But his big brother must never sign up for the Army; he would a thousand times rather see him emigrate to America.

Fredrik would come home for a visit next Sunday and then he must warn him. Elmer Sandin had lent him a book, *Bloody Insanity*; Fredrik must read this book and then he would not sign up. Even with the promise of becoming a policeman afterward, he would never sign up when he had read that book.

Fredrik came home on Sunday and Valter saw his father take him aside and speak to him for a long time. But his brother was adamant—on Monday he went to the minister for his papers; his America-journey must take place according to plan. Valter felt easier and his worries were lightened. Fredrik was wise and did not fall for persuasions; Valter need not lend him *Bloody Insanity*.

And one morning Fredrik was ready to depart. In the yard he
said good-by to his parents and brothers while Aldo Samuel waited
with the red mare and the wagon. And those left behind stood for
a few moments and looked after the wagon, as they had done when
the others departed. Everything was as before when someone emigrated, not much different.

But this time Mother cried.

Soldier-Sträng lost weight that summer; he grew pale and weak,
and his eyesight failed; his posture was no longer that of a soldier.
The unquenchable thirst remained with him and burned like a fire
in his body, and perhaps it was this fire that undermined him and
consumed his strength. He drank and drank and was forever thirsty.
The fluid only passed through his body. He became like a dried
apple in spite of all the drinking. After a few moments' work he had
to sit down and rest, and cold sweat appeared on his forehead.

"I sit here like a lazy fool," said Father.

Balk-Emma made a concoction from moss blooms with a pungently strong odor. Such medicine was used for internal ailments;
it was black-brown, with a bitter taste. The sick man drank this,
mornings and evenings, but it did not help him. He remained
thirsty, weak, wasted, his eyes hollow. He no longer took his long
steps, and his tall body had lost its soldierlike bearing.

128 Sträng was ill.

Soldier-Hulda was afraid that he suffered from some consuming illness and wanted to send him to the doctor. But Sträng said
that he would wait until the maneuver in the fall; then he could ask
the Army doctor and this would not cost him anything. But at last
he gave in to his wife's urging and went to a doctor in Kalmar. He
returned with the information that he suffered from diabetes; he

must not eat sugared food. He would be cured if he took the medicine the doctor had prescribed for him and ate the foods the doctor had advised.

No one in the neighborhood had heard about diabetes before. No one knew whether or not it was a consuming and fatal disease that Father had. He had only asked the doctor if it was contagious: it was not.

"You mustn't worry," the soldier comforted his wife and children. "It isn't contagious."

This was fortunate; diabetes, then, was not so dangerous as tuberculosis or consumption, which everyone was afraid of as soon as one coughed or had a pain in the chest. One of Kalle-Miller's daughters had died of consumption the year before, and now one of her sisters had the disease. And Soldier-Hulda had warned Valter not to get so close to any of Kalle's boys that they could breathe in his face. But Father's diabetes would not contaminate anyone.

Sträng realized that he had got the sugar into his blood by eating too many sweets; he had always liked sweet foods; he would occasionally buy a piece of candy, and one time he had brought home a whole sugarloaf when he returned from the maneuver. And he had liked the sugar pears from the tree in their yard; he had eaten as many as a bucketful at a time. His wife thought that he must surely have caught the disease from the sugar pears, and Sträng himself felt that he had eaten them too ravenously; perhaps the sugar in them remained in his body. This year, too, the old tree was loaded down with the sweet fruit, but in the fall he would be careful and leave the pears alone. All he could do was look at the tree with longing.

Valter was afraid of diabetes every time he ate a pear, but he could not stay away from the tree.

Things had just begun to improve for them at the time Sträng got sick. Now their situation got worse again. He could no longer work as before. The grass on the moor remained uncut; it was just too much for him to harvest it, and with insufficient fodder they were forced to sell the heifer. Luck and bad luck shifted, there was nothing one could do about that, said Hulda.

Sträng hoped to be well again by the time he had drunk the medicine and eaten the food the doctor had prescribed for him. But it was not easy for his wife to furnish the food written down on the paper. It was mostly expensive food, upper-class food, unobtainable for people like them. It was easy for a doctor to sit and write down what they should eat, said Hulda.

Sträng complained that his eyesight grew weaker. He could hardly see to sharpen his scythe during the harvest. He could not see if he held the edge right to the grindstone because he only saw black before his eyes. Gunnar must learn to sharpen the scythe, even though he barely could reach the grindstone.

"Watch the edge!" admonished the father. "Don't get cross-edge!"

Father pulled the grindstone while Gunnar sharpened. It seemed topsy-turvy to Valter to see his father on his knees pulling the stone; this was child work. Father had been debased into child work, and he must have felt ashamed over it himself, for he said:

"Darned if I am not a fool!"

By sitting on his knees while pulling the stone he also got a pain in his back. Father was no longer the strongest man among them. Both the scythe and the ax felt heavy in his hands. When he tried to split a log he always missed the natural cleavage, as he could not see the fissure in the wood. He was unable to file the saw, and he worried greatly about the approaching fall maneuver; he would hate to complain to the Army doctor—a soldier was supposed to endure some inconveniences. But a military man must be able to see the gunsight, and this he could not do unless his eyes grew better. Perhaps they might use him for other, easier tasks because of his bad eyes.

When the order arrived, Soldier-Sträng packed his knapsack as usual and polished his gun. He filled his copper flask with home-made beer and took along an extra three-gallon can of buttermilk to quench his thirst on the journey.

Soldier-Sträng drank as no person had ever been known to drink.

The autumn term of school started, and Valter was excused with only Friday attendance. It was bad enough that school took him away from the factory a whole day each week. School was a nuisance to children of his age. Gunnar, too, now went only on Fridays. He was the best in the whole school—he could read like a bishop and write like a bookkeeper, said Miss Tyra. And he was better at arithmetic than the teacher herself: when difficult problems were encountered in the book, too difficult for the teacher, then they were passed by until Friday, when Gunnar would solve them. Valter admired his brother's great gifts. But Gunnar was peculiar in some ways: even though he was thirteen years of age, he was not interested in politics, and he had not yet seen through the religious humbug he had been taught in school. In those fields Valter was far ahead of his brother.

On the cover of a large notebook he had written: CONTAINS TRUTHS. All truths he had so far discovered were written down in numerical order. He had copied a few lines from *Why I Am a Freethinker*, and these made Truth Number 6: "There is no God. God has never existed except in the brains of ignorant people where the upper-class put him to keep the under-class down. Nature is a majestic, incomprehensible mechanism in which everything happens as it happens because it cannot happen in any other way, and is what it is because it cannot be otherwise."

This piece about God occupied less than half a page in Valter's book, sufficient space for something that did not exist. But he was not quite rid of God as yet—he had to read his Catechism and Biblical History Fridays. During the religious hour he participated as if he hadn't seen through the religious humbug. But secretly he felt superior, the one who knew more than the others; he felt sorry for his teacher, who was led astray and knew less than he.

And he couldn't help putting questions to her: How could the water at the wedding in Cana turn into wine? How could Jesus give sight back to the blind man? How could Jesus awaken from death the widow's son of Nain?

"These were miracles," explained the teacher.

"Why do no miracles take place now?"

"Because no Saviour lives on earth."

"Why is there no Saviour now, Miss Tyra? Why doesn't someone go around and heal the blind and resurrect the dead?"

Miss Tyra grew impatient. "We ignorant creatures must not question everything."

"Oh, well, I beg your pardon, Miss Tyra."

This was only pretended respect with Valter. But it was true, as the teacher had said: To question or search for truth was indeed forbidden. All who belonged to the under-class must retain their superstitious beliefs to keep them submissive and patient. Only the minister and the reactionary farmers made decisions about the school and about what must be taught.

And there was punishment for denying God. Sandin had shown Valter a list enumerating the penalties:

Denial of the Pure Evangelical Teaching:	50–100 crowns fine
Denial of life after death	150 " "
Denial of God	175 " "
Denial of all the above at the same time—	25% reduction

The price list was some years old; perhaps it was cheaper now. But in times past it had been still more expensive. Then only rich people could afford to deny God and a life hereafter. By and by the poor were given this privilege. When Valter grew older and earned more, he would deny. He would save enough money to deny all at one time. Or perhaps he would begin with the Evangelical teaching, which was cheapest; it was like buying something at a sale, for only fifty crowns.

In school he had not dared say anything as yet. He wondered what Miss Tyra would do if he told the truth. Could she fine him a hundred and seventy-five crowns? But it was not honest of him to sit here and pretend he didn't know the truth.

And one time when the lesson dealt with the Tenets he decided to speak up. It said in the First Tenet about God: "He supplies me daily and abundantly with food, clothing, house, home, etc., and with all those things I need for my daily living." This was nothing but lies. Only the upper-class had "things abundantly." He himself had worked for his food for several years, and now he worked in the factory for five öre an hour. He could no longer keep his silence before Miss Tyra.

When he was asked to read the First Tenet, he said that he knew the piece by heart and asked permission not to have to read it, as he didn't believe what it said about God.

"Are you a denier, Valter?" exclaimed the teacher in horror.

"I can't say that God supplies me abundantly."

"What are you saying!"

"Because he doesn't, Miss Tyra. Not by a long shot."

He was ordered to stand in the corner for the rest of the period. Obedient and pious girls on their benches looked with terror in their eyes at the little denier. But he felt no shame, he was not ashamed before anyone, be it the teacher or the comrades; not for one moment did he lower his eyes.

He experienced a pleasant inner joy over the punishment he unjustly suffered because of his denial.

The teacher asked him the next time if he believed now. He denied it.

"You work in the factory and are led astray," said Miss Tyra. "It's the fault of the factory." Tears came to her eyes.

Each Friday he was asked to remain an hour after the other children had left. The teacher wanted to ennoble him by this.

He could have pretended and said that he had begun to believe in God again; then he would have been let out. But then he would have been a "freethinker-humbug." And this would have been no better than a priest-humbug. He wanted to be a truthful, sure, honest denier, not frightened by the threat of authority.

Soldier-Valter stayed after school and passed the time by writing a novel that filled a large notebook. His novels at this time were intended as part of his class fight; they would further the workers' liberation. They were glowing with the slave's hate of the tyrant, with the have-not's hate of the well-to-do. For a few years he had been childish enough to make counts and other upper-class bloodsuckers the heroes in his novels. He felt ashamed when he thought of this. But he hadn't understood before. The nobles were indeed among the worst oppressors. Now he read installment stories in *The People's Will:* "The Slaves at Molokstorp" and "A Crowned Nincompoop and his Mistress." At last he had learned how to write.

In his new, enlightened period he wrote a novel entitled *The Bloodsucker Count of Gyllenholm, Swedish Original, by Valter Sträng.* In it was no trace of his earlier childishness. In it were no noble, justice-loving counts who married beautiful, innocent, poor daughters of the cottage people. In it was nothing but unadulterated truth.

Soldier-Valter was put on probation by Miss Tyra, but he did not change. He continued to deny. He denied persistently that God supplied him "daily and abundantly with food, clothing, house, home, etc., and with all those things I need for my daily living." But when he recited the First Tenet fluently by heart, she was satisfied and let him go home with the other children. She no longer insisted that he believe what he read. The teacher forgave him and blamed the factory.

Valter hardened and grew strong in his freethinking because of the persecution he had suffered through being put in the corner and kept after hours. Now he was convinced and sure in his belief: God did not exist. And if He did not exist, nothing could belong to Him. Thus his soul and body belonged to himself, not to anyone else.

Soldier-Valter owned something and was something himself. He could do with his soul and body whatever he pleased.

Soldier-Sträng was to arrive home from the maneuver, and Valter drove with the Alderman to the station to meet him. At home, the cottage had been tidied and cleaned up for his arrival. Valter had raked many basketfuls of leaves from the yard, cleaned the cowstall and the pigpen. Everything was in order for Father's return. Mother had taken out the carpets and beaten them and had hung newly starched curtains at the windows.

It was evening and dusk had fallen when the train came. Soon Valter discovered his father among the arriving soldiers—his head was above the others. Valter hurried up to him. Father remained standing in the place where he had stepped off the train, and Valter approached him from the side and grabbed his hand before Father saw him.

"Is that you, Gunnar, who have come to meet me?"

"No!"

"Oh, Valter! All right, boy?"

Father had mistaken him for Gunnar. But it was rather dark.

The Alderman came up to greet Father:"Good evening, Sträng!"

"Is that you, Aldo Samuel?"

"No. It's Johan Alfred."

"Well, good evening, Johan. Did you get the trunk?"

"It's right here."

"Oh, right here."

Corporal Hellström, with his big beard that covered his whole chest, was standing next to Father and speaking to him. He had a more commanding voice than other soldiers, being sheriff as well as corporal.

"Can you manage to get home, Sträng?"

"Yes, indeed. Both my son and the Alderman are here to meet me."

"Fine! Good-by, then, Sträng!"

"Good-by, Hellström! And thanks!"

Corporal Hellström left, and the Alderman picked up the trunk and carried it to the wagon.

Father's face had changed. His cheeks had sunk in, and he had lost several teeth; there were big black holes between his lips when he spoke. But, then, he had had diabetes when he left, and he had written that he had been on sick leave.

"Are you all right at home?"

"Yes, Father!"

"That's good. Then let's go to the wagon."

Sträng held his son's hand so hard that it hurt Valter. In this way they walked hand in hand to the wagon. Father stumbled a few times, even though he walked slowly. Valter had never seen him take such short steps with his long legs.

The Alderman picked up the whip from its holder and the wagon started rolling. Valter sat behind, on his father's trunk. He had been promised a mouth organ on Father's return from this maneuver. Anton and Gunnar had already received mouth organs, but they played only seldom. Valter had borrowed his brothers' instruments and had already learned to play the "Fire-Polka Waltz," the "Fisherman's Waltz," and the polka about "Father and Mother and Petter." He had been thinking of the mouth organ as they drove to the station and had been expectantly happy. But now, as they drove home, a feeling of depression had come over him.

There was something wrong with Father. His face had changed in some way. And he asked such strange questions: Was it Aldo Samuel who drove? Even though Johan Alfred had been standing in front of him. And then the question about the trunk, when the trunk was right next to him. And why had Hellström asked if he could manage to get home?

Yes, something was wrong with Father. He was in uniform as always when returning from a maneuver, his voice was the same, and his hand was the same as he held Valter's. Yet something was wrong.

At the first farm they reached, Father wanted to get down to have something to drink. He was so thirsty that he was almost beside himself. The driver went to the well and brought back half a gallon of water, which he drank.

And he was barely across the threshold of the cottage before he asked for something to drink. Hulda had saved buttermilk for his return; he was pleased at hearing this and emptied a quart pitcher—in one long swallow, it seemed.

Father was as thirsty as before. Valter watched him empty the pitcher, watched his big Adam's apple roll up and down his neck as he swallowed. But there was something else the matter with Father this evening. Mother had recoiled at the sight of his face in the dim lamplight. She had almost cried out; her mouth had opened in consternation, but she had kept her silence. Perhaps she had been shocked at seeing his caved-in cheeks, the empty holes where his teeth had been.

She fetched another pitcher of buttermilk for her husband.

"How do you feel, Nils Gottfried?"

"Not too bad, thank you."

"I hope it's nothing serious."

"We'll talk about it later, Hulda."

Father felt in his pocket and pulled out the key for the trunk padlock. He opened it and gave Valter a mouth organ in a red box, with pipes on both sides. Gunnar's and Anton's mouth organs had pipes on only one side. On this instrument two people could play at the same time if they stood facing each other and blew simultaneously. It was an elegant instrument, said Father, the latest model.

They all sat down to supper; Hulda had made dumplings, which had always been a favorite dish with Sträng. It was holiday food, but now he had no appetite and ate only a small helping. His wife said she would not have bothered with this fine food had she known he was not hungry.

Yes, something was definitely the matter with Father. Maybe all of them realized this; at least Mother knew, Valter could clearly see that.

Perhaps it mightn't be too serious.

But Father had stumbled as he stepped across the threshold. And he had had trouble opening his trunk—he had been unable to find the keyhole. He could not find the door when he wanted to go to the kitchen. He no longer had the aid of his eyes to guide him. His eyes were glazed, staring vacantly. *Father's eyes could not see the one he talked to.*

He spoke to Mother as if she were standing at the bureau, while actually she was busy at the stove. He spoke to Gunnar as if he were next to him, while in reality Gunnar was sitting near the door. And when he wanted to go to bed he walked toward the wrong wall. Then all knew how things were with him.

Gunnar and Valter had looked at each other several times, but had said nothing. Valter sat with his new double mouth organ in his hand; he had not yet blown a tune on it.

When the others had gone to bed, Father and Mother were sitting in the kitchen; they would talk afterward. He was all right, Father had said, but they would talk afterward. Mother had beaten the carpets and starched the curtains, but what use was this now? Father had not noticed it.

It was not well with him, it was quite serious.

And Valter knew. He knew why Father had mistaken him for Gunnar, why he had held on to his hand as they walked to the wagon, why he had stumbled at the station and here at home, why his eyes failed to see the one he talked to. And Valter had raked the yard, cleaned away all the fallen leaves, cleaned out the cowstall and the pigpen. It mattered not now, for Father would never see it. And he had been given a mouth organ of his own this evening, but he could not lift it to his lips, could not blow a single tune on it. What did it matter now?

Valter knew: Father had lost the light of his eyes.

CHAPTER VII

Soldier 128 Sträng came home from the maneuver almost blind; after a few weeks he was totally blind.

The Army doctor had said that his diseased eyes were the result of his diabetes. A film had grown over his eyeballs. The film was so thin that it was noticeable only through a magnifying glass, but it would continue to grow until his eyesight was lost. In due time it would ripen, and then it could be removed by an operation and his sight would be restored. The film might ripen in a short time, or it might take a very long time. It might be within a few months or perhaps it would require years before the operation could be undertaken. The blind soldier could do nothing but wait until that day arrived. Such was the opinion of the Army doctor.

Sträng could, however, see the difference between night and day. The light from the window seemed to his blind eyes like a weak, yellow streak, and this streak indicated to him when it was day. He must remain inside and keep quiet, but he grew restless from sitting in the cottage. During the daytime he observed the place of the yellow streak and learned his way to the door. He could manage to get out into the yard, where he felt his way with a stick. Alone he would go no farther than the gate. But he helped his wife in the barn, and he could carry in wood and water even though he was clumsy and had to walk slowly. But he was in no hurry these days; he had nothing to do except to wait for the film to ripen, the film that had grown over his eyes and robbed him of daylight.

Inside, he would sit in the rocking-chair.

"Here I sit like a blind potato," said 128 Sträng.

"Luck comes, luck goes," sighed Soldier-Hulda.

She could not help complaining to neighbors over the bad luck that had befallen them. But Sträng complained to no one as he sat in his darkness. How would it help? What would it bring him? Not the smallest crumb. He was blind as a mole, but one could do nothing about it. One must suffer and be patient and wait and hope that it would pass. And it would have its passing when the film had ripened. And they had a house, and food on the table. He had not been dismissed from service, he was still the village soldier and consequently entitled to live in the cottage. Beside his number in the Army roll, a notation had been entered: "Sick on the village." A blind soldier could not aim at an enemy, but when the film on his eyes had ripened he would get his sight back and then he would return to the service.

Now he must find some occupation while sitting here waiting. In his youth he had learned to bind nets. He sent for string and made a net needle from juniper. He had his hands, healthy and limber, and they had not forgotten to tie meshes. His hands did not need the aid of the eyes, they could handle needle and string by feeling only, they could still tie meshes into nets. And his occupation with this shortened the blind man's day.

Valter realized that he and the others worried more over Father's blindness than Father himself who suffered with it. Father never showed any sign of being depressed. In his *Instruction for the Infantry* the soldier was admonished to endure with patience inconvenience, trouble, or privation, and never to give in to despair, never complain. It was easy for the officers to instruct thus, and perhaps Father had never read it, for he never opened the book. Yet now, in his blindness, he followed it.

Sometimes, though, Father must worry. He would lie awake nights, and perhaps then, when no one was aware of it, he suffered from the loss of his sight. When Valter lay in bed at night and stared into the darkness, he could imagine how it felt to be blind. It was only black, a bottomless, impenetrable blackness. So it was to be without eyes: there was nothing. Nothing all around. Perhaps there were creatures without eyes. Fish living in the deep forest bogs might just as well be without eyes. They had nothing but the black mud to look at, nothing else. A blind person was like a fish in a mud pool. Or like a mole, dug down deep in the earth. Black, black, nothing else.

Valter lay in the dark and stared and thought and imagined until he was seized with fear that he would go blind. His eyes were open and staring, yet he saw nothing. Then he arose and stole on light feet outside. But when he opened the door ever so little, it began to lighten around him. All he had to do to lose his fear was to open the door a little. He was not blind, he had only imagined he was. In one wink he could see that it was snow-light outside, that stars glittered in the firmament above the cottage. He sighed with relief and crept into bed again. He lost the darkness as soon as he peeked through the door; it did not follow him outside.

But Father. If he went out on the stoop, the darkness went with him. He could walk out into the shining sun in the middle of the day, and the same darkness followed him and enveloped the road he took. Father could walk as far as he desired, yet the darkness would pursue him persistently. He might travel all the way to America, and the darkness would accompany him on the journey. If he walked all around the globe, it would be with him. He could never escape it, never run away from it, never hide from it, never discover a place where it wouldn't find him, where it wouldn't engulf him. He could go where he wanted and do what he wanted, but he could never shed it, never shake off his companion, his new comrade.

Father and the darkness were inseparably joined together.

Darkness had become his father's comrade, and Valter had no comrade in the forest; he must still work in the factory. Mother needed his earnings more than ever now that Father earned nothing. He would a thousand times rather have gone in the forest, with Father, under the open sky, than be penned up within the soot-black walls of the factory.

Some nights he would sleep in the factory to avoid walking home in the evening and back in the morning. He slept near the stoke-hole, and Joel-Nightstoker would cover him with an old horse blanket to keep him warm. He could sleep until five in the morning and share the coffee that Joel always brewed about that time. It was nice and quiet with Joel in the factory, except after payday when the chemist got drunk. His name was Jonas, usually called Pot-Jonas, and during the night he prepared the glass-mass that would go into the melting-pot and suffice for a day's blowing. The chemist was a stumpy man, his body square, with thick neck and long arms. His face was a tangle of bushy, red beard from which peered a pair of narrow, angry eyes. It was he who "knew the secret of glass, it was he who mixed the glowing-red glass-brew for all of them. He kneaded the dough in his troughs, a dough of sand and soda-lime and red lead and potash, into which he poured arsenic and other deadly powders. It was a frightening thought that

Pot-Jonas had death in his laboratory, in those jars. Once he had stuck a jar under Valter's nose and asked him to taste it. Valter guessed what it contained. Since then he had never dared go into the chemist's laboratory.

Some nights Pot-Jonas—more ornery and disagreeable than usual—locked himself in with his dough and his *brännvin*, but his mixture was always ready on time in the morning. The owner himself was said to be afraid of the evil man in the laboratory.

Joel-Nightstoker did not drink. He had been a member of the Lodestar, the local temperance union, for many years. In his youth he had been a blower, but when he joined the temperance lodge his conscience forbade him to blow liquor glasses. He had blown thousands upon thousands of *brännvin* glasses in his day, which he now regretted deeply. He could no longer make the tools by which the drunkards ruined their lives and dug their early graves. But he stayed on in the factory as stoker, a poorer job with less pay. For twenty years now he had walked around the furnaces as night watchman, even though his thoughts often wandered to another part of the factory—the lamp-chimney furnace; here he could have worked with a peaceful conscience.

The drinking-glass was a Devil's tool, an instrument of vice, but the lamp chimney was a harbinger of light, aiding humanity.

On his bed near one of the furnaces Valter would sometimes awaken during the night and listen to the licking fire tongues as Joel-Nightstoker fed the flames in his eternal walk around the furnaces. In that oven, so close to his bed, glowed hell itself in its many hundred degrees of heat. Joel guarded this heat, which must not rise too high nor sink too low. He was familiar with the furnaces and knew what the crucibles could stand. Not one log too many, not one too few; then he resumed his infinite wandering, from stoke-hole to stokehole. Hundreds of miles he had walked through the years, nourishing, guarding the furnace fire, tending the hell that burned in there.

To Valter there was no other hell than this—the furnace hell, the factory. "It was good luck for cottage children that factories were so close." But he did not like the factory; Ljungdala was hell.

He had learned to carry glasses without too much trouble; that was easy. But there was so much else belonging to the factory: he did not like to "learn manners."

He had risen to cooler under Master Sjölin. He cooled simple drinking-glasses intended for the under-class. He handled fine, delicate glasses into which drinks would be poured for the upper-class—wineglasses and cognac glasses from which the rich drank their expensive liquors. He handled glasses for people on all levels of society—glittering, elegant carafes for the tables of the rich and noble, simple coffee bottles for the wooden-shoe people in the cottages. He might stand and admire a wineglass just received from the stem-maker or the Master, he might imagine how an upper-class lady, with jewelry-laden fingers, lifted the glass to her beautiful lips, which quivered sarcastically or haughtily.

During the dark winter mornings the factory was lighted by the furnace fire and by the glowing glass on the blowers' pipes. Their occupation created its own light; they moved their pipes back and forth, down toward the floor, up against the ceiling; the pipes were in constant swinging motion, and their red glass-balls shattered the factory darkness. The melting mass in the crucibles glowed like a red wine, a hot wine, the hottest of wines. With the assistants' aid, it was poured into the forms, and the pipes turned it into solid objects. Like musicians, the blowers walked around in the factory and played on their pipes. No tune was heard, no melody, but from the soft mass figures were formed, taking shape obediently when breathed upon by the blowers. At the touch of their pipes the glass came to life, grew, changed form every moment. The blowers gave life to the mass with their breath.

A blower could play what he wanted on his pipe. He blew life, he created with the air from his lungs, he was a Lord Omnipotent to the red wine in the crucibles. A carrier or a cooler labored with the finished glass and ruled over nothing. But Valter wanted to try the pipes during his lunch hour, he wanted to play this instrument according to his own desire, unhindered. He wanted to create what no one had done before; he thought of lions and elephants, fishes and ships. One's thoughts might encompass all the things that existed on this earth, and also things outside the earth; mammals and fishes and ships did not suffice—Valter would try suns and moons and stars; he wanted, above all, to make those things he could not reach. But when he played the pipes, neither suns nor moons nor heavenly stars were successful; the objects he created resembled nothing that a human eye had ever seen—only grotesque pieces of glass which were thrown back into the refuse box to be melted again.

Master Sjölin suggested that it would be better if he tried preserve jars; it would not take too many years to learn to form a pickle jar.

Night guests would come to the factory. With approaching winter, almost every night some wanderer from the road would seek quarters near the furnace warmth. These were the steady vagabonds of the road, walking from factory to factory, one night in Boda, the next night in Johansfors, tonight in Ljungdala, tomorrow in Kosta or Orrefors. There was "Old Aseptin," who sold Aseptin fluid, which healed all illnesses except consumption, and even consumption in mild cases. The blowers washed their cracked and burned hands in the Aseptin. The old man had wandered about since his youth, one of the road's elders, a veteran among hobos. There was Marta's Klas, who sold almanacs, songbooks, celluloid collars, and fortune letters, which he carried in a number of small bundles on his back. There was the tinner from Långasjö who had been in Kalmar prison because he had castrated the man who stole his wife. And Salomon Bunte, who sang ditties and played an accordion— a true minstrel of the road.

All these were regular night guests, returning to the factory at definite intervals. But also unknown guests arrived, strangers from far away. Some wanted murderer or some thief might ask for night quarter; no one announced his crime if he sought shelter. Joel-Nightstoker would sometimes look at their hands: if a man had been in prison, there would be marks on his wrists from the handcuffs.

All wanderers were admitted to the factory, except gypsies, whom the owner expressly had forbidden shelter: to harbor a gypsy in that parish cost a fifty-crown fine.

Valter slept among the hobos, and this made him realize that he did not belong to the very poorest. He had a home in a cottage, he had a mother who prepared his lunch box and mended his clothes. The hobos had no home, not even a shed. They "borrowed home" every night, and everything they owned they carried in a box or a bundle. They wore all their clothes at the same time, torn clothes, worn through behind and at the knees, and from their shoes the toes peeped out without shame.

These were the road people, the lowest among the under-class, the paupers' paupers.

Valter was frightened when some of the strangers came, and he would look at their wrists, wondering what marks from handcuffs would be like. But none of the wanderers bothered him, none among them seemed to think that boys must "learn manners."

When the furnaces were banked for the Christmas holidays an ale party was to be given at the factory. The day before, they worked overtime, emptying all the cooling-pots. When Valter was ready to go to bed, he found Pot-Jonas near the furnace where his bed was. It was the day after payday, and Pot-Jonas's breath stank from *brännvin*, his eyes peered *brännvin*-bleary from his bearded face. He leered at Valter with a meaningful grin; he stuck his index finger into his mouth and pushed it slowly along his lower gum—he was removing his snuff cud.

Valter quickly suspected the meaning and turned to run. But the chemist had grabbed him from behind and now got hold of his neck with one hand while he pressed two fingers from the other hand against the boy's mouth. And between the fingers he held the cud he had just removed from his own mouth. He tried to press his old cud into Valter's mouth.

To force little boys to chew something that had been in one's own mouth—that was to teach them manners. It was very useful to them, they learned manliness, and it was entertaining fun for the grown-ups as well.

"Don't fight me, little one!"

He was only giving the little boy a taste of tobacco—was that anything to fight against? Valter closed his lips desperately. Pot-Jonas's rough fingers pressed still harder and separated his lips. The sticky, wet cud with its bitter tobacco taste nauseated him; he felt like vomiting. He opened his mouth and yelled for help. Pot-Jonas took this opportunity to get his fingers into the boy's mouth. Valter tried to spit out the tobacco, but part of the cud was already inside. Then he bit into the finger; in self-defense his teeth closed in terror.

"So you bite, you little devil!"

Now it was Pot-Jonas who yelled, as he quickly pulled out his injured finger.

His steamy, bearded face was close to Valter's, and the *brännvin* fumes flowed from his open mouth.

"You bite like an alley cat, you bastard! I'll teach you manners!"

He held up his index finger, dripping with blood, and looked around for some weapon, while his other hand held Valter securely by the neck. He would once and for all teach youngsters due respect for their elders who meant well when they instructed them in the art of chewing.

How to free himself? He must get loose at any price. Pot-Jonas was choking him, he saw stars before his eyes.

Then he kicked out. He kicked as hard as he could, and he hit Pot-Jonas right between the legs. It took. It took so well that the chemist groaned with pain, forgot himself for a moment, and let go his hold. Valter was free, and he ran.

Pot-Jonas did not pursue him; he stood still and felt his groin and swore one continuous oath. The kick had hit the sensitive spot, and Valter's wooden shoes were heavy and sharp-toed.

"You devil's brat of a bastard bitch!"

Now began a race around the furnace, a wild chase. Valter first, Pot-Jonas after. An ornery, furious man chasing a terror-stricken child. Valter threw off his wooden shoes and ran in his stockinged feet to escape. There was no place to run except round the furnace, there was no help except running. He was lighter and quicker than Pot-Jonas, who was drunk as well as clumsy. Turn after turn, and the man did not give up; he was wild, roaring like a bull. Valter must run until he fell, there was no help. Pot-Jonas would undoubtedly kill him because of the kick. He had spat out the cud, but it tasted as if it were still in his mouth. That devilish Pot-Jonas!

The chase around the furnace went on until Joel-Nightstoker happened to come in. He jumped in front of Pot-Jonas with a log in his hands.

"Let the boy alone!"

"That bastard bites and kicks!"

"Let him alone or I'll kill you!"

Joel raised his log over Pot-Jonas's head, and his threat sounded unexpectedly courageous. Pot-Jonas stopped in his tracks; he had never expected interference from little Joel.

"This is none of your business."

"Let the boy alone or I'll crush your skull!"

Pot-Jonas seemed to consider this. He was at his bravest with small boys. But Joel might hit him. And while he thought about this and argued, Valter made his escape from the furnace room. Then Pot-Jonas went into his laboratory, limping, dragging his legs, swearing at boys who had no manners.

Valter hid under some hay in the stable near by; Joel found him and brought him back to his bed near the furnace. Joel comforted him, Joel had saved him. He had discovered a comrade in Joel-Nightstoker, Joel was the comrade.

Valter kept spitting for several hours before he could go to sleep. He began spitting as soon as he woke up the following morning. He spat the whole day while he performed his duties. He spat the following day, he kept on spitting for several days. He tried to spit out the degrading, the disgraceful, the utterly nauseating taste of Pot-Jonas's cud. He seemed to have a lingering taste that he must rid himself of if he were ever to feel like a decent human being again, if he were to continue to live. It seemed as if the taste would remain with him for the rest of his life, as if finally at death he would still retain this humiliating taste in his mouth. He continued to spit for days. He spat in his dreams, he spat out thousands of cuds, but always one remained.

Soldier-Valter had not yet learned manners. He did not want to learn manners—he kept on spitting.

CHAPTER VIII

There was talk of a strike at Ljungdala. The blowers and their assistants demanded higher pay. The unrest spread to neighboring factories.

The political tension between Master Sjölin and Elmer Sandin had increased nearly to the bursting-point. Master Sjölin would address his assistant: "You damned sossy!" Master Sjölin himself had been a socialist since 1893, when he had helped organize the first local at Kosta. In 1902 he had gone on strike for suffrage and lost his job for it; it was then that he had moved to Ljungdala. Here, too, he had started a local union, but not all the workers had joined. He hated the Young Socialists, who ruined the chances of success for the decent workers. Their leader, Hinke Bergegren, had been thrown out of the party last year, and at this joyful news Master Sjölin had treated everyone to *lousbeer*. There was only one leader in the party he respected, a man all workers could trust, a man who knew when to fight and when not to fight: Hjalmar Branting. Master Sjölin knew him personally; they had met at the national conventions, and they were intimate enough to use first names.

One day at lunch Elmer Sandin pulled out a copy of *The Fire-brand*, a weekly for the Young Socialists. While Sjölin sat on his master's chair and ate his sandwiches and drank his beer, Elmer Sandin read to him:

"*The People's Friend Branting.* After the opening of a new play a brilliant crowd always gathers in Grand Hotel's elegant ballroom, where the crystal chandeliers shine as ostentatiously as they do in the Royal Palace. In thousands of workers' homes a piece of bread is divided among hungry children, but in these lofty chambers the participants drink sparkling wines and chilled champagne. And in this assemblage can always be found the editor of the *Social-Democrat*, Hjalmar Branting, with his wife, washing down the day's tribulations with sparkling champagne. In these glittering salons there is no shortage of liquors, flowers, or life's abundance and there is ever present 'the people's friend' with his silk- and jewelry-bedecked 'queen' who insists on being brought to the table by some minister or foreign diplomat. 'The people's friend,' Mr. Branting, and his 'queen'—"

Master Sjölin jumped up from his chair, his face red, his shiny skull scarlet. "Gimme that rotten sheet!"

He jerked the *Firebrand* from the assistant and crumpled and squashed the paper into a ball, which he jammed into his pocket; he would use it as it deserved to be used the next time he needed to go out.

Sandin was taken by surprise, but he said proudly: "Forceful actions are no arguments. Nor are insults."

A piece of bread stuck in Sjölin's throat in his excitement. He coughed and cleared his throat. "Forceful actions! What about the dynamite the sossies have used to blow up factories! What kind of argument is that?"

Master Sjölin's whole head was so red that Valter feared it might burst into flames. The lunch hour was ended and the blowing commenced again, but the master did not forget what his assistant had been reading about Branting; Sandin was unable to do anything right for him that day; however anxious he was to please, the master would find fault and yell at him:

"See what you did! You sossy bastard! You and your ilk should work in hell!"

Sandin worked as if nothing had happened, but a fire glowed in his eyes which all recognized. Valter did not dislike Sjölin, who was perhaps the kindest of the masters, though a little short-tempered. But Valter's feelings were with Sandin; all Young Socialists who fought the fight of freedom must suffer abuse. This they all understood, and no one was surprised. Valter was among the persecuted, and he wanted to be among them. Sandin had told him: Only the important ones were hated and reviled.

Elmer Sandin had thick, black, curly hair that fell in soft waves over his ears. He had the longest hair of anyone in the factory, and bald-headed Master Sjölin could not stand the sight of it:

"Why don't you cut off your hair so your toes don't get tangled up in it!" he would say.

The owner had forbidden meetings of the Young Socialists in the factory, and now its members gathered in Sandin's attic room. There they fought The Religious Humbug and The Joke About Heaven and, first and foremost, Militarism. Boys who might be thinking of volunteering were warned, threatened, and persuaded to desist. A few members of draft age were kept away from induction. Things happened in this club.

Banda's Valfrid had been discharged and was home again after half a year in the Army. Something had gone wrong with his head, and now he brooded. Valfrid had always been sensitive, and he had been unable to take military life. The thought of three years' enlistment had broken him. He had got it into his head that those three years would never come to an end. At last he felt convinced that he would have to serve for eternity. No one in the Army had been able to change that conviction. He was sent to a hospital and his head was examined, but he was not pretending; he had actually gone crazy from the confinement of the service. He had been sent home with a discharge, and now he still believed that he would have to serve forever and could never be freed from his contract. There was no more joy for Valfrid.

Now Soldier-Banda could see what the forty crowns had brought him. He had sold his son to the service, and when the Army had robbed the boy of his sound mind he was returned to his father.

Soldier-Sträng had this to say: Kalmar Regiment could not be blamed if a man was weak-minded.

But to the club at Ljungdala, Valfrid became a warning example: If you want to keep your senses, don't join the service!

The club sent for a new broadside from the Agitation Committee Against Military Service. The members waited for a while, then were advised that the police had confiscated the broadside; its writers had been jailed. The work was indeed hard. Sandin wrote once more and ordered the anti-military pamphlet; in their club no one would be afraid to distribute it. He also sent for the anti-military insignia. This was difficult to sell outside the club, as many people believed that it was against the law to display it. Valter bought an anti-military pin. It was a red, circular plate with a line around the edge on which was stamped the legend: *"Down with Militarism! For Peace and International Fraternization!"* On the red field was a gun, broken in two. A pair of solid workmen's hands held the broken pieces.

The Sword to be broken. The united, strong hands of organized labor to break it. The day would come when all the training-fields would be strewn with broken guns—the accomplished aim of the working-class. Valter's hands would help to liberate the world from the Sword.

He put the pin in his jacket lapel; he wore this jacket only on Sundays. The pin cost fifty öre, and he valued it highly; if he wore it at work, he might easily lose or damage it; it might get sooty from the smoke in the factory. He saved his anti-military pin for Sundays and holidays. And it looked nice on his Sunday coat. Thus, he carried the pin with the broken gun both as a decoration and as an emblem of his belief and purpose. There it sat, a red, glowing spot on his chest, easy for all to see. This red sign was like a red heart, an extra blood-red heart on top of the real one. It indicated to all who saw it where his real heart belonged, for what ideals it beat. It was his sign of faith, and his pride.

His mother looked at it and said: "Have you been decorated, boy?"

Yes, the red pin looked good, it gave light to the jacket lapel, it was almost like a medal. But Mother must have realized that it was not the sword-medal, which Corporal Hellström displayed with much bragging when he wore his uniform. And the one who carried this medal would in due time participate in throwing on the dunghill the sword-medal and other childish military insignia. The one who carried this sign was also a soldier, but a soldier of the broken gun.

Father could not see the red sign on his breast, and perhaps this was just as well—now he needn't explain. Nothing was more difficult than to explain things to Father.

On the wall of their home hung the Crown gun, model '96, above the bed where Valter had come into the world. It had hung there since the year he was born. And Soldier-Sträng's blind eyes could not discover that his youngest son had grown into a soldier who carried, not the gun belonging to the Crown, but his own gun.

It was Saturday afternoon, the work in the factory was coming to an end, when a whispering message circulated among the club members: the agitation pamphlets had arrived.

After work, five of the small boys accompanied Sandin to his attic room. They were Kalle-Miller's boys, Ernst and Teodor; Banda's Edvin; Sven, the son of the section hand; and Soldier-Valter. All understood that now there was something to be done, something of utmost importance. Sandin was highly mysterious, speaking in short sentences and in a very low voice. He took out a package that he had hidden in his closet, and pulled off the strings with trembling fingers. On the outside of the package it said only MERCHANDISE, as if it might be a package from a mail-order house. But the boys all realized that this parcel did not contain shirt fronts, wallets, combs, or brushes. The "merchandise" turned out to be a bundle of red posters. They were posters like the ones the police had confiscated earlier. The parcel contained unlawful merchandise.

The five young club members looked grim with determination as Sandin handed a poster to each one of them. Valter read his poster:

THINK FIRST!—THEN ACT!

The great thinker Leo Tolstoy has written an appeal to the soldiers of Russia. We bring his appeal to the Swedish soldiers also.

This is what Tolstoy writes:

"Suppose you are brought to a mill or a factory, and you see from a distance a great crowd of people. The governor, the sheriff, the bailiff, and others approach the crowd and make speeches.

"At first the mass of people are quiet, then they begin to cry out, louder and louder, and the authorities disappear. You might guess that these people are farmers and workers in revolt, and that you have been brought here to suppress the revolt.

"The authorities approach the crowd many times, and retreat. The cries become louder and louder, and you see military officers consulting with one another. You are ordered to load your gun with live bullets. You see before you people like yourself, from whose midst you were taken when you enlisted; men in blue jeans, short jackets, wooden shoes; women dressed like your mother or wife.

"First you are ordered to shoot over the heads of the crowd. But the crowd does not disperse; the yells grow more intense, and you are ordered to shoot in earnest into the crowd.

"You have been told that you are not responsible for your shots. *But you know that you and no one else has killed the man who stumbled in his blood back there, you know that he would still be alive if you had not shot him.*

"What would you do?

"It is of no use that you today turn your gun aside and refuse to kill your brother. Tomorrow the same story will be repeated. And therefore you must, whether you wish to or not, search your conscience as to what this is that forces you to shoot on your defenseless brethren.

"It is a lie that the commander alone is responsible for your actions, and not you.

"Can your conscience be with someone other than yourself? With the sergeant, the corporal, the colonel, or anyone else?

"No! No one else can decide what you should do or not do, because *man is always responsible for his actions!*"

Comrade, remember your duty to your fighting class-brethren!

The Anti-Military Agitation Committee

All the members of Valter's club read the poster, solemnly and silently. Valter had never read anything by Tolstoy, the great thinker, whose thoughts were allowed in Russia but forbidden in Sweden.

These printed words were words of open truth—that must be why the poster was hated and suppressed.

"Swell!" said Sandin.

All helped to count the number of posters received. There were exactly five hundred, as they had ordered, said Sandin. The appeals were printed on thin, poor paper and must be handled carefully or they would fall to pieces.

"What's that noise?" Sandin opened the door and peered out into the dim corridor; he felt sure he had heard someone. He closed the door and lectured the boys: This was dangerous business, they could never be too cautious. The poster "Think First!—Then Act!" had been confiscated under the criminal code, chapter 8, paragraph 3. Birger Swahn, who had ordered the printing, was in jail for one year and three months, and two of his friends had been sentenced to a year each for distributing the appeal. And according to Swedish law, anyone having anything to do with the poster was liable to a maximum of six years' imprisonment.

"How old are you?" asked Sandin, looking from one to another of the young club members.

"I'm eleven, nearly twelve," said Valter.

"I'm the same," said Banda's Edvin.

"I'm a year older," said Ernst.

"I'm fourteen," said Sven.

And Teodor was just twelve.

"None of you is over fifteen?"

None of the five had reached this age.

"That's fine. You must distribute the posters. You're under age and not liable to punishment."

At the word *punishment* the boys looked at one another. Ernst turned a little away, Edvin's eyes twitched, but the other three remained fearless.

Sandin divided the posters in five piles, a hundred in each, and named the places where each of the boys should operate. Tomorrow was Sunday, a good day to begin. Valter got the church green as his place: here he must distribute his appeals after the service.

"Remember to keep quiet! Not a word must leak out! You don't know where the posters came from! You didn't get them from me! You understand, boys?"

They understood. They knew nothing about the posters, they had not received them from Elmer Sandin in Ljungdala. This was like a conspiracy, with oath and all; they liked it.

But Banda's Edvin kept silent and did not pick up his bundle. "I dare not," he stuttered.

"You're a coward! You're as old as the others!"

"I'm afraid of Father. He'll beat me up if he ever learns."

"He need never learn!"

"But if he should—"

"Dare you go alone to the privy?"

Edvin started to cry.

"I'll take his posters," offered Valter.

"That mother's suckling couldn't do it, of course!" said Sandin. "I'll get another boy." Banda's boys were all feeble-minded; better not get Edvin mixed up in this.

Valter trudged homeward with his hundred red posters well hidden under his shirt. He carried the forbidden words of a great thinker at his heart. A great thinker thought great thoughts, and these thoughts had reached him on the poster. Fly-leaves they were also called; this paper flew in secret like a red bird over the country. It was dangerous to let the bird out to fly, it was a confiscated and criminal bird. Because this bird sang the song of truth. It sang the truth to the comrades in uniform, in butcher uniform. They must learn to think before they obeyed orders. Nothing was more dangerous than to tell people to think.

One hundred of these dangerous red birds were entrusted to Valter, and he would let them loose tomorrow at church. They would fly out in freedom over the parish with their message of truth. He was not afraid, because the one who did the right had nothing to be afraid of, come what might. He was proud that he— little as he was—had been entrusted with something for which older comrades sat in prison. And he decided to show his worth, even though under age.

He put the posters under his pillow and told his mother that he intended to go to the church in the morning. She was surprised: usually he did not go to church. He corrected her—he had not said he would go to church, he had said he would go to the church. Beyond that, he let her think what she wanted. They must know nothing about the posters at home. The appeal was directed to his father also, but even if Father had had his sight, Valter would not have given him one. He was not worried about Father, who would never shoot at a comrade.

The winter Sunday was bitterly cold, with a wind that bit the nose. Valter tramped the church road, his hands deep in his pockets, miserably cold. He wore a knitted sweater, but the wind cut right through it, making it feel as thin as a cobweb. But against his chest he carried a bundle of papers which helped to keep him warm.

He arrived at the church as the bells rang for the service to begin. But his errand could not be attended to until after the service. Then people would come out onto the church green and stand in groups for a few moments, talking of the parish gossip, before they returned home. He looked for churchgoers from Strängshult, his own village, but didn't discover anyone who might know him, and this was good luck. He was a little afraid of Corporal Hellström, the bailiff, who usually attended church. Sandin had urged them to be on their guard against the sheriff and the bailiff. Black-bearded Hellström had been to his home many times and would recognize Soldier-Sträng's boy. Perhaps Valter had had the good luck to choose a day when Corporal Hellström lay in bed sick.

Valter went into one of the church stables and sat down. Here among the horses it was warm and comfortable, with the smell of horse manure, oats, and horses. He thought over how he would go about his business. He must be careful not to do anything foolish. He must think first, and then act. It would be foolish of him to walk out onto the church green and holler: Come here! Come here! I'll give you an anti-military fly-leaf! "Think First!—Then Act!" Then he would get rid of the whole bunch quickly, but after a few minutes everyone would know what it was all about, and someone would send for the minister and the county councilman. That would ruin everything. A fool would go about it in that way. Not he—he would act much more wisely. He would not go around and distribute the posters to just anybody, without discrimination. What use would there be in handing them to old men or women who never would hold a gun in their hands? Why should they be asked not to shoot on their fighting class-brethren? No, he would choose men of military age, those who had just completed their service or boys about to be called. And he would sneak silently from one to another, thus preventing his actions from being noticed. Silently he would liberate his forbidden red birds, and no one would know a thing until they had all flown on their way.

Soldier-Valter sat in the stable and thought, then he acted.

The service was over and the congregation was trickling out to the green. First came a group of older, mourning-dressed parishioners; there must have been a funeral. Then Valter spied three young men in uniform, in polished boots and spurs. They must be cavalry recruits home on leave. He approached them and handed each one a red fly-leaf:

"This is for you! With my compliments!"

The soldiers stared in embarrassment at the papers. One of them, more bright-looking than the others, whispered something to his comrades. Then all three quickly pushed their papers into their pockets. They must have realized that the appeal was forbidden; perhaps the bright-looking man had recognized "Think First!—Then Act!"

It had started well. Valter's courage grew. He repeated his performance with a few farm boys who were leaning against the churchyard wall: "This is for you! With my compliments!"

One of them said with a vacant stare: "What is it?"

Valter did not answer, but left them quickly. Such fools! "What is it?" They could read the paper and find out. They should be capable of that much thinking. But farm boys were not enlightened like factory workers, nor were they as keen.

Valter mixed with the crowd, walking about casually with his hands in his pockets but with his eyes wide open: as soon as he saw a man of the right kind, his right hand moved quickly away from its pocket to his jacket, where the forbidden birds were hidden against his heart—zoops! a bird had flown. It had taken only a second, and before the recipient realized what had taken place, Valter was somewhere else. There was a great crowd at church today—he moved from one end of the green to the other.

The old dean came walking from the church and entered the parish house. Valter omitted to hand him a fly-leaf. He also ignored some of the broad-legged farmers who, with an air of owning the world, followed the dean to the parish hall; they were, of course, hardened conservatives, and the great Tolstoy's thoughts would be lost on them. He would not waste his valuable papers—he thought first and then acted.

In vain he looked for people who might be workers in the neighboring glass factories; they were not church-going people. The workers came here only for some parish meeting, and it looked as if some meeting was to take place in the parish hall today.

Suddenly his heart seemed to stop: Corporal Hellström came walking toward him, his beard flowing, his bailiff cap with the yellow band on his head, the sword-medal on his coat. He was not sick, then; he was at church as usual. What bad luck! Valter hurried aside before Hellström saw him.

Now he must be more careful and take it easy for a while; the bailiff might soon leave. Valter slid into the stable, pretending he was looking for someone to ride home with. A fat, kind farm wife, eating her lunch, looked at him with curiosity.

"You look sick and hungry, little boy."

She handed him a piece of bread with a good slice of salt pork sausage. It tasted so good that he swallowed it almost without chewing.

"You must be from one of the factories, of course. They are always so pale, those glass boys."

The farm wife seemed intelligent; he shook hands with her and thanked her for the food and made her in return a gift of one of his fly-leaves, "Think First!—Then Act!" In so doing, he broke his original plan—the old woman would never be fit for military service, would never be tempted to shoot down the working-class. But she looked friendly and good-hearted, and as she sat alone in the stable he wanted to cheer her with Tolstoy's thoughts. It might do some good, one never knew.

He still had two thirds of his bundle left. He got an idea: he put papers in the horse blankets and the hay sacks, he hid them in sleighs and sledges outside the stable. This was less risky, and the fly-leaves would be found later and read at leisure. But he no longer could be sure that they reached the right people; this was really a gamble.

He still had half left. He looked around the corner of the stable and wondered if he hadn't better hide the rest of his criminal papers at home, for the time being. A youth some years older than himself came running in his direction. He came up to Valter with one of the red papers in his hand.

"Are you handing out these?"

Valter need not be afraid—the boy wore the broken gun and the black club tie, he was one of the Young Socialists.

"Yes."

"Are you from Johansfors factory?"

"From Ljungdala."

"I'm a member of the Boda club." He spoke hurriedly and tensely and pointed up the church green. "You're in trouble. How many left?"

"About fifty."

"Someone reported it. The bailiff is looking for you."

Near the church wall Valter could see Corporal Hellström with a cluster of men around him. They spoke loudly and gesticulated, one of them pointing toward the stables. One of the papers must have reached the wrong person, and now everything was lost.

"I'll help you!" said the Boda man. "Gimme your bundle! I'll distribute them at home."

Valter put a few of the posters inside his coat and gave the rest to the older boy. Now "Think First!—Then Act!" was in safe hands.

"Run before they recognize you!"

Hellström was already approaching with long strides, followed by a group of sturdy, forceful farmers.

"Run and hide in the forest!"

Valter disappeared behind the stables, and with a few jumps he reached the forest. The snow lay deep and unmarked but solid enough to carry his light body. Now he ran like a stag, fell and sank into the snow as deep as his armpits, got up and was on his way again. Then he reached a well-tramped timber road and ran until his insides seemed to be burning with heat and caused a pain in his chest. He stopped and listened, but no one seemed to be following him. He slowed his pace, turned off across the wastelands, and reached the highway. He was two miles from the church, and no one was pursuing him. He had managed to escape.

He returned home, tired but satisfied with his church visit. He had liberated fifty of the dangerous red posters with Tolstoy's appeal; they would now preach their truth and enlightenment. They would light up the parish. And he had done a deed for which many of his comrades were in prison. He had today done something that called for at least one year in prison. He was well pleased with his Sunday.

A few days later, at lunch, Elmer Sandin called him aside and showed him a piece in the *Småland-Posten*:

A SOSSY'S DEED

A correspondent from Uppvidinge writes us:

"After church services last Sunday a painful occurrence took place. When the churchgoers gathered on the green, several among them were handed a Young Socialist pamphlet called "Think First!—Then Act!" which has been declared illegal and confiscated. Disturbing the church peace, sad to relate, was a misguided youth who, according to observers, was not yet of confirmation age. The authorities were notified and took action against the sossy's daring as soon as it was discovered, but unfortunately the scoundrel had managed to run away and escaped this time the punishment he so well deserved. He probably belonged to one of the glass factories in the neighborhood."

It is high time precautions were taken to prevent a repetition
of similar outrages on the very Sabbath near God's House.
And may the Lord protect us from these organized hordes of
lawbreaking, hating, misguided, useless scoundrels.

Soldier-Valter, the soldier with the broken gun, had begun his
fight.

CHAPTER IX

Soldier-Sträng kept busy at his net-binding frame. He tied large and small meshes, thousands and more thousands of meshes; his hands found their way in the dark. He made strong nets from "bear thread" which no fish could manage to tear. When he finished a net sixty feet long, he began on a new one. He sat working in the evenings and was not interrupted by the falling dusk, for darkness was already with him; no lamp need be lit for his sake.

"A blind man saves on light," said Soldier-Sträng.

He sat in the rocking-chair with the water pail and a scoop next to him so he needn't rise each time he had to drink. He sat and waited for the film to ripen, until it could be cut away from his eyes and let in light.

The cottage's old gray cat lay on the floor next to the rocker and kept him company in his darkness. Sometimes the farmers in whose employ he was would come to visit their soldier and inquire about his sickness and his blindness. He would hand them the certificate from the Army doctor: "Soldier 128 Sträng, due to cataracta diabetica, is presently incapable of military service, attested by my hand." But they were no wiser after reading the paper, for no one understood the name of the disease. They worried about the work on his place—who would take care of the field while the soldier was sick? The farmers feared that the village might be made responsible for the tilling and harvesting of the plot. Thus, they had reason to be concerned. But their blind soldier comforted them and replied that he would be responsible for the sowing this spring; his son Anton was now sixteen and could work like a full-grown. He was employed in the stone quarry at Hermanstorp, but he had been promised time off to come home for the spring work and for the harvesting. These were comforting words to the villagers from their blind soldier.

Sträng was supposed to eat nourishing dishes, and Hulda tried to obtain fresh food for him according to the doctor's prescription. He should eat fresh meat, and this was difficult to come by now in winter. When Aldo Samuel slaughtered a newborn calf, Hulda bought a piece for the sick man. Gunnar and Valter ogled the calfmeat on their father's plate. It did not surprise her that the boys were greedy for the juicy, delicious-smelling meat. But they never asked for a taste of it; they would not steal food from their blind father.

Hulda let her husband believe that they all were eating meat, and this was difficult, for the blind one had his suspicions. He listened to his wife's and his sons' chewing before he touched the food on his plate.

"Eat!" said Hulda. "This is nourishing food."

"Are you eating meat, all of you?" wondered her husband.

"Of course. I told you so."

"You too, Hulda?"

"Yes—I've told you several times!"

Hulda and the boys were eating potatoes and salt herring with their bread.

"Gunnar?" asked the father. "Are you eating meat?"

"I? Yes, I am."

Gunnar was chewing his herring and had no answer ready. But his mother stared into his eyes.

"Yes!" Gunnar hurried to explain. "Of course I have meat!"

"He's eating well," the mother added.

"Gunnar needs it; he's working in the mill."

"He's got a piece—do you believe me now?"

"The boys need nourishing food. They are growing."

At last the blind man tasted the meat that Hulda had cut into small pieces on his plate.

"You must eat well, Valter. You work in the factory."

"I've a big chunk in my mouth, Father," said Valter. He had his mouth full of bread, and he chewed as he thought he would have done had his mouth been full of meat.

"That's good. You have to grow, boy."

"He's growing too fast," said the mother.

"So much more food does he need," retorted the father. "Will you have another piece of meat, Valter?"

"I can't eat any more, Father."

"I wonder—" His son did not sound very convincing.

"He has had enough," assured the mother.

"Yes, I'm full up!"

"You don't want any more at all?"

"I don't want any more!" said Valter firmly.

"There, you hear," said Hulda. "He's satisfied!"

"It's awfully good meat!" Valter added and smacked his lips to be on the safe side.

This performance had to be repeated at each meal before the father began eating the meat that had been bought for him. Calf steak was served the diabetic man day after day, and at last he asked his wife with some surprise:

"Do you still have some of that piece of calfmeat left?"

"A little."

"It must have been a big piece."

"It was a whole quarter," replied Hulda, forced to tell a lie.

"Hm. I thought you only bought a small piece."

"It was a fourth part of a milk-fed calf."

"Hmm. I thought it was a newborn calf."

"Aldo Samuel had a big milk-fed calf."

"Well, then I understand how the meat lasts," said the blind one thoughtfully. "But where did you get the money for a whole quarter?"

One single lie will help nothing.

"I had saved some from the lingonberries. I picked and sold a lot."

"You didn't mention that to me."

"I forgot all about it."

Sträng had managed his house well while healthy. Hulda was credulous and easily taken advantage of; he could figure things better, and Hulda had been glad to depend on him. And he knew that she could never hide money from him. Because of this, he now had something to think about.

Next time Aldo Samuel came to visit, the blind soldier asked the Alderman: "Have you slaughtered a big milkfed calf recently?"

"No. Only a newborn calf."

"Did Hulda buy a piece from you?"

"Yes, you know I sold a piece to her."

"I know. Was it only a small piece?"

"About eight pounds. I couldn't let her have a whole quarter."

Sträng had received information. From eight pounds of calfmeat, all four of them had eaten for several weeks. It would have had to be a big calf for a quarter of it to suffice such a long time. Hulda was discovered.

The soldier spoke to his wife: "You spoke the truth to me while I had my sight. Why must you lie to me after I'm blind?"

"For your own good. You must eat well."

"I don't want better food than the rest of you."

"Then you'll never get well."

"Well or not, I'll never eat meat while you others look on. I'm not that sick. Remember what I have said."

Now Hulda had to remember. She could do nothing else, once he had told her. It was not a good deed to lie to a blind man, but she had done so with the kindest intentions. But she should have known how her husband would take it. She knew Nils Sträng, she had been his wife now for twenty-five years.

After Sträng's order, the remainder of the calfmeat was divided equally among the family members at the next meal. The meat was juicy and easy to chew, but it didn't taste so good as Valter had imagined it would when he watched his father eat it alone. It was wrong to be greedy for food that Father needed to get well; it was worse to eat some of it. But Father wanted it that way. He shared what he had. They were no longer comrades in work, but Father remained the same comrade.

Spring came, the yard turned green, the wagtails arrived, one by one, and the starlings came in flocks. During clear April days with sun bathing the yard, Sträng would move his rocker and his net out onto the stoop. He could discern a pale yellow light and he felt that it was the sun. He liked to sit in the warmth and know that the sun was still there. Between him and the sun was the obscuring film before his eyes which must ripen and be cut away. He waited. Soon he would journey to the doctor and find out how many days of waiting were left.

One Sunday when the sun was shining he asked Valter to walk with him a bit; he wanted to go to his fields.

Valter held his father's hand and walked beside him. He walked in the wheel track and let Father walk on the even edge of the road. The blind man carried his stick in the other hand, but he hardly needed it when Valter was with him. They walked slowly. Father stopped now and then when his breath gave out, and Valter too stopped. When walking together from work in the forest, Father had never left him behind; he would never leave his father behind now.

Once when Valter had been little, they had walked together through the wastelands and Father had held him by the hand. He remembered the spring day when they had gone to the Big Field. Today they walked the same road together and the same sun shone upon them. But now it was he who led Father by the hand.

He lent his eyes to Father to show the way. But he pretended he was not leading him; he walked as if he were just holding his hand for the fun of it. If his father stepped too close to the edge of the road, he pulled on the hand casually, as if he just happened to.

They stopped at the Little Field—Father had asked him to tell him when they reached it. Sträng stumbled a few steps and felt for the stile. His hands recognized the posts he had cut and split in the forest, posts he had put up and removed hundreds of times. A stone lay close by the stile opening, and the soldier put his foot on it and nodded, remembering: he had intended many times to blast that stone out; perhaps he wouldn't be able to now.

Valter told him that the edge of the ditch was covered with the early-blooming hepaticas.

"Yes, yes—they grow here in spring. Yes—"

Sträng walked a few steps, and then bent down and felt the ground with his hand. He rose, a little embarrassed, with wet earth on his fingers; he had not gone far enough to reach the edge where the flowers were. Valter climbed the stile noisily, pretending not to have seen his father's movement; he could have told him not to bother with the hepaticas when the wastelands were full of them; he felt the need of comforting his father for the failure.

The blind man sat down on the stone at the stile.

"Keep quiet a moment, Valter! Listen!"

His son stopped the noise of the stile posts and both listened. Something was ringing in the air high above them; they heard a clear, distinct sound. Valter looked up in all directions, but saw nothing, not the smallest little speck under the bright sty.

"The lark is above the field," said the father.

Somewhere above their heads they heard the clear singing. Valter recognized the sound from earlier springs, but however much he craned his neck he was unable to discover the singing bird.

"Do you see it?" asked the soldier.

"No. I don't see anything."

"She's right above."

Valter could truthfully say that he did not see the lark singing above the field, however much he strained his eyes, and it pleased him that he could say this. This time he had no advantage over Father, this time they were equals: neither of them could see the lark.

"Don't you see the bird yet?"

"No, Father."

He was glad he could repeat the assurance.

The clear note of joyous birdsong reached them from above, streaming down from the heavens over the small gray field that lay naked and threadbare after the winter. It was a light, ringing sound that streamed over them, played by nothing visible; it was the air itself under the heavens which played for them.

The soldier turned his eyes upward and "looked." It was as though the blind one believed he would discover the lark that his seeing son had been unable to locate. He listened and "looked" for a few moments, sitting on the stone expectantly. Then he rose, as if suddenly something had come to his mind, and they continued their walk through the wastelands.

Valter avoided looking at his father's eyes. They no longer shone with recognition; they were not the eyes he remembered. He did not see Father in them.

They met Banda's Valfrid, who looked down at the ground and walked by without greeting them. His mind was clouded, there was no object in speaking to him. If spoken to, he would answer that he was in a hurry, that the service required all his time. He worried over his foolishness in signing up with the Army for time and eternity. He had his discharge papers, stating that he was free from the service forever, but this did not help him. Nor did it help to tell him he was free, not even when his own father, Soldier-Banda, told him so. Valfrid would only answer: He was in a hurry, the service required his time. Valter turned and looked after him. Valfrid continued his walk, staring at the ground, brooding. Militarism had taken his mind.

Valter glanced at his emblem, which today adorned his Sunday jacket; the words flamed in red: "*Down with Militarism!*"

The soldier and his youngest son walked side by side on the road, and darkness walked with the soldier.

The wheel tracks had dried after the spring rains, but water still ran and foamed in the ditches. Between the Little Field and the Big Field they met a group of boys who were out on their Sunday activities. They stopped and gaped at Soldier-Sträng and Soldier-Valter, who walked along holding hands like a pair of small children. Valter looked rigidly ahead and pretended that he was not aware of their insults. He wanted to get by the group as quickly as possible. But Ossian Flink was among them, and he was always one to pick a fight; he turned and walked behind Valter, tramping on his heels; he need not be afraid of the blind soldier.

"Are you out grazing your father?" teased Ossian.

Valter threatened him with the closed fist of his free hand.

"You should have your mother hold that hand, babyface!"

His father stopped and asked whom they had met. At this, Ossian took to his heels, but did not forget to turn and thumb his nose.

"Were they boys from the factory?"

"No, just some brats," retorted Valter, enraged.

His father asked no more questions. Valter had been insulted because of him. Flink's boy had wanted to ridicule him, but it had hit Father. Ossian was such a fool; he had thought he could make Valter feel ashamed because he held his blind father by the hand; so hellishly dumb was he. Perhaps Valter had mentioned some time that he and Father were comrades in the forest, and that Father was so strong he could carry a twelve-inch log on his shoulder, and that his aim was so good he could hit the smallest speck eight hundred feet away. Valter had been childish in those days and had bragged a little. And now Ossian wanted to get even with him, since Father had turned blind. That was how stupid he was.

At the Big Field the soldier stopped again and leaned against the stile. His nostrils narrowed as he inhaled the earth's smell from last autumn's furrows; they now lay pale and cracked in the sun.

"It's time to harrow."

He could smell the condition of the field. It was time to begin spring work. But he must borrow a team from the village, and the farmers must attend to their own fields first; the soldier-acre came last. Now Anton must come home and help with the sowing.

"It'll be awfully dry before we get the team."

He sounded worried about the spring work. And Valter heard him mumble a word that hurt him deeply: "Feeble."

For the first time Valter heard what his father thought of himself: "Feeble." He was leaning against the stile and knew from the smell that his field was ready for sowing, and he mumbled: "Feeble."

Father had never let a word of complaint escape him. It was bad to be diabetic and blind as a mole, but Father always said to Mother and to all of them that things could have been worse. He could have had consumption and contaminated them all. That would have been worse. He could have done something evil and been put in prison, with his good name ruined for all time. That would have been worse. He could have lost his mind and been penned up in the insane asylum like an animal in its stall. That would have been worse.

"A soldier must always have a courageous heart and never in adversity become a victim of despair—"

But now he had said that he was a "feeble" person, and his youngest son had heard it. He had mumbled the word too loud. Valter played with the stones in the ditch, giving the water a freer flow. He must say something to Father now. He could say that it wouldn't be long before the film over his eyes was ripe and could be cut. He could say that the doctor would surely cut it away this summer. It might not be long before he had his sight back. The film would surely ripen fast when its time came. But it wouldn't ripen fast enough to permit Father to harrow the Big Field this spring. Father's worry concerned the spring work, and this gave Valter his cue. He poked the earth with a stick and said that the field was not dry yet; it was all right if the harrowing waited awhile; the moisture was still in the ground. When he poked with his stick like this, he realized that there was no need to hurry with the sowing.

So spoke the son who had his sight.

A young spruce stood close to the stile, and the soldier felt its trunk with his hand. Someone had in mischief made an ax cut, and his fingers happened to touch the deep wound, from which pitch oozed. The tree was injured and its wound bled. The gluey pitch, the spruce's running red blood, stuck to the blind man's fingers. He mumbled—this tree ought to be felled, and it was a pity for such a young tree, its glory gone.

At the edge of the field grew a wide pussy-willow bush, its buds ready to burst. Valter broke off a twig and handed it to his father, who held it under his nose and smelled it. He felt the soft yellow buds with his fingers. It was like touching downy baby birds in their nest.

"The willows are a-bursting, yes—"

Then once more he felt the wounded, pitchy spruce. A tall, healthy spruce in its growingest years was bleeding, wounded deep in its life, and there would be no joy with that tree any more.

Feeble.

His father had not answered when Valter spoke of the harrowing of the field. Valter didn't know what more he could say. He kept poking in the ditch with his stick, helping the water along in its stream; it was fun to watch the liberation of anything pent-up.

A long silence ensued. The soldier remained standing by the injured tree. Then he took a few steps by himself toward a juniper.

"Are you here, Valter?"

The juniper answered nothing, but the boy hurried to him. "Here I am!"

"Wondered if you had left me."

"I have been standing here."

"It was so quiet—that's why I wondered."

They resumed their walk. Valter held on to his father's rough fingers. How could Father imagine he would leave him! Before, when they had walked together—while he was so little—Father had never left him. He would never leave Father.

On they walked, past the Big Field. 128 Sträng and his son walked side by side over the soldier-acre this April Sunday. Red-hued birchtops stretched high toward the clear, bright spring sky, the larks sang over the gray earth in the Big Field and the Little Field. The sun flowed down over the wastelands until the eyes hurt. But with the soldier walked darkness, following him like a steadfast friend. Darkness had become his inseparable companion and comrade.

But Soldier-Sträng had another comrade—his son, who lent him some of his light.

CHAPTER X

The summer of 1909 began with lock-outs and rain and much talk about the Czar, and ended with the big strike.

The Czar of all Russia, "the world's greatest tyrant," came to Stockholm to visit Sweden's King. A sossy—Hjalmar Vang—was to shoot the Czar, but couldn't get close enough; instead he shot a Swede, General Bäckman, and then himself. Many sossies were thrown into prison.

The lock-out was society's latest deviltry. The word itself was given the widest interpretations; the workers would be locked out of the factories, said the simple folk, the idiots. To be locked out was the same as to be fired, driven away from the job even if one wished to work. It was robbing the worker of his self-respect, making him feel useless and superfluous, said Elmer Sandin. Mr. Lundevall, the owner of Ljungdala, tried the new method: one evening in July he ordered the furnace fires extinguished, and no one knew when they would be lit again. Now Joel-Nightstoker could take a rest from his eternity walk—his fires were killed because of the lock-out.

But other happenings were brewing. Not many days passed before the workers hit back: General strike! General strike! was the

call echoing through the country, on everyone's lips, heard everywhere. They must fight, the deciding battle had begun at last, the
Great Fight was on.

And it was then that the great calm descended. When the big
battle began, it grew quiet and peaceful. Now all furnaces shut
down, all factories closed their doors, all sawmills came to a stop,
all machinery wheels slowed to a standstill. No glass boxes were
packed, no glass wagons rolled, the roads lay silent. Now it was
apparent how much commotion and din work had caused, now,
when the calm descended, when the battle began. The glass workers were idle, picking berries in the wastelands, fishing in the lakes,
walking unhurriedly in clusters. In the evenings they gathered at
the railroad station, talked of the Great Fight, looked at the trains,
which rolled as before on the shiny rails—the only noise to disturb
the calm. The railroads were not involved, and this was bitterly
disappointing.

Valter no longer went to the factory. He participated in the fight
by resting from his job, a wonderful fight he hoped long to enjoy.
He did not feel that he was missing anything, he felt that he had
been liberated from something. This was the best summer so far in
his life.

But Mother was short of money when she wanted to go to the
store, and Father could no longer have the nourishing food he was
supposed to have.

Now Valter had plenty of time to hate the "enemy." Mr. Lundevall
was his nearest enemy. Lundevall had never done him any wrong,
had never said an unkind word to him, but to Valter all employers were personified in Mr. Lundevall. His big belly represented
all employers' bellies; it grew in size until it became one immense
capitalist pouch, containing all that the upper-class had stolen.
If Valter doffed his cap to that "thief belly," he doffed it to the

whole upper-class, to the enemy. Therefore, he walked the road proudly and did not greet Mr. Lundevall. For the battle was on, the Big Fight.

This summer was fought the Battle of Calm and Stillness. And they walked silent and quiet, those who knew what it cost.

During those misty, rainy summer days Soldier-Sträng sat inside at his net frame. Meshes were tied and grew into whole nets, and the soldier's cat lay on the floor and watched as if expecting the nets to catch fish for him here on dry land, inside the cottage. On the bureau stood the pictures of the America-relatives; there stood Albin, Ivar, Dagmar, and Fredrik, looking down on their blind father in the rocking-chair. Nothing had as yet been written to them about the film over his eyes.

Sträng had been to the doctor once more, but the doctor had said that the film was not yet ripe. It would be a while before it could be cut. He could only sit and wait for the light.

Balk-Emma said it was nothing but cataracts in his eyes. If they could find a sty-cutter, he would get his sight back at once. It was no more difficult than lancing a boil. But there was no one hereabouts nowadays who could perform the sty-cut; in the old days they used to stand around at every fair, but it was different then.

Sträng sat and waited. Outside, the swallows flew like arrows, crisscrossing the yard in all directions, disappearing under the cottage roof. They built their nests against the bark under the sod. Toward evening the crickets played in the grass. On the pear tree the August fruit turned yellow, the good, sweet sugar pears that melted like lumps of butter in one's mouth and were now forbidden the diabetic invalid.

Valter started school again. One evening as he returned home he saw his father on the bench under the pear tree. He whistled as he walked toward him, so his father would understand that he was back.

"Come here, Valter!"

Father stretched his hands toward him, felt along his thighs, his back, his shoulders, until his hands rested on his head.

Valter was a little surprised at Father's action; later he would remember that evening.

"Have you grown any?"

"Two inches since last year."

"You seem narrow across the shoulders."

Now Father's fingers were on his cheekbones.

"You have no flesh on your face. Are you a pale-face?"

"No, I'm not pale," assured Valter.

"Are you telling me the truth?"

"I am. My face is almost red."

"You should have more flesh."

"My jaws are fat, Father."

All boys working in the factory were called pale-faces. And he, too, was undoubtedly a pale-face, but he hadn't thought about it. Now he would have liked to swell up and grow fat for a moment, for only a few minutes while Father felt his body. He could not deceive Father's fingers: he was pale and skinny.

But if Father could have seen himself! The sick man's face was close to him, and Valter could see the deep furrows in his cheeks, the black rings under his eyes, the pouchy skin hanging empty below his chin. All his front teeth were gone. Father was forty-five years of age, the youngest in his platoon. He was younger than Banda and Flink and Hellström and Lönn. But this last year his face had turned old. He was as thirsty as ever and drank as much as before. And he mixed vinegar with the well water to make it quench his thirst better.

Nothing had been right here at home since Father had become ill. There was not the same order as before—Mother could never take Father's place.

"It's a long time since I last saw you," said Soldier-Sträng to his youngest son.

It had been a year. Since Father had left for the maneuver last fall. He knew from the mark in the doorpost that he had grown two inches since then, and he would have liked to show this to Father. He would have liked to show him how big and tall he now was. But he couldn't.

He sat down on the bench beside his father. The swallows were flying close—in circles, diving down, twittering, sailing on. They had their sight; their eyes were so sharp that they could shoot like arrows into their narrow, invisible holes under the roof sod. Here under the pear tree, their wings brushed by Father, who sat in darkness. If Father had the eyes of only one swallow, if he could have borrowed one pair of their eyes. Then he could have seen his youngest son, who had grown two inches since last year.

The crickets played in the grass. They sounded like the playing of a violin, a violin with strings of grass, which had only one melody, knew only one tune, and played it every evening. It was a peaceful August evening with shyly approaching twilight; Valter was to remember it later.

Father took him again by the shoulder.

"I would have liked to see you once more."

His eyes were turned on Valter; for a moment he imagined that Father saw him as before.

There was something strange about Father this evening. Valter felt it the whole time. Father said he wanted to see him once more.

But the film would soon ripen and be cut away, and then he could see him as many times as he wanted. Why, then, did he speak of "once more"? That was the strange thing.

"Anton wants to go next spring."

Sträng's hand remained on the thin boy-shoulder. Valter's eyes looked questioningly at his father: Yes, Anton would go to America next year. But before that time the film on Father's eyes would ripen; before then he would have his sight back. Father would undoubtedly see Anton before he emigrated. It was a long time till next spring.

"But you and your brother will remain," said Sträng.

Yes, Gunnar and he would be left. And Valter had a suspicion that his father was worried about something concerning him and Gunnar. He sat quietly on the bench; Father must not think he was in a hurry to leave him. And Father wanted him to remain.

"I hope one of you will stay at home."

Mother was calling Valter—it was milking-time and he must fetch the cow from the wastelands. But he remained sitting beside his father, he couldn't leave now.

Sträng's voice had grown hoarse and clouded lately, and sounded broken. Now, suddenly, it came clear and strong as he said:

"She'll need someone—one of you."

A swallow shot by. He noticed the change in Father's voice, and this struck him more strongly than the words. His mother called again, and he must leave at once, with half his thoughts on Father's words, wondering what they meant. He had spoken of *someone* who would need *someone.* Yes, that was what he had said.

The cowbell tinkled back in the road; the cow was at the gate, waiting to come home. She would stand there toward evening, rubbing her neck against the gate until all the hair was gone.

"I hope one of you will stay home—one of you two."

Someone must stay at home. One of two. But Valter's thoughts lingered only a moment on the meaning of this. His mother's calls urged him to hurry—the cow must be milked immediately.

There was one date that Valter Sträng in years to come would ever hate and abhor—the 29th of the month. That day was never again the same to him as other days of the month. The very number became obnoxious to him, it seemed to irritate him even with its sound as it came around each month. He never would expect anything nice to happen to him on that date.

The 27th of August was a Friday. He returned from school in the late afternoon. Mother and Gunnar were carrying in the rye from the Little Field. They gathered a few sheaves in a bundle, tied them together with a rope, and carried the rye on their backs to the barn. It had been poor drying-weather, and the rye was heavy. Valter was hungry and went to the kitchen for a piece of bread, as he often did when Mother was out. In the living-room he saw his father's chair standing empty. Father had gone to bed with his clothes on. Valter went over to his bed.

Soldier-Sträng lay stretched out on the bed, his blind eyes staring at the ceiling. He was not sleeping. When Valter asked if he was worse, Father gave a nervous laugh. His mouth opened, exposing the holes where teeth were missing, while he laughed.

Not for many a moon had Valter heard his father laugh so heartily. Perhaps the doctor had come and told him that the film was ripe. It should have been ripe long ago, according to the doctor. Something must have happened, Father must have received joyous news to make him so happy.

Valter attempted to smile back. He spoke louder so that his father would be sure to recognize his voice. But again Father did not answer, only laughed some more. His eyes were on the ceiling as if he saw something funny up there and couldn't help laughing.

Valter took a step backward, the smile frozen on his lips: Father did not answer him, only laughed. And he had never heard him laugh like that before. In fact, he had never heard anyone laugh like that.

He ran to his mother in the Little Field.

"Father has gone to bed!"

"To bed? He was just outside."

"He's laughing!"

"What do you mean, boy? Laughing?"

"He keeps laughing and doesn't answer me!"

Valter had never seen his mother's face so filled with concern. She dropped the sheaf from her hand and ran back to the cottage. Gunnar and Valter sat down, each on a stone; they avoided looking at each other.

A moment later their mother came running back.

"We must send a message to Carpenter-Elof!"

"Why Elof?" asked Valter.

"That you wouldn't understand. Gunnar, you run! Your legs are fast!"

Gunnar started off. Mother went back to the house. Valter was left alone in the Little Field. There were still a few shocks of rye to be carried in. He spread the rope on the ground, placed a few sheaves in it, pulled the rope tight, and swung the bundle onto his back. The sheaves were taller than he, and the heads dragged on the ground as he struggled homeward. The burden grew heavier with each step; he must take a sheaf or two less next time, he thought.

The sun was going down behind a cloud bank, which meant that it would rain tomorrow. Now he must carry in the remaining shocks alone, as Gunnar had gone for Elof and Mother was staying with

Father. When he had gathered the last sheaves in his rope, he saw Gunnar on the road with Carpenter-Elof. The old man went inside and remained there. Mother, too, was inside, but Gunnar came out and walked toward the village.

Mother had not sent for the doctor, she had sent for pious Elof. Valter knew why, it wasn't that which bothered him.

He threw the last rye sheaves into the barn, then fetched the tethered cow from the clover stubble. Mother would milk it some time when she got to it. He was hungry—he had only eaten the slice of bread he had cut in the kitchen on his return from school. His stomach rumbled and burned. But he did not like to go inside. He picked up the ax and began chopping juniper for the pig's bedding, only to have something to do; and Father wanted the pigpen clean. But his hunger increased. He went to the barn, crushed some of the rye heads between his fingers, and put the kernels in his mouth; they were at least something to chew on, and the taste wasn't bad.

He walked toward the wastelands; there were lingonberries on the tussocks, and he ate a few. He didn't like to go inside the cottage. Carpenter-Elof had been called in, and he knew why. Father had not laughed because he had seen something funny on the ceiling: Father was blind. He had laughed anyway, and Valter was beginning to understand why. Mother had sent for Elof.

It was not long ago that he and Father had been sitting under the pear tree. But tonight Valter could find peace nowhere. He walked hither and yon; he couldn't go in. His father was lying there and had not answered him; he had laughed with his open, toothless mouth.

Pious Elof had come to talk with Father. But suppose Father wouldn't answer him either?

It was almost dark when Valter finally went inside. His mother reproached him for having stayed out so late. He ate cold rye porridge with milk and bread in the kitchen. His mother said it would be best if he went to bed; Gunnar was already undressed and in bed.

At Father's bedside sat Carpenter-Elof, an old, white-haired man with bent shoulders. His pants were shaggy and yellow from sawdust and shavings—he had come directly from his carpenter bench. His face was turned toward the soldier in bed, and Valter could only see his back. A carpenter rule protruded from his hip pocket; he had been busy on some work, but had left immediately to come and talk with Father. He must have felt it was urgent. Father no longer laughed; he lay silent and immobile, but Valter could hear his breathing.

Father's net frame was missing; Mother had moved it out into the hall. Father had been working on a pike net for Valter; it was half finished.

He undressed and crept into bed next to Gunnar. The tin lamp had been lit and stood on a chair near Father's bed. Elof sat with the Bible on his knees and read by its light, slowly, emphasizing every word:

"And it was about the sixth hour, and there was a darkness over all the earth until the ninth hour.

"And the sun was darkened, and the veil of the temple was rent in the midst.

"And when Jesus had cried with a loud voice, he said, Father, into thy hands I commend my spirit: and having said thus, he gave up the ghost."

Elof helped people die.

The oil lamp at Father's bed spread a poor light, its flame not much larger than a glowworm. Valter could not go to sleep, but listened for the sounds in the dark. Once he heard that Father wanted to get out of bed and Elof prevented him. Mother went to the kitchen for homebrewed beer, which he drank. Once he heard Father laugh.

But except for that, the voices he heard were those of Mother and Elof.

"He recognized me a moment ago," said Elof.

"May God make him conscious!" replied Mother.

"Has he thought of his salvation?"

"He hasn't said anything, but we must believe he has."

"He has had time for preparation."

"He has been alone much, with his nets."

"Then he has had time."

"All day long."

"I believe he has been thinking, then."

"But if he shouldn't have," said Mother, "he might still—The thief on the cross—you know, Elof—he, the thief—"

Valter didn't hear what was the matter with the thief on the cross. Mother suddenly broke into sobs, and the rest of the conversation was lost. He wondered what the thief could have to do with Father, until at last he fell asleep.

Elof went home early Saturday morning. Soldier-Sträng lay with his eyes closed and slept with heavy breathing. Mother told Gunnar and Valter to move quietly so as not to awaken him, but although they created considerable noise a few times, they did not disturb him; he did not sleep as one sleeps at night.

Father's hour had come. Word was sent to Anton at the quarry. Mother told Gunnar and Valter to move the rye from the threshing-barn floor, where they had piled it the day before. They knew what this meant: the dead were always laid out in their coffins on the threshing-floor. They must begin their work at once; tomorrow was Sunday, and the floor might be required today. Gunnar and Valter busied themselves with their work and said little to each other; their father's name was not mentioned. There was nothing to be said about him, beyond what Mother had said: his hour was come. By evening the threshing-barn had been cleared and swept.

Carpenter-Elof returned at dusk. Now he was dressed in black wadmal, as if ready to attend church. But his carpenter rule still stuck out of his back pocket.

Sträng was still unconscious; he had not awakened during the day; he did not even awaken to ask for something to drink. Hulda had several times poured raspberry juice into his mouth, but his throat refused to swallow; the juice came out of both sides of his mouth and ran down his neck in two long runnels, red as blood.

This night Hulda and Elof in turn would sit with the dying man. Anton had come home. Valter went to sleep earlier than last night, but was suddenly awakened by some noise. He thought it was about midnight. The feeble lamp was still burning on the chair near Father. He heard voices and realized that the voices had awakened him. A few times he could distinguish Father's voice—strangely hoarse and broken and very low, but Valter's ears were good.

"What time is it?" asked Father.

"Almost three," replied Elof. "You're conscious, Sträng."

"Yes . . . yes . . . Did you light the lamp, Elof?"

"Can you see the flame?"

"Sure, I can see."

"Do you recognize me, Nils Gottfried?" asked Mother.

"You are my dear wife."

Mother sobbed.

"Jesus has died for your sins, Sträng," said Elof.

"Do you want anything to drink?" asked Mother.

"No, I'm not thirsty."

Mother was crying.

"Don't be sad, Hulda," Father comforted her.

Elof was reading: "—And Jesus said unto him, Verily I say unto thee, To day shalt thou be with me in paradise."

"I'm not sad. Nor am I thirsty," said Father.

Valter rose silently and pulled on his trousers. Anton and Gunnar had also awakened. But now it was quiet at Father's bedside. Mother and Elof stood motionless and looked at him. Valter walked up to the bed, his brothers behind him. Father had closed his eyes except for a narrow slit that showed the whites, in which a reflection from the lamplight played. He lay still, on his back, with his hands crossed over his stomach. But his lower jaw moved up and down, ever slower. Finally it dropped down and did not move up again, leaving his mouth half open; in one corner was a red spot from the dried raspberry juice.

Carpenter-Elof said that it was exactly a quarter past three when the soldier's life came to an end.

The sun would not be up for a few hours; Hulda sent Anton to summon Balk-Emma.

Elof pulled his rule from his pocket, opened it, and measured Sträng. Now Valter understood why he had brought his rule, even though he wore his Sunday-best wadmal suit. He would make the coffin. As Father now lay, he seemed longer than in life; it was a long coffin-measure Elof took this time.

Hulda said: Father had regained his consciousness before the end and then he had had his sight. By saying that he recognized her, he had meant that he saw her. And he had seen the lamp on the chair. The film had at last ripened, but it had hardly broken before his time was up. That was how strangely things happened.

Carpenter-Elof folded his rule.

"He died in light," he said.

Dawn was slow in coming this Sunday morning. Balk-Emma arrived, and she helped Mother wash Father and put a clean shirt on him. She came when people were born and when they died. Then Father was to be moved, and all must help. He wasn't so heavy, however—he had lost a lot of weight. They took the top from the bench and placed Father on it. A couple of rollers from the loom had been placed under the top to facilitate carrying. Anton and Gunnar carried the legs end and walked ahead, Emma and Elof were at about the middle, and Mother walked last at the head. Valter was not needed. It was a cumbersome burden, after all, and they walked slowly.

Placed on the bed lid, the dead man was carried to the threshing-barn, which Gunnar and Valter had put in order the day before. Valter walked behind the others across the yard, following his father to the barn.

Emma and Elof left, and when Mother had milked the cow and let it out to graze, she put on her Sunday clothes: if she managed to reach the church before service began, the minister would announce Father's death today. Anton decided to go with her to church; he would stop by at the Sutaremåla tailor's on the way home and get measured for a black suit for the funeral.

Thus, Gunnar and Valter were left alone at home, but Gunnar said there was hardly a Sunday feeling today. He went to the hazel-bush and cut himself a fishing-rod; he wanted to try for pike with bacon rind. Valter could have gone with him, but didn't feel like it. He remained alone at home this Sunday.

Inside the cottage everything was much the same as ever. Father had been carried out to the barn; his rocking-chair stood empty, his net frame had been put away. His wooden shoes stood in their usual place near the door as if waiting for his feet. On the wall hung his jacket, and above the jacket the gun. Everything was familiar, yet nothing was the same. It was so empty, and he felt empty inside. On the windowsill lay the mouth organ, the red one Father had given him. Valter put it in his pocket and strolled out.

He walked about the yard. He walked as if he were inspecting the soldier-property. He looked over the fields and at the crops, he walked by the cow in her pasture. He picked up fallen pears under the tree, but remembered diabetes and did not taste them. He tried first one thing and then another. But the day was long. The sun stood still and burned the stones and the earth. The cat followed him everywhere and miaowed. Young swallows, hatched and brought up this summer under the cottage sod, swarmed and twittered. He could have imitated their sound on his mouth organ, his hand now and then made the motion to bring it out from his pocket. But he did not play.

He arrived at the closed barn door, and then he stopped short and held his breath.

He had not accompanied Gunnar in his fishing because he could not leave Father alone at home the first day after he was dead. Father had never left him; today he did not wish to leave Father.

He stood outside the barnhouse door and tried the word: *Dead*. *D-e-a-d*. It came suddenly to an end at the last letter. He was up against a wall no one could climb. *D-e-a-d*. On the *d* his tongue locked itself, with its tip against the roof of his mouth. *D-e-a-d*—no, it was impossible, however much he tried. It was the end, the end for all time. He came to a stop again and again when he tried to say the word, and in the same way he came to a stop when he tried to think about it: dead—never more. No one could understand it.

The film over Father's eyes had ripened, but not before he was dying. There had been light around him when he died, the oil lamp had spread its light on him. And he had not wanted to drink—the thirst had no longer plagued him. His last words had been that he was not thirsty any more. I would have liked to see you once more, Father had said that evening under the pear tree. His eyes had closed just as the film burst. But he had seen Mother.

It was a beautiful Sunday, a long Sunday, the longest he ever could remember. Children from the village walked by on the road, jumped about noisily and laughed; he stole around the corner to hide from them. He was annoyed at their noise—such brats! No sense! A hen emerging from under the barn floor where it had laid an egg irritated him with its eternal cackle. The pig, gulping at its trough, annoyed him. The swallows, flittering about, annoyed him; they would soon leave and cared about nothing. Nobody cared about anything, neither people nor animals. Not a single creature understood that from now on it would never be as it had been in their home. Never as it once was.

It was a long Sunday. But he did not leave Father.

At last Gunnar returned with a huge pike strung on an alder branch, and at last Anton and Mother came from church. At last evening came. But when Valter had gone to bed that evening, with his father still on the bench top in the barn, at last it came; he had not shed a tear all day long—Mother had cried during the night, and Anton and Gunnar in the morning—but now in the evening he cried more than any of the others. He cried over the inexorable, the irrevocable, which he was old enough to understand in its un-understandable cruelty. He cried over this: never more. He cried over that which from now on forever would separate him from his father out in the barn. He cried over that which no one can change, which has no changing. He cried over the word *eternity*.

Mother gave him camphor drops on a lump of sugar to make him go to sleep. And he finally went to sleep from his crying. The last thing he remembered on this day was the red juice spot he had seen in the corner of Father's mouth.

So ended the 29th of August, this evil, hated date—when he became fatherless.

The funeral took place the following Sunday. The villagers whom Sträng had represented followed their soldier to the grave. Six of 128 Sträng's comrades arrived in brushed uniforms and polished buttons, with swaying plumes of horsehair in their caps. They were to carry the coffin. They were the same soldiers who had come to the Christmas parties—fat Banda, Valter's godfather; Corporal Hellström of the long beard, with his shiny medal; little Bäck of Bäckhult; Flink from Sutaremåla, who had been put on probation; Nero of Bökevara; and Lönn from Hermanstorp, who now, since Sträng's demise, was the tallest in the platoon. The last soldier to represent Strängshult village was to be brought to his resting-place.

The black hearse with two white horses had stopped on the road outside the gate, which was too narrow for it to pass through. The coffin, Carpenter-Elof's creation, rested on sawhorses in the yard with the funeral guests gathered around it. The lid had been removed for the participants to view the mortal remains of 128 Sträng of Uppvidinge Company.

The soldiers stood in a group, talking among themselves.

"I predicted last fall that Sträng would never do another maneuver," said Banda.

"He has reported for the last call," said Corporal Hellström and twisted his long beard-ends, which parted over his chest to display his shining rows of buttons.

"Sträng was a young man," said Lönn.

"Forty-five," reported Banda. "No age at all."

"A fine man in the days of his strength," said little Bäck.

Hellström nodded. "Serviceable."

Valter stood squeezed in among the soldiers and felt very little. He wore his blue suit—one of Gunnar's old ones which he already had outgrown, but he must wear a dark suit today. And he had not put his anti-military pin on the lapel—it didn't fit at a funeral, as it was red. Not a red speck was allowed at a funeral. He had washed himself with soap, combed his hair, cut and cleaned his fingernails. After great trouble his mother had managed to button his stiff, straight collar, which was too small and chafed and hurt his neck. If he lowered his chin ever so little, the collar cut into his flesh like a sharp knife; he was forced to carry his head higher than was his custom.

Soldier-Banda patted him on the shoulder. "High-spirited! My godson! He holds his nose in the air! That's right, boy! You're a soldier's son!"

Banda was so damned foolish he understood hardly anything; it was because of his collar that Valter was forced to carry his head high at Father's funeral.

Carpenter-Elof began a psalm, and the six soldiers came to an agreement as to which position each of them was to take when the time came to carry the coffin; each two soldiers of the same height became partners. Bäck and Flink, as the shortest, took their places first, Banda and Nero carried at the waist, and Lönn and Hellström, who were the tallest, came last and carried at the head.

It turned out to be a long funeral cortege, as each farmer had brought his own carriage. Aldo Samuel was Alderman this year, and Sträng's family rode on his wagon, pulled by the red mare. Hulda wore her black silk kerchief, tied firmly under her chin and pulled forward until her cheeks were barely visible. In her fingers she held a small bouquet of daisies and resedas which she had picked from the bed under the cottage window. The three sons had pooled their savings and bought a small wreath for their father; it was made of white and black glass beads. A glass wreath was the most endurable to put on a grave, Mother had said; it would not wither away. Each boy had chipped in three crowns.

The village soldier rode for the last time along the road, and in front of each farm chopped spruce twigs had been spread on the road. But after the cortege had passed through Strängshult, the village the dead man had served, they encountered twigs only outside soldier-cottages.

The churchgoers gaped curiously at the six soldiers in uniform and plumes. Today 128 Sträng was of some importance in the parish; all these soldiers and farmers and horses and wagons were in motion because of him. And now the minister and the organist and the sexton were to perform their duties because of him. But they were paid for it, thought Valter; it mattered little to them whether his poor, blind father was dead or alive.

The coffin had been lifted from the hearse and placed on boxes at the church gate, and on either side of it stood three soldiers waiting. Valter stood next to Mother, near the coffin, and Gunnar and Anton were close by. But he was not very conscious of his surroundings any longer.

The minister and the organist emerged from the sacristy. They stopped at the gate and doffed their tall hats simultaneously. The organist took up the psalm: "I walk toward death wherever I walk—" He had a forceful, clear voice that affected one strangely. Now the bells tolled, ringing thunderously from their lofty position in the steeple. Valter had a feeling that the earth trembled under his feet with the heavy din from the bells. He shuddered, with an icy chill that passed through his body. The sound of the bells streamed down from the heavens, enveloping the church green with an overpowering vibration. For a moment he wondered if perhaps God did exist after all; then he felt the narrow collar chafing his neck and he held his head higher.

The minister and the organist walked down the churchyard, and the six soldiers lifted Father's coffin and walked behind them.

Mother walked, he walked beside her, his brothers walked, and all the others walked behind. The minister and the organist led the way and all walked. The organist sang. The bells tolled heavily. Three soldiers walked on either side of the coffin, with soldier pace according to their habit. Father's comrades they were—Father had walked many miles in step with them. Six men from the fifth platoon of the Uppvidinge Company. The soldiers walked, all walked. Only Father was borne. The bells thundered, the soldiers' feet—in their black, newly polished shoes—tramped heavily on the gravel of the churchyard path. Now they lost step; the brass plates in their caps glittered in the sun, the horsetail plumes swayed, swayed at every step: one, two, one, two. The bells tolled and Father was carried. All others must walk, but he was borne.

And the organist sang that they were walking toward death.

The late village soldier was carried to his grave, and Soldier-Valter walked after him, beside his mother; he walked straight, head high. The narrow, starched collar cut and chafed his neck and made him carry his head high when he followed his father to the grave. He was dressed in Sunday best, brushed and combed, and his hands smelled of soap. In front of him walked two tall soldiers, four long legs moved in step, four of the Crown's sturdy pants legs with yellow stripes. Corporal Hellström had a brown spot below the knee on one of his pants legs. The soldier feet tramped slowly, step after step, six soldiers bearing the seventh. And the churchbells tolled in rhythm with their steps: one, two, one, two.

A broad plank had been laid over a ditch. On the plank stood the sexton, waiting for the coffin. Here Father was to remain. The collar chafed and pinched around the neck.

The coffin with Father was lowered and gone. The minister picked up a toy spade and threw down some earth. The organist sang, the minister read. Valter heard the sound of the words, yet heard nothing of them. The daisy-and-reseda-bunch fell from Mother's hand. The six soldiers put their heels together at the edge of the grave and saluted. The Alderman and the other farmers tipped their hats. The bells stopped ringing, and it grew strangely silent. Mother spoke to the sexton about the black and white bead wreath, and he promised to put it on the grave after he had filled it. Valter had contributed three crowns as his share in the wreath, and the thought came to him that this was six days' pay in the factory. He felt ashamed that he remembered this here at Father's grave. But Father would have understood, and it concerned no one else. A bead wreath lasted, it did not wither away like other wreaths. His six days' pay would lie here with Father.

Soldier-Valter stood at the grave and stared in front of him. He held his head high—the collar around his neck was high and narrow.

In the afternoon the funeral guests gathered in the cottage. Soldier-Hulda went to the kitchen, with her work apron over her church clothes, and busied herself with the food, aided by Balk-Emma. She wanted to make the funeral as decent as a soldier-widow could afford, and she treated her guests with peeled potatoes, veal, meatballs, and stewed pears. The farm wives from the village had brought funeral gifts consisting of sugar cakes and sweet cheese. Corporal Hellström was in charge of the *brännvin* and poured drinks for the men. In the absence of wine, *brännvin* served as the mourning-drink. The small soldier-cottage was crowded; some of the guests had to sit in the entrance hall and in the kitchen, and those unable to find room inside sat down on planks and bench tops in the yard.

They ate mourning-food and drank mourning-drinks. Valter lost his appetite the moment he tasted the food. This was feast food he knew not when he might again taste such—but his appetite failed him. Must he stuff himself because Father was dead? Must he eat more than was good for him because Father had been buried today? A sugar cake was served, brought by one of the guests; on top of the cake was a big, black, baked cross. Mourning-food must be black as sorrow itself, and perhaps one ought to force oneself to eat it. The women praised the cake with the cross: eggwhites and sugar had been mixed with coloring, so suitable for a funeral. And both men and women walked up to the cake and cut themselves pieces of the cross, which grew smaller and smaller. Last in line Valter walked up to the table, but he could not taste the sugar cake, he could not eat of the black cross, he could not chew and swallow his own black sorrow.

He withdrew to a corner, where he listened to Flink and Bäck speaking of 128 Sträng and praising him: He had been an honest and decent comrade. Valter felt friendly toward the two soldiers, even toward Ossian's father. Flink had been put on probation and perhaps he was already improved. Then their talk shifted to other subjects: *Brännvin* had grown so terribly dear in these strange latter days. Recently it had risen to twenty-eight öre a quart, even in a quantity of thirty quarts or more.

"If you order only twenty quarts, those devils ask ninety öre," said Flink.

"But that's the best quality, of course," said Bäck.

"Tyringe *brännvin*—I always order Tyringe *brännvin*."

"Cognac has gone up to one fifty."

"Cognac is for rich people."

"But ninety öre for *brännvin*!"

"People should refuse to pay it!"

Valter listened awhile, but they made no more mention of his father. He listened to the farmers a few minutes. They were discussing the sale of Fågeltuva bog to some men from Kalmar; the bog was said to hold a million crowns' worth of peat, and the villagers had sold it for only twelve thousand. None of the farmers spoke of Father; they ate with enjoyment the mourning-food.

Corporal Hellström poured *brännvin* generously; the men's voices had grown louder, and they no longer sat solemnly on their chairs. *Brännvin* was a mourning-drink today, but a mourning-drink that could be imbibed until it brought gladness. So it seemed. Banda was the loudest of all. He told stories from the maneuvers at Hultsfred and laughed at his own stories until the laughter rang under the rafters.

Valter had returned from school one evening and had found his father in bed laughing. Since that evening no one had laughed in this house. It seemed unreal to sit here now and listen to Banda laugh. He felt ashamed for his godfather; he denied him. A godfather was supposed to be in God's place. But when God didn't exist, no godfather was needed, at least not one to sit and laugh at the funeral of Valter's real father.

Corporal Hellström looked at the gun on the wall and said that they must now return that gun: it belonged to the Crown. But he said nothing about Valter's father; none of the guests made further mention of Father.

Valter wished it would be over, that the guests would leave. His head felt heavy above the sharp, narrow collar; he wanted to go to bed. But he had no place to sleep while the guests remained and filled the cottage. And they would eat all the mourning-food before they left. Dishes were emptied, one after another; the big black cross of eggwhite and sugar had already been devoured. The black sorrow was swallowed and gone. Thus they honored Father in his

grave. Or did they honor and praise Jesus by swallowing the cross
on the cake?

At last Carpenter-Elof started up an evening psalm; it was growing late and the guests would leave. The women found the empty
dishes and bowls in which they had brought their gifts, and each one
took Hulda by hand and said good-by. The soldier-widow thanked
the guests for having honored Sträng and his survivors: her mate
had received a funeral above his position and possessions; she wished
to thank them. Some even shook Valter's hand.

Banda pinched his ear in godfather fashion. "Right you are! Your
nose to the sky, boy!"

Banda, his godfather, the stupidest of all the soldiers! Why had
he never been put on probation!

Then all the guests were gone, and suddenly a strange stillness
and emptiness and forlornness descended over the cottage. After
all the din and noise from the many people crowded together, the
silence seemed eerily frightening. Valter had wished the guests to
leave, but now that they had gone everything about him seemed
desolate, as if he were standing all alone in the center of the big
Fågeltuva bog. It was as lonely as it must be in Father's grave. Someone should have stayed, some guest who did not mourn. At least
old Balk-Emma. They should have had someone with them. Now
it was only they, they themselves to share the sorrow. That was
what made it so strange. All—all had gone, and here in the cottage
only sorrow was left behind.

Valter went outside. A bright moon shone over the yard. He
walked toward the barn. It was almost like daylight with the bright
moon, yet deserted and desolate. Only a few moments ago the yard
had been filled with people. And now it seemed to him as if they
suddenly had been deserted by all, as if no one would ever come to
see them. Only sorrow had been left, for them to share.

The barn door stood open, and he peeked inside. The threshing-barn was empty. In there, too, were desolation and emptiness. The moon shone down on the threshing-floor, which lay clean-swept and shiny. He had swept it himself, the day before Sunday the 29th.

He lingered a moment: We were comrades. He never left me behind. I would not leave him.

He returned inside and found his mother in the kitchen, in a bent-down, sitting position on the sofa. Her eyes were closed; she had gone to sleep where she happened to be sitting, with her clothes on. Beside her rose a pile of unwashed dishes, and on the floor at her feet lay the pieces of a broken dish; she had been holding the dish in her hand and had dropped it when she went to sleep.

Valter spread a shawl over his mother's shoulders and left her there. Gunnar was already in bed. On the wall hung the Crown gun with the yellow strap. He recalled Hellström's words: the gun must be returned.

He had been born under that gun. They might as well return it. He carried his own, broken gun and did not care to see another in the house. But this—returning the gun—meant something more: something more must be returned. Father no longer earned their right to live in the cottage. The cow, the pig, the field, the waste-lands, the moor—all must be returned. Their whole home must be returned to the village. The cottage, the walls around him, the roof over his head, the floor under his feet—all must be returned. The village soldier was no more, and finished for himself was that part of his life when he had been Soldier-Valter.

He had lost his home. His home must be given back to those who had lent it to Father. And great changes would take place in his life now that he no longer was Soldier-Valter.

He thought this over while he undressed. At last, with the combined strength of both hands, he managed to tear off the narrow starched collar that his mother with great trouble had fastened round his neck in the morning. He moved his head freely as if liberated after a day in neck-irons. He felt a soreness under his chin, and looking in the mirror, he discovered that the collar had chafed the skin in a broad red ring around his neck.

So this day finally had given him a blood-red ring around his neck—Father's endlessly long funeral day, when he had been forced to carry his head high from beginning to end.

CHAPTER XI

In the rolls of Uppvidinge Company a notation was entered after soldier Nils Sträng's number: "Deceased at home."

And in the spring of 1910 the soldier's widow moved away from the soldier-cottage. She returned to her mother's old shack in the wastelands at Trångadal. This cottage had stood unoccupied since her mother's death and was in bad repair; and it was much smaller than the soldier-cottage. A little-used roadway led through the wastelands to the place, but the last stretch of it was barely a path through the untouched wilderness. The cottage perched on a hill that had once produced grass but had later been used as a garden. Thickets of birch, willow, and aspen now covered the hillsides. Behind the hill, bogs and moors stretched far away, their black pools gaping between the tussocks. Trångadal had a beautiful location; if its inhabitants could have found sustenance from wild-growing trees and filmy pools, they could have lived well.

But the cotter people must buy every crumb of food. Hulda missed her previous home—she missed the bread from the field, the milk from the cow, the pork from the pig. Now she felt that she must have been rich while she lived in the soldier-cottage. Then she had sent baskets of food to the cotter women; now she herself was sitting in a cotter shack and was the recipient of food baskets from generous farm wives in the village. It was a great change. She worked as a day laborer on the farms during summer and did weaving and spinning for the farm wives in winter. Gunnar kept his job at the sawmill, and Valter remained at the glass factory; both boys carried home their full pay and gave it to their mother. Anton had left for America shortly before they moved to Trångadal; the three remaining family members must somehow get along in their new circumstances.

Soldier-Sträng's survivors had become cotters. They had moved into Grandmother Mathilda's shack, and no one could live in smaller quarters, thought Valter. They had sunk a step lower into the underclass. Below them was now only one group—the hobos, the people of the road who carried their possessions on their backs and borrowed night shelter near the furnaces of the glass factories.

Work had been resumed at Ljungdala, but the pay was the same as before the strike. The strike fund of the local unions was long ago spent, the Great Fight was over, the workers again tipped their hats to the owner. Socialists and Young Socialists quarreled and blamed each other for the inglorious result: the Socialists had given in with the promise from the upper-class of the right of suffrage, the Young Socialists were rattle-brained fools who had ruined their chances by dynamiting some factories. The membership of the local union had decreased, for some blowers had moved to other factories. But the Young Socialist leader, Elmer Sandin, remained. Under his tutelage Valter was educating himself to become a hater of religion and militarism; his ultimate goal was to be a social revolutionary.

Persuaded by Joel-Nightstoker, who had proved himself a true comrade when Pot-Jonas attacked him, Valter now joined the Lodestar, the local temperance union. This gave him access to their library and brought him in contact with new comrades whose ideals he shared.

He was now as tall as Gunnar, though his brother was broader over the shoulders and stronger. Gunnar had lost his freckles, but Valter's still remained; Gunnar had lost his front teeth, but Valter still had his. Gunnar was better-looking, but this he did not envy his brother. Gunnar wrote a hand as fine as a teacher's and he could count as well as a bookkeeper; indeed, he was taking a correspondence course in bookkeeping, and it was not simple Swedish bookkeeping but Italian double bookkeeping. Miss Tyra, the teacher, said it was a shame that he must work in the mill, so gifted as he was. With education, he could become a minister. These words of the teacher's pleased his mother greatly. She thought that Gunnar deserved the praise; she always agreed with Gunnar. As a child he had been obedient and easy to bring up, and now when he returned from the sawmill in the evenings he would carry in water and wood without being asked. And she had borne a son who could have become a minister; a greater joy could hardly be imagined by a mother.

In Valter's eyes his older brother had only one fault, but it was a grave one: he was almost sixteen and not yet class-conscious. He did not care for politics. In other matters Valter got along well with him. Gunnar was his brother in a greater sense than were his other brothers. The older ones had come and gone before they left for America and he had never had time to get to know them intimately. But now Gunnar and he were alone with Mother in the little shack at Trångadal. Only the two of them were left, and they must stick together.

Their spare time the brothers spent together. Sundays they would go fishing in the tarns and pools near their home. They took the net their father had tied during the last weeks of his life and strung it across the pools; then with long sticks they would chase the pike against the net. In the smaller pools they stirred up the water until it was muddy and thick; the pike would then become disturbed, their fins and tails breaking the surface, which made it easy to catch them in their hands. From alder bushes each boy made himself a forked stick on which to string the pike, through the gills; when both forks were full, they felt satisfied with the day's catch. They picked and ate wild strawberries, blueberries, and raspberries and when they had eaten their fill they would stretch out in some sunny glade and lie gazing at the drifting clouds. These were moments when intimate secrets were shared, when plans for the future were spun.

Their confided desires did not encompass kingdoms, imperial thrones, or Rockefeller's riches; more immediate matters were at hand.

Gunnar desired: (1) a gun, a breechloader with ready shots that could be put in in a second; (2) enough money to buy their old home; they would then move back and earn their living from fishing and hunting; (3) one thousand crowns to give to Mother so she needn't do day labor in the village; (4) enough money to buy new teeth for the front of his mouth.

Valter desired: (1) a bicycle, nickel-plated all over, with freewheeling and gears; (2) an overcoat that he could wear to the Lodestar meetings—all temperance members came in overcoats during the winter, and, besides, he would look more grown-up in an overcoat; (3) a book in which all truths about the world and life were enumerated, thus relieving him of the necessity of buying any more books.

They would lie for hours in the glade under the sailing clouds, their ability to wish never ending. Their confidences would take them beyond this world, into the next world. Valter denied a life hereafter, but at times he was a little unsure. He didn't like death either, he would have liked to deny it, too. He had so many times tried to get by the word *dead*. He had tried to go on. A life other than the one he now was living was not easy to comprehend. But he liked to believe in a life somewhere where all were equals, where some needn't slave in a factory all year round while others did no work at all.

Gunnar had begun to see through the religious humbug; he no longer believed in the devil or in hell. But he believed in God and a special life hereafter on one of the stars; there must be something for all those who wanted to live. He wanted to live to be a hundred years old, to see what happened in the world.

Gunnar was such a deep thinker that it made Valter feel dizzy: If this earth had not been, nor its people, if no life and nothing else had existed, if the firmament above them had not existed, no clouds, no sun, no stars, nothing, neither below them nor above them, neither dark nor light, air or water—then nothing would have existed. Not a drop of water, nor a particle of earth, not the smallest streak of light, not even darkness. Nothing. This was impossible to comprehend, a ghastly strain on one's imagination.

"Can you imagine Nothing?" asked Gunnar.

Valter closed his eyes and thought. No, he couldn't. He thought until his head felt giddy, but he couldn't think away from himself and everything else on earth and imagine Nothing. At the very attempt he felt depressed, thwarted, a great futility facing him. Nothing. No. What luck that something did exist, that this earth existed, he said to Gunnar.

"Yes, it is terrible to think of oneself away from here."

Gunnar had gifts. He was too good to become a minister, a black-frock, suppressing the workers with the humbug of heaven.

They hung their net to dry on some trees in the forest, and when they discovered broken meshes they thought of their father, who had tied the net during his last summer. It wasn't two years since he had died, yet his name was seldom mentioned. Mother sometimes spoke of him: "When Father was alive—" "Before Father took sick—" "When Father grew blind—" But few others referred to him any more; he was forgotten on earth because he lay dead below it. These meshes had been tied by Father's fingers, which now were only decayed bones. Yet—every pike they caught, Father's fingers helped them catch, for he had tied the net that snared the pike. Thus, he was not dead, he was with them at their fishing. And when they discovered broken meshes they said: If Father had been alive, then he could have mended the holes for us.

Soldier-Sträng was alive for his sons. On his grave lay their bead wreath, and the grass grew over it. But the beads did not wither away.

And it was because of his father that Valter made occasional visits to his old home. Here he encountered all that was left of the dead one: here lay the ground he had tramped, the stones he had broken, the fences he had built, the many objects his hands had touched. On these visits Valter experienced something akin to closeness to his father. And he liked to sit on the board under the pear tree where he had been sitting the last time his father spoke to him—that evening when they had talked to an end with each other, end for all time, for eternity.

Eternity. Father was supposed to be dead for eternity. No, the infinity of death was not acceptable, he could not acknowledge it. He turned the idea, twisted it: for eternity. A hundred years hence, in the twenty-first century Father would still be dead. A thousand years from now, at the beginning of the thirty-first century, Father would still be equally dead. And after a hundred thousand, after a million years, the same: dead. And the same would be his own lot: dead for the millions and millions of years to come.

This was impossible to accept. No one could be satisfied with this one life only. Father's life had lasted forty-five years; if his own were to be no longer, he would already have lived a third of it. This was a miserly allotment compared to the time without end in which he would be dead, that eternity when he would be nothing. Nothing. Gunnar with his sharp thinking was right: It was frightful to try to imagine oneself as nothing. To have less life than a fly, not even the life of a worm. Less than a worm. Nothing. Never to live more.

With these reflections it would have been easy to cry, if he hadn't been too old to cry now. He must, *must* get further than this puny bit of life which didn't suffice. He must get by, *he must strive further*. He couldn't endure otherwise, couldn't leave things as they now were.

Carpenter-Elof thought that Father in his last moments had received forgiveness for his sins and now was in heaven. He had been forgiven for twenty-five years' devoted military service, for having worked at miserly pay for the village farmers. The simple-minded might believe this. Father was neither in heaven nor in hell; he slept the thrall's sleep after the many miles of tramping at maneuvers, after the thousands of cords of wood and posts he had cut in the forest. All Valter's ancestors slept the same sleep. He had seen the marks they had left in the fallen-down places and overgrown clearings in the wastelands. They, like Father, had been thralls, slaving for other people more fortunately situated. They had been soldiers, cotters, farmhands, day laborers. They had received no education, had never learned to read or write. They had lived in ignorance, in obedience to priest and sheriff, and their lives had been poor and bleak.

But he, Valter, was informed, he had learned to write and read, he would take revenge for his ancestors: he would become a class-fighter.

This was his irrevocable decision; he would educate himself for his mission as class-fighter. He had never confided a word of this to anyone, nor would he ever. He didn't want it said that he was incapable; he didn't want to be dissuaded by comrades. He was starting on the lowest rung of the ladder, it would be a long climb for him, many hard years to reach his goal.

In Ingersoll's *Free Thoughts* he had found a paragraph that encouraged him greatly:

> "It has often been said of one man or another that he was born
> to the poorest, most humble parents, yet in spite of this drawback
> became a great man. This idea is a mistake. Poverty is generally
> an advantage. Most of the intellectual giants have been nourished
> to strength at the breast of paucity. On the other hand—it is
> difficult for the rich man to resist the thousand temptations
> of pleasure."

So had Colonel Ingersoll written, and why couldn't these words be confirmed by him, Valter Sträng, when they had been confirmed by many others before him? He, too, had been nourished at the breast of paucity, and that was why he was strong. Poverty had its own pure, strength-giving mother's milk to offer its sons. The children of rich parents could not share this, and consequently they grew up spineless and weakened by their pleasures. It was only right that the upper-class should reap some harm from its riches while the under-class gained advantage from its poverty.

He decided to accomplish something great that no one before him had accomplished. Perhaps he couldn't become one of the very greatest men in the world, perhaps not a Kropotkin, a Rogert Ingersoll, a Victor Hugo, August Strindberg, Leo Tolstoy, Karl Marx, Jack London, or Maxim Gorky. But there were places near those men, immediately below them, and such a place he would reach. However, there were temptations even for the poor, and he must steel himself so as not to fail in his calling.

When he combed his hair in front of the mirror, he examined his face. He had seen youthful portraits of great men, and in his mind he compared these with his own looks and wondered what conclusions he could draw concerning his calling. His eyes were blue, open, and penetrating. He didn't like the color, because it was so common, but his eyes could look through humbug. His nose was straight, but too long and too big; his nose came from his mother's side—all his mother's brothers in the America-pictures had large, clumsy noses. The mouth was just the right width, the lips a little too thick. His chin ought to have been stronger, more protruding; that would have been a sign of energy, persistence, and power of decision; all forceful men had strong chins. But criminals, too, had strong chins; perhaps his chin was all right the way it was. His forehead was broad, but he wished that it had been somewhat higher. All leaders and thinkers had high foreheads; Karl Marx had had one of the highest in the world. The thinkers of the upper-class, naturally, had low foreheads. His own brow was perhaps not high enough for a deep thinker, but he would use it tenaciously the way it was. His hair was blond and straight; he wished it had been black and curly, but there was nothing he could do about that. His eyebrows were thick, and darker than his hair; they rose in great arches above his eyes quite elegantly. But the misfortune of his face was the multitude of freckles. Both forehead and cheeks were strewn with them. In winter they almost disappeared, as if frozen away, but in summer his whole face bloomed, a luxuriant freckle-field. When he grew older he would wear a full beard to hide the freckles; great men often wore full beards, in appropriate dignity.

Such were his looks. He was not handsome, but neither was he ugly. Not repulsive, at least. Many boys were much uglier than he.

But what did his looks matter? What mattered was not the freckles on the brow, rather what was inside it. What mattered was his character. What mattered was his ability to harden himself against temptations.

During the meetings of the Lodestar he had been aware of one danger: he wasted too much time and interest on the girl members. He would talk to his "sisters" during the folk dances, and this was necessary recreation—to gain strength for the temperance work. But he didn't feel at ease with the girls; he tried to act funny in their presence, to say something that would attract their attention; he wanted to show his best side. He knew that he said and did many things only because of the girls. At such times he looked through himself and was annoyed at his behavior.

Concerning the sexual relationship between man and woman he knew about all he needed to know. He had read *Woman as a Sexual Being* and *Woman as Virgin, Wife and Mother*, and in these books all truths about women were explained with great clarity, easy to understand. He had understood everything. It was interesting reading, of value as knowledge in the same way that he once had learned the multiplication table. But a man educating himself for the mission of class-fighter ought not to have sexual relations. He had read about leaders and thinkers and had found that the ones who had done the greatest work were those who had avoided distraction in marriage and family life. If you wed your life to high ideals, you must not bind yourself to a woman. Such a relationship took too much time.

To be sure of remembering this discovery of his, Valter wrote it down in the notebook called TRUTHS:

"A class-fighter must live alone and steel himself against women. He must keep his hands free."

At Ljungdala things were going downhill. The small factory could not compete with its bigger neighbors. Soon they lost their contract for drinking-glasses, leaving lamp chimneys as the most important order. When a contract for shoe-polish jars was announced, the workers knew that the end was near; making shoe-polish jars was a blower's most degrading task. In a few weeks the news spread that Mr. Lundevall had petitioned for bankruptcy; the factory was closing.

The Ljungdala factory buildings remained standing for a few years—black, ghostlike, silent, deserted, empty. Then they were razed; spruce seedlings shot up in the ground, and the forest began to reconquer the place where the factory had stood.

To the small boys the factory had been a school in which they were to "learn manners." Valter had fought, had not wished to "learn manners." But from his comrades he had learned something else: he had discovered the truth about himself and his class. Ljungdala Factory had produced drinking-glasses and lamp chimneys—products for darkness and light. The old factory had been a hell, but in his dark hell he had been enlightened.

CHAPTER XII

The eerie Fågeltuva bog with its frightening vastness was no more; it had been drained and a peat factory built on its edge. Valter got a job in the peat factory as wire-cutter. The wire was used for baling the dried peat, which was sold to farmers for animal-bedding and fertilizer mix. Here he was paid one crown and twenty-five öre a day, and the work was easy enough. But while he was baling, his eyes and ears were so filled with peat dust that it took much time to clean up when he came home in the evening. At last he had finished school, which had interfered so greatly with his work in the glass factory. But he was not yet rid of God and the church and the minister: this winter he was being prepared for his confirmation and first communion.

Once a week he walked the six miles to the church. The religious instruction caused him no trouble; the minister was old and nearly deaf and seldom heard the replies to his questions, but always gave them a favorable interpretation. During his time of preparation Valter must also attend church on Sundays. Perhaps he would not have considered the minister detestable if he hadn't preached every Sunday against socialists and glassworkers. According to the minister's words, God must be the enemy of organized workers, and here it was demanded of Valter that he serve and praise this enemy.

There were sixty-five boys in his class, all sons of farmers or factory workers. The factory boys smoked cigarettes, the farm boys chewed snuff; three or four among them—including Valter—did neither. The factory boys were intelligent and class-conscious, the farm boys dull and old-fashioned, refusing to mix in politics. During their free moments between lessons Valter sometimes attempted to inform them about God and class-society, but they guarded their ignorance jealously, anxious to keep it. Most of the boys came to class on bicycles; Valter walked with Ossian Flink, who also had no bike.

During Valter's preparation for his first communion, the *Titanic*, the world's largest steamship on her maiden voyage across the Atlantic, hit an iceberg and sank. Consequently, many of the prospective emigrants that spring hesitated. Later, toward summer, Sweden's greatest author, August Strindberg, died. During his last years he had often said that his pen would be used exclusively for the working-class. Now the reactionary press insisted that the last book Strindberg had asked for was the Bible, and that he had died with the Bible pressed to his heart. Valter felt sure that this was a deliberate upper-class lie.

The confirmation would take place at Whitsuntide. He ordered a black confirmation suit, bought black gloves and white tie. What an idiotic custom! But, however he decked himself out, his soul would remain a freethinker's. It was only that he must be dressed like the rest of the class in order to be admitted to the communion—in order finally and for all time to get rid of God and church.

He had worn his leather shoes to class all winter long; the soles were worn quite through, and he would need a new pair for the confirmation. But the suit had taken all his pay from the peat factory and he had nothing left for shoes. His mother was in a great quandary: What could he wear at the communion? Could he use Gunnar's shoes? Gunnar's shoes were brought out and tried on Valter's feet, but they were too narrow and too short. Gunnar had unusually small feet for his age, whereas Valter's were unusually large for his age. He could push only half his foot into his older brother's shoe. It was out of the question. Otherwise, Gunnar would willingly have lent his shoes and stayed home for the holidays.

The year before, Albin had sent some money from America and Hulda had bought a pair of button shoes; these she now handed to Valter.

"Try my shoes, they're bigger."

The button shoes had been a pair the storekeeper had been unable to sell, and he had offered them to Hulda at a greatly reduced price; they were of a style long out of use, with extremely long, sharp toes. Valter tried them on. They almost fitted him, except for the empty space in the long toes. Everyone could see that they were women's shoes.

"They're new and shiny," said Hulda. "They're just right."

"But you can't go barefoot to church, Mother."

His mother had said that she wanted to be present at his confirmation.

"I'll stay home," she said. "It's the only way out."

"No. You keep your shoes."

"But you're the important one, boy. You're to receive holy communion. You can't go to the altar in stocking feet."

"I can wear my wooden shoes."

"That would be blasphemy."

"Why aren't wooden shoes good enough? Christ Himself walked barefoot."

"That might be. But a confirmant must have decent footgear. Holy communion is a serious business."

Valter strolled a few times across the floor in his mother's narrow-toed shoes. Yes, they fitted. But he wasn't satisfied.

"They're so black and shiny," she said. "Why aren't they good enough for you?"

Valter kept silent. He felt ashamed to wear his mother's shoes. But he felt still deeper shame in feeling ashamed of it. Shouldn't that which belonged to his own poor mother be good enough for him? And was it anyone's business what he wore on his feet? Need he pay attention to his comrades? It concerned no one if he went to the altar in wooden shoes. But he wouldn't have been admitted in his wooden shoes. The guests at the Lord's table must be well dressed, because most important of all in the religious humbug was the outward appearance. No, why should he be ashamed to wear his mother's shoes? He was participating in the confirmation only to get it over with, and what he wore on his feet meant nothing. Having looked through the religious humbug, he need not be afraid of going to church in his mother's shoes, even though they were old-fashioned and had been lying in the store for twenty years.

But at the confirmation the year's class of girls would also be present. He was not pleased.

"One can see they are women's shoes," he said.

"Lengthen your suspenders," suggested Gunnar. "Then the pants will hide the buttons."

He followed his brother's suggestion, and when he lowered his pants as far as his suspenders would allow, no one could see that he wore button shoes. But the long, narrow toes he was unable to hide. He decided, however, to master the toes—to spite the pure Evangelical Lutheran Church. Yes, he would borrow his mother's shoes.

The examination was to take place on Whitsunday and the communion on Monday, which was Second Whitsunday and also a religious holiday. Valter appeared at church on Sunday in his new suit, with his first gloves, and in his mother's shoes. Today he didn't wear his black club tie, he wore the white one. He had tried his anti-military emblem on the lapel, but had removed it when his mother said it was too red to wear in church.

Mother's shoes were light on his feet, easy-walking shoes. And his pants were lowered so much that none of his comrades noticed that he wore women's shoes; as he marched with the others into the church, he had forgotten about his footgear.

The confirmants stood in a group outside the altar rail and were questioned about the tenets; afterward they would all in unison, in the presence of the congregation, confess their faith. At the question of the Trinity, Valter remained silent while the other boys replied in the affirmative. The other freethinkers among the boys, those from the factories, were of the opinion that it was of no consequence what they promised at a confirmation in which they had been forced to participate; those who forced them must take the responsibility. But Valter could not make himself lie and say in front of the whole congregation that he believed in God and the Son and the Holy Ghost. And in the unison answer the old semi-deaf minister would not notice if one boy kept silent, for he couldn't check and see that all mouths moved at one time.

The answer from the girls was stronger and clearer than from the boys. They promised loudly and definitely that each one of them would through prayer and vigilance profess her faith and prove it in her living. Yet, many of the girls Valter knew had long been waiting for the confirmation to be over, to permit them participation at the dances that had already begun for the summer. Perhaps more than one girl would lose her virginity out in the hills even before

Midsummer. But at the moment they all stood in their white dresses, their eyes modestly lowered in front of the minister, and from their voices it sounded as if they had made up their minds to stay at home and read the Bible every Saturday and Sunday night throughout the summer. Some might mean what they said, but many voices were false.

The boys knelt at the altar railing. Valter was barely down when he heard a suppressed giggling beside him. Next to him on his left knelt Ossian Flink, and he it was who had giggled. Valter cautiously turned his head to see what had amused his comrade. Ossian was poking his neighbor to the left with his elbow, slyly showing him something: Valter's feet.

When he knelt, Valter had pulled up his pants, exposing his mother's button shoes in their entirety. Ossian and the boys near him were red-cheeked from attempted suppression of their merriment. Valter was discovered; now he could not escape Ossian.

After the confirmation, as they gathered on the church green, Ossian came up to him, and before Valter suspected his intentions he pulled up one of Valter's pants legs.

"Look, kids! Valter wears his ma's shoes!"

Valter could only pretend that he was unconcerned; he mustn't let on in the least.

A group of girls had come out, among them the most beautiful ones. They looked at his button shoes with the long, narrow toes, and put their heads together and tittered.

Ossian completed his work:

"Hurry home with the shoes! Your ma might need them! Suppose she has a date tonight!"

He felt the blood rush to his face, and he trembled inside. But he must show nothing. Not here on the church green, among all the people, on a day like this. But tomorrow, when all was over, tomorrow, when he was rid of minister and church. Tomorrow when they walked home.

He felt the girls' smiles, but forgot them when Ossian referred to his mother. Those words about his mother, that was dirt in his face. And thrown in front of his comrades, both boys and girls. It could be washed off in only one way, with only one thing. Tomorrow, on the way home, tomorrow, after he was through with the minister and all that.

Thus, he did not say one word to Ossian Flink about the incident as they walked home together after the examination on Whitsunday. And the following day, Second Whitsunday, he went to his first communion in his mother's shoes and made no attempt to hide them by lowering his pants. It didn't matter now. Nothing could be worse than what Ossian had said about Mother.

After the communion, gifts of books were distributed to the youths, Valter receiving a psalmbook that his godfather Banda had bought him and a book of sermons and a Bible from his mother. "In Remembrance of Your Confirmation." How silly that his godfather and Mother hadn't pooled their resources and bought him a pair of shoes instead!

He walked homeward again, silent, tense, with his three books under his arm. They were still a small group of boys together, cotter boys with neither carriage nor bicycle, but on the last part of the road he and Ossian would be alone. Then it would happen. The very last moment, at the parting of the roads.

Valter walked homeward from his first communion and awaited his moment. In his company walked Ossian Flink, tall, almost taller than he, but crane-necked and factory-pale; he looked almost consumptive. At each branch road the group of communion boys thinned out. When he and Ossian were alone, Ossian would be friendly and agreeable; he always was when they were alone.

At last the other boys had left. Ossian and Valter walked toward the Sutaremåla road-parting, where Ossian would turn off. Arriving there, Valter stopped still. Slowly he put his confirmation books on a stone at the roadside. Then he pulled off the black gloves, the first gloves of his life, and began turning up the right sleeve of his confirmation suit.

Ossian became apprehensive; he smiled ingratiatingly. "It's warm today. Let's go for a swim."

"No. But you mentioned my mother yesterday. Now we'll talk about it."

Ossian nervously looked in different directions. "You're not going to fight? Don't be silly . . . Look at those squirrels! Let's try to catch them!"

Ossian pretended he had just caught sight of some squirrels in the top of a hazel bush; he bent down and picked up a stone from the road. Then Valter understood the meaning of the squirrel hunt.

"No weapons! Only our fists!"

Ossian grew even paler. "What do you want?"

"Did you think I would forget what you said?"

"Nonsense! I was only joking. Can't you take a joke?"

"Why did you have to mix my mother into it?"

"But, Valter—you and I are friends!"

"Put down your books!"

"We—we can't fight—on the way home from church."

"Only our fists—no weapons!"

"If you hit me, you devil, I'm going to tell the minister."

"I'm through with the minister."

Ossian was backing away toward the road leading to his home. Valter pursued him with quickening strides. Then Ossian turned quickly and took to his heels, Valter after him.

"Are you afraid, you bastard!"

Valter made a couple of long jumps and was beside Ossian. He gave him a hard blow with his fist on the side of his face, as hard as he was able to. The victim yelled and ran even faster homeward, holding his hand over his nose. Valter pursued him, but his anger was so great that his breath grew short and he could not keep up with Ossian. Then on the gravel he noticed blood that had trickled from Ossian's nose as he ran. Well, in that case, perhaps it was enough.

He turned and walked, panting, back to the main road, where he had left his books. He turned down his coat sleeve and sat down on a stone to rest. His right hand felt numb; it had been a fine blow, quite sufficient.

He had beaten up Ossian, given him a hell of a blow. But, thinking it over, he was a little concerned about his comrade's blood-trickling nose. In the under-class fight for independence, violence might eventually be needed, if nothing else succeeded. But the blow he had given Ossian could hardly be counted as a class-fight. Ossian was a worker like himself, and disagreements among class-brethren must be solved peaceably. Violence was permitted only against traitors. But Ossian was an organized glassworker. Had he the right to hit him?

Ossian had made fun of his mother's shoes; in so doing, he had made fun of Mother herself. Undoubtedly Valter would have had new shoes today if it hadn't been for their poverty. If Father had been alive, if they had still lived in their old home, he would have had his own shoes, the modern American type with broad toes. These old-fashioned button shoes on his feet—well, it was because of their poverty. Indeed, poverty personified glared at him from his feet. It was nothing but poverty Ossian had made fun of and laughed at—his own poverty, his parents', the whole class-poverty. Ossian had thus made an unfair attack upon his class-brethren. He had been a traitor—not a big one like the strikebreakers, but a small one, a nasty little traitor. And these little ones were in some ways as bad as the big ones; they were of the same ilk.

In proving to himself that Ossian had been a traitor, Valter felt justified hitting him.

He found his sermon book, Bible, and psalmbook, picked them up, and walked slowly homeward. He was returning from his first communion, well satisfied with his day: he was even with Ossian.

And on this Second Whitsunday he had forever rid himself of the minister, the church, and God.

His imagination was always at work. Ever since the old man with the cart and a sackful of children's heads had come to the house, he had known that he could imagine almost anything he wished. But he seldom wrote down his imaginings now that he had grown older. Most of his fantasies were childish things he ought to have outgrown. It was fun to imagine, but imagining must have a purpose.

He wrote a story to further the temperance work. It told of a drunkard's conversion. The drunkard had a wise dog, which he sold to get money for liquor. The dog would not stay with its new owner, but ran back to its old master. The wise animal through this action tried to persuade him that he must return the purchase money instead of squandering it in the saloon. The drunkard was so deeply touched by his dog's behavior that he bought it back, and from that day on never touched liquor.

The weekly *Brokiga Blad* had a story contest for children under sixteen. Valter sent in his story; he wanted it printed and read so that it might move the hearts of drunkards throughout the land.

After a few months he read in the paper that "The Drunkard's

Dog" had received prize number eighteen. Twenty prizes in all were distributed.

When he told his mother about having been awarded eighteenth prize, she took it much more calmly than he had expected. She knew that he invented stories and wrote them down, but she had never thought that any publisher would bother to print them. But perhaps, now that there were so many papers, it was difficult to find things to fill them.

"What is the prize?"

Well, the first prize was fifty crowns, but he didn't know the size of the eighteenth—perhaps fifteen or twenty crowns.

"Twenty crowns!" exclaimed Hulda. "That isn't possible!"

It wasn't reasonable that he should receive—for a silly story he had invented—as much as she received for a whole month's work for the farmers. She just didn't believe it.

Valter thought to himself that he would show Mother; he would buy a present for her with the money he received. Her old silk kerchief was torn to tatters; he would buy her a new one with the prize money. He would show her what he could earn with his writing.

One day a long roll arrived in the mail, addressed to "Mr. Valter Sträng." He had expected a postal money order, such as Mother got from America. He opened the parcel and unrolled a chart, as big as the map of the world in school: "Our Edible Mushrooms." There were mushrooms of all types and colors, and with the chart came another paper, beautifully decorated with flowers and green wreaths. In the center of this paper his name was printed in big red and green letters. This paper was called "The Winner's Diploma," certifying that he had received prize number eighteen. There was also a picture of the house where the paper was printed.

Hulda felt the thick paper of the chart; she was only mildly interested in the diploma.

"Where is the prize?"

He explained: no money had arrived; the prize for his story "The Drunkard's Dog" consisted of the mushroom chart.

"Edible mushrooms?" His mother peered at the chart. Did the people who had printed it believe that anyone besides cows would eat mushrooms?

Valter replied evasively that perhaps the chart was meant as a wall decoration; it had so many colors—red, white, gold, green. And he hung it on the wall over a tear in the wallpaper. Didn't his mother think it looked nice? It covered the torn wallpaper and lit up the whole room. It served the same purpose as an expensive oil painting.

But Hulda had little use for the chart with the cow mushrooms: it hung on the wall as a shining example of the futility of her son's writing.

"What about the twenty crowns you mentioned?"

"The diploma has a certain value," said Valter, hurt.

"Who'll give you anything for that paper?"

"I wouldn't sell it for twenty crowns."

"You wouldn't get half a crown."

"There are other things than money in life."

"All that paper is good for is the privy."

But Valter thought his prize story would now be printed and read by thousands of people. Perhaps some miserable father who brought his pay to the saloon might read it and turn away from drinking. Then his children would get better food and warmer clothing, and his wife would not be beaten up every time he returned from the saloon. Valter had done a good deed with his story. Perhaps some old drunkard would write and thank him for his happy family life after giving up drinking. Perhaps the wife of some reformed drunkard might write and bless him. One single letter from a woman who had escaped her former miseries would be worth more than the fifty crowns of the first prize; his mother ought to realize this.

"The Drunkard's Dog" had been his first contribution to the temperance work, and now he began to devote much of his spare time to the lodge. He went to the Brethren's Evening and to the Sisters' Evening and to the Postcard Evening; he strove to be a strong member. He was elected to the entertainment committee and read instructive stories. He was beginning to be noticed in the Lodestar. And he began to be careful about his dress; he sent for a celluloid collar with a three-year guarantee; for three whole years it need not be washed, only rubbed off with a handkerchief; now he was always neat around his neck. He had begun to part his hair all the way to the back, and he tried with a red-hot wire to curl a few locks around his ears. All the boys who wanted to be up with the times had fat curls above the ears for the cap to rest on. But Valter never managed to get any curls, however much he tried; his hair remained coarse and straight. When he burned his ear on the glowing-hot wire, he finally gave up trying. After all, it was not the kind of thing for a person of his interests to do.

But he wanted to look his best because of the girls, and particularly because of one—a brown-eyed girl named Agda, whom he thought more of than the other "sisters." She had helped initiate him into the lodge, she had whispered words of confidence in his ear. He was sure that she was not so superficial as the other girls, but was capable of deeper thinking. As yet, he had not been able to exchange thoughts with Agda; she was the most difficult one to talk to. He could be clever and funny with the other girls, but when Agda was present nothing funny came to his mind.

He asked her to be his partner in the folk dances as often as he decently could. Agda was round and plump and felt soft under his hand, soft as velvet. She might wear a cotton dress, yet she felt like velvet to the touch. He chose her for the dances only to be allowed to hold her waist for a minute. At such moments he was silent, solemn, unable to say a word. If he said anything, it sounded so silly that he regretted having spoken. "On the hillside, near the spring, on the hillside, near the spring, There my friend awaits me now, there my friend awaits me now." Agda's brown eyes shone as she sang and danced, and he imagined that the friend on the hillside was none other than himself.

But Harry, the son of the section hand, was Agda's beau. And this was the sad thing about her: she had a beau who had become a drunkard while still very young. Four times he had been received into the lodge, and four times he had been expelled for drinking. Yet he was still Agda's beau. How could she continue to go with a boy who had four times broken his vow?

Valter wanted to warn her against Harry. But he was afraid that she might think he wanted to take the place of her beau, which wasn't at all the case; it was only for her own sake that he wanted her to ditch Harry. If Harry loved his liquor more than her, he ought to be sent on his way. In the lodge library he had come across a novel in which a young woman let her fiancé choose between herself and a glass of Madeira; the fiancé could not resist his drinking-desire and took the wine. So Agda ought to let Harry choose. She should put a glass of *brännvin* in front of him and say: Take me or the *brännvin!* No, Valter was not interested in Agda; he was quite satisfied with holding her waist while they danced. He only wished she had a fiancé worthy of her.

"The Drunkard's Dog" was finally printed in the paper, and Valter was asked to read his story at a meeting. Now the members eyed him with new respect: he, one of their youngest lodge brethren, had written something that was printed! How had he managed to accomplish this? The story fitted exactly in its place in the paper, it was neither too long nor too short. How could he have figured it out so well? What kind of paper had he used? What kind of hand-writing that could be read by the printer?

Valter knew no more about the art of printing than did the others, but he answered mysteriously and evasively. After that eve-ning he was considered an equal with the older, respected members of the Lodestar.

He had felt Agda's eyes on him several times during the evening, and on the way home they happened to be in each other's company. For the first time they walked along the road alone, one on either side of the road. He could not have endured it if she had walked on the same side as he. He was filled with tension, his vest felt too small.

Tonight he understood why it was difficult to talk with Agda; to her he could not say anything unimportant, anything silly, as he did to the other girls; to her he must talk of his great ideals, about man's high purpose in life, about deep things. Nothing less with Agda. With her it must be a real exchange of thoughts. But it was difficult, almost impossible, to find the right words for high ideals and deep thoughts, words that would be worthy of the fine thoughts he harbored. Because his thoughts were finer than all the words that existed, he must keep his silence in her company. And he would a thousand times rather keep silent in her company than use ordinary words such as he used with others; she stood so high above the others.

But something had to be said—it was half a mile to Mr. Ros-mark's home where she worked as maid, and he couldn't keep silent all the way. He spoke of the new regulations for the lodge; as long

as he kept to the temperance field, he wouldn't say anything silly he
need regret. But the regulations lasted only about a hundred paces.
Then he walked silently again along his side of the road. He looked
up at the stars and wondered if he should say something about
them; this was a high subject, worthy of her, but it was difficult to
say anything deep about the stars.

Agda was tired, she yawned loudly.

"They had guests at Rosmark's last night," she said. "I was up till
three o'clock."

He was glad she kept talking. It had been a big party, liquors
of all kinds had been served, and she had washed over a hundred
glasses of different kinds before she went to bed; that was why she
was sleepy tonight.

"A hundred glasses!" he exclaimed, greatly wrought-up.

"Yes, and it wasn't the first time either."

In Valter's heart a feeling of compassion and tenderness grew
for her; she was one of the suppressed, she had to stay up nights to
clean up after Rosmark and his drinking-companions; her night's
rest was ruined because of pleasures and debauchery among the
upper-class.

Agda was forced to serve liquor and wash the glasses used by
the drunkards, and he asked her kindly if she didn't suffer from this
kind of work. Agda replied, with unexpected calm, that it didn't
bother her much, as it was permitted for members to serve liquor
if their employers ordered it; she was so accustomed to it now
that the thought of alcohol never entered her mind; she must have
opened hundreds of bottles during her four years with Rosmark—
more bottles than any other member, she felt sure. She wished,
though, that drinking people would use the same glass for different
kinds of liquors, as this would give her less to wash up afterward.

"They have a heck of a lot of dishes," she concluded.

"Yes," he said, "they're doing an injustice—an injustice to the working-people."

He couldn't forget the hundred glasses; Agda must wash and dry drinking-glasses until late in the night, she who was so much better a person than those who soiled them. She was a temperance fighter with a high goal, and yet she had to serve these superficial people who had no ideals and who lived only for their pleasures. In order to earn her living she must uncork all the bottles with the disgusting contents, though she herself was an idealist. She was a heroine, the lodge's feminine ideal personified.

He was about to start a discussion of the details of class-injustice when they reached her employer's house. Instead, he shook her hand like a man of the world, bowed a little, and said good-night.

"Sleep well!" he added, a little surprised at his daring. He hoped she wouldn't believe that his thoughts followed her to her bed. No, she must understand that he thought too highly of her for anything like that.

He held Agda in high esteem. What happened a few nights later was therefore inexplicable. He couldn't explain it, explain why it concerned Agda: he dreamed he was about to have sexual intercourse with her.

He woke up and felt ashamed. The moment before it was about to take place, Agda had vanished from his arms.

He looked in his bed and understood what had happened. How fortunate that he had read books and gathered knowledge! He need not, like many others, believe that he had some venereal disease. He had heard about boys who became frightened at similar discoveries and went to see a doctor. He knew that it was natural for healthy boys of his age. He had read in a Medical Adviser that it would be well to avoid stimulating books, dirty stories, insinuating references. But it had happened anyway, it seemed.

Agda's connection with the dream caused him to have a bad conscience. But his dream had not been conceived in his mind while awake; he had never desired her in that way while awake; he couldn't help what came to his mind while he was asleep. Yet, against his own will, he had dragged her down with his evil desire. He had dragged her down in his dream. After this it would be difficult to look into Agda's innocent, trusting eyes.

By now the paper with his story must be spread to thousands of homes, and thousands of families would read "The Drunkard's Dog." People would surely read it to the end, and then they couldn't help seeing the name of the author at the bottom. By now his name was mentioned in thousands of homes. To think of this was a great satisfaction.

But no letters from reformed drinkers or their happy wives came to him. Perhaps the drunkards felt ashamed to write him and expose their wretched earlier lives. He could appreciate their desire for silence. Or perhaps they felt that he was too young—only fifteen; their letters might fire his vanity. He must never succumb to vanity when he did great deeds. He knew how dangerous sudden success might be to a youth. He reminded himself of his decision to steel himself, to harden his character against the big head.

"The Drunkard's Dog" was to have unexpected consequences for Valter. His ability to write was now known to all members of the temperance lodge, and at the quarterly meeting in October he was elected its secretary, to succeed Joel-Nightstoker.

Never before had the Lodestar had a secretary so young that he had barely passed the confirmation. And Valter wanted to show himself worthy of the honor bestowed on him, digging himself into the temperance work with ever increasing fervor. At the meetings he asked to be heard more and more frequently, he offered suggestions for the work, he proposed questions for the discussion evenings. At his initiative, a fund was started for work among nonmembers. Temperance posters were sent for and plastered on every available wall and gate along the roads:

LET THE GLASS ALONE!
To save your health,
To improve your mind,
To ease your conscience,
To enrich your purse,
LET THE GLASS ALONE!

CHAPTER XIII

His quest for comrades continued. He had his "brethren" and "sisters" in the lodge, but they were not class-conscious. He sought comrades in the class-fight. Comrade and socialist were one and the same thing. *Comrade* was a powerful word; worker comrades throughout the world would save humanity. And salvation was not realized through the shedding of innocent blood, as the Christians believed; rather, shedding of innocent blood must be stopped to realize salvation.

Brother also was a great word. Valter had a real brother at home, but he would soon be gone. Gunnar had received his America-ticket from Anton and would emigrate in June. Anton had promised to get him work with the railroad in Duluth, Minnesota, where he himself had a job.

A worker's homeland was where work was available, where the best wages were paid. Here in Sweden one was born and grew up, and, once grown, one went to America. "There are brats to spare," Dagmar had said when she left. No one could say that now; after Gunnar left, there would only be Valter with his mother in the cottage.

Soldier-Hulda was running short of children; but they returned from America in pictures, which were lined up on the bureau for general admiration. There was Albin with his American wife and two children; he worked in a garage in St. Paul. Ivar lived in Chicago and was a salesman, traveling much; he had married a Norwegian girl, but they had no children. Dagmar had married a Swedish farmer in North Dakota and had one girl; she had sent home four pictures of her daughter. Fredrik was unmarried and had a hardware store in Oakland, California, and it seemed as if he earned more money than the other children. He and Albin sent money to Mother every Christmas.

Now it was Gunnar's turn to travel on the White Star Line— "the favorite line of the Swedes." Gunnar, his last brother. Valter took it hard. He also had his share in this emigration, as he had written Anton asking for the ticket without Gunnar's knowledge; Gunnar had wanted to sign up with the Army, and the only way to save the brother from "The Sword" had been to arrange for his emigration. But the parting seemed difficult as the day approached.

Gunnar had been part of his childhood in the soldier-cottage, a part that now would go to America on the White Star Line. Valter would be fishing alone on Sundays; there would be no one to help stretch the net across the pools, and two were needed—one at each end of the net.

Gunnar also was the only one he could speak to about Father; there must be two for that.

The last evening Gunnar was at home the two brothers walked over to their old cottage. Since the new military laws had gone into effect, the village was no longer required to furnish a soldier, and the old place had been sold to Johannes of Kvarn, who already owned three hundred acres but needed a few more. The cottage was not lived in and would soon be in ruins. The fields were now used for grazing. The barn had been razed, and the cellarhouse was caved in; the well was half filled with debris. The cottage still stood, but the chimney had crumbled, and the sod on the roof had washed away, exposing the birchbark under it, which now rattled in the wind. Hardly a pane of glass was left in the windows.

The soldier's sons walked about in the yard where they had grown into consciousness of their own existence in the world, with nostalgic thoughts of their home, which through no fault of its own had been neglected, ill-used, and degraded. They were warmed when they encountered some object still undisturbed. They stepped cautiously over well-known stones and with feeling hands touched trees and bushes. Behind the cellarhouse the cowslips were in bloom, and Gunnar picked a few to take along on his journey; he liked those little delicate flowers.

A woodcock came flying like a trembling black cross against the light June sky, and Valter saw it disappear behind two towering spruce trees. It was his childhood twilight bird, still flittering here. The bird's sudden appearance and disappearance over the yard had once awakened in him the first wonder at life's mystery. The bird's flight across the yard was as short as man's life. Who are you? Whither do you fly? Whither? Whither? It was the question he had asked when Father lay dead in the threshing-barn, that Sunday while he walked outside the barn door. Whither? Whither? Toward a disintegration that was inexorable. To oblivion that never ended.

But he himself existed in the fleeting moment of the flight.

Before they left, Gunnar turned to the cottage.

"I'll buy back the place when I come home!"

All the relatives in America had at one time or another written that they would come home to visit. The children had written that they would come home to see Mother. But Gunnar kept insisting that he would come home and stay home. As soon as he had earned enough money "over there" to buy their old home, he would come back and lift it from its present disgrace. This he always said most earnestly, and neither Valter nor his mother doubted his intent.

Gunnar had been quiet and serious-looking these last days before the America-boat would leave. There was also another reason why he seldom smiled or laughed this last year: he had suffered so much from toothache that Lind, the tailor, had had to pull out all his teeth; Gunnar was not anxious to show his lack of teeth. As soon as he arrived in America and earned enough money, he would have new teeth put in. Both Albin and Fredrik had written that they had bought new teeth. But Gunnar was serious because of the emigration also.

Mother had been against his leaving, but after the arrival of the ticket she had said nothing more about it; in silence she had helped him get ready. She was closer to Gunnar than to any of the other children; he had such great gifts—she could never forget that it had been said of him that he might become a minister if he could get an education. She would have liked to keep him in Sweden; the ones in America she would never see again.

Gunnar was to leave on the evening train, the night express, on the first Saturday in June. Aldo Samuel's wagon could not fetch him at the house, as the last stretch of the road was too narrow. Gunnar must therefore begin his America-journey walking. He and Valter carried the trunk between them, while the mother walked behind with the suitcase. She had put on her black silk kerchief tonight—it was a solemn occasion. Gunnar wore his new blue America-suit, with the bunch of cowslips from their old home pinned to the lapel.

The path was narrow, and one of the brothers had to walk ahead with his end of the trunk while the other followed. The road to

America was narrow, said Valter. There would be so much more room on the Atlantic, replied Gunnar.

A cuckoo sang in a spruce top, and Valter wondered if there were any cuckoos in America. Gunnar didn't know how the western hemisphere fared in that respect, but he would always remember this farewell cuckoo at Trångadal which sang for him on this last evening at home as he began his America-journey.

They reached the broader road where Aldo Samuel's hired hand waited with the spring wagon and the old red mare. They loaded the trunk in the back, and Gunnar took the suitcase from Mother. Valter would accompany him to the station, but Mother would turn back here. Gunnar would say good-by to her now.

The driver sat on the right side of the seat and waited. He need not rein in the horse—the old mare stood drowsily in the shafts, her head down. There was only the handshaking left before the wheels would begin to roll.

It's like following one's children to the grave. She had uttered those words once, and now she wore her black silk kerchief.

The driver waited. No one said anything. Hulda had walked up to the head of the mare and patted the animal on the neck near the harness hame. Some white fluid trickled from the corners of the mare's mouth, but she no longer stood champing foam; Aldo Samuel's red mare had grown old. She no longer chewed the bit; by now she had given up trying to chew it to pieces.

"How old is the mare?" asked Hulda.

"About fifteen."

"Hmm. Yes, I guess you're right. Fifteen. Well—"

They had always hired Aldo Samuel's mare when anyone left. The red mare had pulled all of them away. She had always been hitched to the wagon that came and fetched and rolled away. There had been different drivers and different wagons, but the horse in the shafts had always been the same. Early morning, middle of the day, late at night—the red mare had always been hitched to the wagon.

Soldier-Hulda was remembering other times. When Albin rode behind her, the mare had still been young. Then she had stamped impatiently in the shafts, chewed the bit, and pushed the wagon back and forth, causing the driver great trouble. That was Albin, that was many years ago. Then she had pulled Ivar and Dagmar, and then she was well broken in and stood more patiently; then she had been in her best years; then her eyes had still been awake—she had pricked up her ears and held her head high. The time Fredrik left she had just had a colt, which ran alongside as they drove away. But when she came for Anton one could already notice that she was growing old; she walked slowly, had to be nudged with the whip. And that had been some years ago.

Now Gunnar drove away with the red mare. Now she was old and tired, did not chew the bit, did not champ foam, did not move a hoof from where she had put it down. Now Aldo Samuel's mare had reached the reliability of old age; her eyes were faded, her head was down as she stood between the shafts waiting.

The mare was old, and Gunnar was the sixth one of Hulda's children to ride away behind her.

"I wish I'd brought a lump of sugar for the mare," said Hulda.

She ought to have had something. Poor, innocent animal, she wasn't to blame for the evil of this world.

"Tomorrow night I'll be on the North Sea," said Gunnar.

Mother looked up at the treetops; it was calm, not a leaf stirring.

"I hope it doesn't storm at sea," she said.

"Never this time of year."

"Better put on your muffler, to be on the safe side."

"Do you think you'll be seasick?" asked Valter.

"Who can tell?"

Gunnar said that he would buy some peppermints when he arrived in Gothenburg; he had heard that they were good against seasickness.

"Well," said his mother, "do you think they'll help? I hope they do. Good-by, then. Well—"

"Good-by, Mother."

They shook hands. The driver pulled in the reins, the old mare lifted her hoofs, slowly, with effort, and the wheels began to roll. Gunnar sat in the front seat; he turned around after they had driven a bit, but the road had made a turn and he couldn't see if she still was there.

At the station, friends of Gunnar were waiting, boys and girls; they hung a wreath of flowers around his neck, completely hiding the small bunch of cowslips from his old home. Decked in his flowers, Gunnar smiled in embarrassment and opened his toothless mouth. He didn't know what to do with all the flowers, he said, but he thought there would be enough water in the Atlantic to keep them fresh. All laughed, Gunnar was so amusing.

The express blew its signal of arrival behind the bend, and the stationmaster came out with his flag; he looked at the bedecked America-farer on the platform. Gunnar shook hands with Valter: he would keep his word, he would come home and buy back their old home.

"Good-by, then!"

"Good-by!"

A youth decked with flowers, an America-farer, up there on the train, the door slamming shut after him. The locomotive releasing its steam over the platform, enveloping Valter like thick fog so that he couldn't see his brother on the train. The hot vapor smarted in his eyes. Then the locomotive drew a deep breath, inhaled and exhaled, inhaled and exhaled, faster and faster, and when the vaporous fog lifted, the whole train had disappeared. Gunnar was gone.

Valter remained on the platform until all had left, until it was empty. He remained there still when the train whistled at the next crossing, two miles farther on.

His brother had gone to America. He walked homeward, his hands in his pockets, his shoulders slumped.

His eyes still smarted. The smart had been caused by the steam, but perhaps not by the steam only or it would be gone by now. His eyes still smarted; they remained dry, though for a moment he had thought—But that had happened hardly a single time since Father's death, and now he was surely too old. He was acting silly and mawkish: Gunnar had gone, but he was still alive; he would only be living in another part of the world. It would be idiotic to feel sorry, idiotic to mourn a brother who lived and was well, even though he was no longer here. He might miss Gunnar, but he mustn't act the weakling because of it.

And nothing happened; his eyes remained dry. To hell! He must become a man, hardened and in control of his emotions. But he must steel himself still more, he had a mission in life.

Fågeltuva bog had been crisscrossed by hundreds of black ditches a yard or so deep, and along the ditches stood the drying-barns. A narrow railroad had been laid on ties—or "sleepers," as they were called—across the bog, and the peat was brought in cars to the factory for pulverizing and baling. A gang of men—the car gang— pushed the cars over the rails, loading the peat at the barns and unloading it at the factory, handling their heavy cars in all weathers, through drenching rain or burning sun, through winter blizzards or sweltering summer heat. This was considered the heaviest work in the factory, and only sturdy, rough men were employed for the handling of the cars. But these men earned much higher pay than the other workers.

An extra man was needed in the car gang, and Valter had been suggested for the job in spite of his youth. The car-handlers earned from four to five crowns a day, and he was anxious to try it. He was now almost six feet tall, and his shoulders had broadened some, though his body in general seemed loose and lanky. He was nearly seventeen, but his mother thought that the peat car was still too much for him. He insisted that he could manage.

The first week would decide if he was to be kept on the gang, and he worried about how his new comrades would receive him as he reported for work.

Kalle Bleking, the gang boss, was a giant of a man; he walked a little stooped—if he had straightened up, he would have been taller than any other man hereabouts since Soldier-Sträng's death. He was also a fighter; it was well known what would happen when he decided to use his fists: three months in the hospital if he used his left arm, six months from the right, and often aftereffects for life. It was inexplicable that a drinking man like Kalle Bleking could possess such strength. Johan Tilly also and August Ling were incorrigible drinkers, and they, too, were respected for their raw strength. Mandus Karlsson was the shortest of the eleven comrades in the gang, but his firm, muscled body made up for his lack of height: he was solid through and through, like a forty-inch timber. The youth Valter was conspicuous among his eleven comrades, who eyed him suspiciously as they pushed out their cars.

"A paleface, hmm—"

"A cookie boy—"

"A lodge boy—"

"That's why he's so pale."

Kalle Bleking had not yet voiced his opinion. The gang boss twisted his mustaches and inspected Valter. The man's eyes were such a very light blue that they could almost be called white. On a Monday morning like this, Kalle Bleking often was sullen and irate because of his week-end drinking.

"A temperance kid, hey? Think you'll last till night?" He turned to the other men. "Which one of you'll carry the boy home to his mother this evening?"

Guffaws and grunts met his remark. A few of the men looked at Valter as though they felt sorry for him. He himself said nothing. Whatever he might say would mean nothing. Only his ability meant something to this gang. And the others might say whatever they wanted, as long as they didn't feel sorry for him. They might deride him for his paleness, for his lankiness, for his temperance work, but they must not feel sorry for him. He wanted no pity. He appreciated the fact that they considered the work hard; it would have been worse had they said it was nothing, something he could handle easily. He was grateful that they gave him no false encouragement. They knew their job. And he thought he detected in their voices a trace of respect for his daring in attempting to join the gang.

The cars were pushed one after another in a row; each car had its given place in the row, and all the men must make the same number of trips in a day. The cars, therefore, could not be pushed faster than the weakest man in the gang could manage; the poorest handler in the gang set the speed and the number of trips. A handler whom the others must wait for dragged down the pay for all of them, as the work was paid for by the car. That was why they insisted on strong men in the gang, and that was as it should be.

Valter had been given a chance. If he was unable to keep up with the others, he would be fired. This was only just; he could not ask that his comrades should be satisfied with less pay on his account. It depended on him whether he would stay and become one of them. No one would help him with the loading or unloading, and no one would help him push his car; it was his own business, it depended on him.

And the north wind and the south wind blew over the bog, filling his nose and mouth and ears and eyes with peat dust, and in between came windless days with time for thoughts other than weather worries. Then he could think of whatever he pleased beside his car.

Many are the sorrows of existence and equally manifold its disappointments. Valter had recently lost a "sister" in the lodge. The warm light from this sister's eyes had long ennobled his thoughts. In her presence his mind had risen to heights that had silenced his tongue. Agda, the marshal who had whispered to him the first secret password when he entered the lodge—she was struck from the lodge roster, gone, lost.

She had managed to hide her condition for rather a long time, but discovery inevitably came, according to the laws of nature. Insinuating remarks had perhaps been made by her sisters in the lodge, but no one had said anything directly to her. At last, however, the undeniable truth stood forth—the marshal was pregnant.

It was not clear who had got Agda with child. Section-hand Harry, her assumed fiancé, denied definitely that it was he, and Agda accused neither him nor anyone else. To her employer she said that the name of her child's father concerned only herself, and that was all she would say to anyone. It was evident, however, that there were many guilty ones to choose from. It had gradually become apparent that more than one man had been allowed to get close to her. She had had older men and boys, and she had made no distinction between lodge members and outsiders. A number of the brethren had at various times escorted her home from the meetings, particularly on dark nights, and among them were trusted high officials of the temperance society.

Valter did not puzzle his brain as to who was the father of Agda's expected child. His mind was busy with other things, inexplicable to him. She had been his particular, well-hidden secret, and this secret was now soiled and tramped in the mud. She had hurt him, violated what he held sacred. His pure feelings were desecrated. He had taken pride in his ability to look through so much humbug in society, but he had not been able to look through the brown-eyed Agda.

She had had intercourse with drinkers and non-drinkers, with old men and young men. What she had done could not be blamed on drinking, for she had not broken her temperance pledges and all the time she had been a member of the lodge, one of its officials. And Valter had chosen her as his partner in the folk dances and experienced a radiation of purity and innocence from her body. He had not felt worthy of kissing her lips, barely even her forehead under the frizzly locks. Once he had had an unclean dream about her—which he couldn't help—and for this he had often in his thoughts asked her forgiveness; each time his eyes had met hers he had silently apologized for an action beyond his control. But that which had been a dream to him had been a reality to her, a raw reality. She had had intercourse with men while perfectly sober. Why hadn't she resigned, at least, while she carried on?

Thus, Agda was a sister lost to him. He struck her from his life as she was stricken from the lodge. He himself wrote the paragraph about her expulsion for failing to pay her dues: "Sister Agda Svensson, not having paid her dues for two quarters—"

And thus he had also seen through female rottenness and vice to its very core, and consequently further hardened himself against temptation; it hurt now, but he would profit for the future.

For manifold are the disappointments of our existence. He had lost a sister whom he had held in highest esteem. But *comrade* was a noble word, and more sacred; his acceptance as a comrade in the car gang must compensate for the lost sister.

They were twelve in the gang, pushing their cars over the bog, and the twelfth in the gang was Soldier-Valter. He had become a comrade among comrades. He had gained this distinction, not alone by his ability to keep up his end of the work, but equally much by his spending of seven crowns for two quarts of *brännvin,* the usual treat of a newcomer at the end of the first week in the gang.

Comrade was a word of pledge—the most powerful word on earth.

CHAPTER XIV

At the quarterly meeting in April, Valter Sträng was elected president of the Lodestar, the local chapter of the temperance society.

Older brethren and sisters had hesitated to vote for him because of his youth, but Joel-Nightstoker had reminded the members that Valter had belonged to the lodge almost four years, that he had remained steadfast in his sobriety, and that—considering his years—his character was reliable; he was already a powerful fighter for the society's aims.

"Brother Sträng is a solid member!" Joel had said.

The gavel was handed to Valter. He said modestly that he was really too young for the post, though within him he felt that he would do honor to his exalted position in the lodge. He had learned how to preside at meetings; he knew the Rules of Order almost by heart, and he was at home with the Bylaws. During the last year he had spoken on almost all questions that came up, and he had made more suggestions than any other member. He had practiced speaking and acquired the use of more and more words. When he walked alone in the forest near his home at Trångadal, he would deliver speeches, ask questions, and give himself murderous answers. He must learn the meaning of words and keep them in mind to use when needed. That was all there was to it. Of course he could preside at meetings; he would execute his office in a way to gain respect. No one must think that he could show disrespect toward the president because of his youth. It was not Valter personally the members must look up to, it was the office he represented.

Nor must he let the elevation go to his head. There would be no change in him when outside the lodge. Defiance in adversity, humility in success—that was how a manly character displayed itself.

The number of members in the Lodestar had decreased in recent months, and now spring was coming with the yearly repetitions of breach of vows among the younger brethren and sisters. Many boys and girls joined the lodge in the autumn, remained members in good standing for the winter, broke in the spring, and applied for new memberships again in the fall. They came to the lodge because they had nowhere else to go during the winter evenings. Valter had raised the question: "Why is the temperance work dependent on the seasons?" and the lodge had decided that each repentant applicant must pay fifty öre to the publicity fund for his weakness. This character-weakness existed in all lodges. During 1912 five thousand members throughout the land had been stricken from the society's rolls for breach of vows—a depressing fact to Valter. In one year alone five thousand Swedish characters had failed; what a disgusting blot on the nation!

There had been a difference of opinion among the Lodestar members concerning dancing. The Bylaws stated explicitly: "Dancing and other degrading amusements are forbidden." Many local chapters broke the laws and danced lustily after the meetings. Many local chapters built elegant dance halls, but when it was a question of engaging a speaker they had not even money for a rostrum.

Others argued that dancing had taken place through the ages as an expression of human happiness.

The members of the Lodestar were split in two factions: those for and those against dancing.

The dance faction asked: Have some members the right to deny pleasure to others?

The non-dancers replied that temperance work was not a pleasure.

But if we allow dancing, we will increase the membership, insisted the dancers.

Those who join because of the dancing will bring little of value to the lodge, persisted the non-dancers.

We will by and by get them interested in our aims, was the reply.

Valter had as yet taken no part in the arguments. He hadn't learned to dance, and he was afraid that dancing might hurt both the class-fight and the temperance work; it might overshadow the great ideals and the high aims of the organization. Yet he did not regard dancing as a sign of low character; he thought that a person inclined to waltzing or dancing *schottis* might well harbor feelings as noble as those of one who wanted games or folk dances after the meetings.

As president, he now devoted all his energy to the spring membership drive. He engaged a speaker who showed charts of a drinker's insides. A great number of outsiders attended, as the lecture was given in the school. It was edifying to view a drunkard's body from the inside, look at his swollen heart, his inflamed kidneys, his enlarged liver. Some of the villagers must have felt that they were beholding their own insides. The speaker had brought thirty-four charts, and the audience looked and listened in silence.

At the next meeting of the Lodestar, eight newcomers applied for membership. It was always good for people to learn the truth.

ITEM 8. A motion was carried to arrange a sunrise picnic with basket-auction at Lake Löften the first Saturday in June. All sisters were asked to donate food baskets and the brethren to offer generous bids for said baskets.

In numerous groups the lodge members made their way through the wastelands toward the lake. There was no danger of stumbling over roots or stones in the transparent June night. After a day of rain had followed a clear, windless twilight. The rain had already been sucked up by the earth, which now exuded a fragrance of growth. A balmy night, exactly right for a sunrise picnic. Blankets had been brought along to ward off the dew on the grass, even though the minutes had failed to recommend this.

The brethren carried the baskets for their sisters as gently as if they had been full of eggs. At the stiles the boys climbed over first and set down their baskets to lift the girls, who couldn't avoid putting an arm around the helper's neck; five stiles on the road to the lake were climbed in this way, with patience.

It was near midnight and as dark as it ever was in June when the members reached the grassy shores of Lake Löften. In a month a load of hay would be mowed and harvested from this meadow, but as yet the blades of grass were tender among the spring flowers. Near the stones gleamed the light heads of the lilies of the valley; bumblebee blossoms and cuckoo breeches held their crowns high, and between them stood an occasional Virgin Mary Hand as a noble lady among the commoners. In the thickets of hazel and alder a timid wild rose opened here and there. Lake Löften's water lay unruffled, black like the forest on its shores. Around the stones in the water rose a nervous bubble—the bleak-carps had begun their spawning.

The boys and girls spread their blankets over the meadow grass and sat down. The baskets to be auctioned off had been placed in a circle around a big stone. The auction was part of the temperance work, as the proceeds would go to the membership drive. Joel-Nightstoker, in his capacity of cashier, would hold the auction; he wanted to wait until it grew lighter so that he would be sure to see the money and give the right change. After the shutdown of the glass factory he had got a job in the new grocery store and knew how to handle money.

It was an unusually still night at the lake. The lilies of the valley gleamed on the ground; the night grew lighter by the minute. By now the cashier was confident of seeing the difference between coppers and silver.

The president must open the auction. It was Valter's official duty, even though he cared little for it. Each brother must bid without knowing who had prepared the basket, and after he had bought it he must share the contents with the donating sister; that was how couples were made up at a sunrise picnic. This kind of game seemed childish to Valter. It was pleasant enough to eat a midnight lunch out in the open with a young girl, but some of the sisters were advanced in years; he might bid on a basket that had been donated by a thirty-year-old woman. And after Agda's departure he had not sought an exchange of thoughts with any other girl member in the Lodestar; he had no reason to believe that the sisters were thinking thoughts that would interest him.

The president climbed onto a stone and appealed to all brethren to be generous in their bids; they had not gathered only for heedless pleasure in Mother Nature's bosom, they had come to increase their membership fund. All bids must be paid at the fall of the hammer.

Tailor-Lind, the choirmaster, began a song: "Keep fighting, keep fighting, if courage you have!"

Then Joel rose and lifted the first basket above his head, standing as straight as his humped back permitted him:

"Gimme a bid!"

He was told to hold the basket behind his back: the bidders might recognize it.

"A bid! Buy a sister in the sack!"

A light joke was permitted at an auction.

"This basket has sweet cheese! Who likes sweet cheese?"

The first basket was sold for one seventy-five. The second was up ten öre, and the third one brought two crowns even. But no brother would pay more than two crowns; the next basket sank to one sixty-five.

"Open your purse strings!" shouted Joel.

Valter was angered by the low bids. Didn't they realize that it was a collection for the temperance cause? And that, besides, they would have the pleasure of eating out in nature in the company of a girl? But many of the brethren were materialistically inclined and counted the pennies. He had to admit that many people he knew outside the lodge were much more generous.

As president, he must set a good example. He started the next bid with two twenty-five.

No one bid higher, and Brother Valter Sträng stood suddenly with a basket on his arm. He looked at his purchase as if not knowing what to do with it. It was a nice basket, not the usual kind made of rough fibers; it had delicate, intricate weaving, and it looked new and little used. Whose basket was it? There was a certain elegance in its narrow handle.

As soon as donor and buyer found each other, they walked away with their basket and sat down to eat. Couple after couple found places among the bushes and the tussocks. Sandwiches, soft drinks, coffee, delicacies were brought forth. Valter stood and waited with his basket. No sister came to claim it. Well, if no one wanted his company, he would be glad to sit alone. He was not seeking female companionship anyway; he could go home now, he had done his duty for the cause.

A hesitant girl approached him, a tall girl, her hair hanging loosely down her back.

"That must be mine," she said without looking at him.

It was Karin Lund, the new stationmaster's daughter. She had joined at the last meeting, when Valter was home in bed with the measles; he had not seen her in the lodge.

The basket belonged to the stationmaster. Valter had guessed that it was not a common peasant basket or one belonging to the cotter people. Such a narrow handle had not been made for rough hands. But it suited well the small white hands of this girl. She couldn't be more than eighteen.

"We'll sit together," she said, and looked up at him. Her eyes were dark brown.

"Well, of course," he replied like a man of the world, with a certain studied indifference that he recently had begun to use with women.

"We must find a place."

"I guess so. Anyplace."

She took hold of the handle, and they carried the basket between them as they walked. It was good luck that she was so tall, just right to carry a basket with a man his size. And he liked the way she let her hair hang down. She was fairer than most girls; she must be spending most of her time indoors. But concerning her soul neither her hair nor her complexion told him anything. Could he exchange thoughts with her?

Where could they find a place? Everywhere, it seemed, the club members were sitting in pairs, a basket between them. The best places were taken. They walked some distance along the shore seeking a tussock; he was pleased to sit a little apart with her, in case she had some thoughts to exchange.

Under a lush hazel bush near the shore she stopped.

"This is the place!"

It was she who had made all the suggestions so far, and he had been the one to agree. She had suggested that they eat together, that they look for a place, that this place be under the hazel bush near the shore. He had not had an opportunity to say anything of importance yet. He could preside at a meeting, he spoke with ease to a group of people, but he found it difficult to speak to one single person, and doubly difficult if this person was a girl. For the time being, he must show his best manner and brotherly behavior.

The darkest part of the June night had passed; full dawn had come, and the dewdrops glittered in its light. The new day boded clear weather, perfect for a picnic at the lake.

The girl spread her wrap on the moist grass, and at her bidding he sat down on it. Then she opened the basket and brought forth its contents. Her checkered cotton dress strained at the waist and over her full breast. As she sat down beside him, her skirt slipped up and showed the calves of her soft girl-legs. The early light played on the wavy hair that hung down her back like an opened sheaf from the field.

She was Karin Lund, the new lodge sister. She might be a year older than he. But he was the president. He wanted to point out his position in the lodge, but in a casual way.

"I didn't preside at the last meeting," he said.

"I joined at last meeting."

"I was ill in bed. I had the—"

He didn't complete the sentence. Measles—it sounded too child-ish; he had got the measles too late; if he mentioned the word to her, she might think him younger than he actually was. And per-haps also she might be afraid of contagion.

"I had a cold," he said.

"Really?" she said, and poked in the basket for some sweet rolls.

"It was a bad cold. As a rule, I preside at the meetings."

The Lunds considered themselves almost upper-class, and he needed the counterweight his position as president gave him. It wasn't a heavy counterweight, but it ought to be enough; the position of stationmaster out here in the country was nothing to brag about. Moreover, he had heard her father referred to as *extra* stationmaster.

Karin had emptied her basket, and now she offered its contents to the buyer:

"Please!"

"Thank you! Thank you very much!"

He bowed lightly in his sitting position.

Beside the sweet rolls, she had brought cookies, sugar cake with strawberry jam, two bottles of lemonade, and, crowning the whole, two great oranges, which at first he had taken to be giant, yellow-colored eggs; he had never tasted oranges.

"Some stuff you've brought!" he exclaimed.

"My basket fetched the highest price," said Karin, without hiding her satisfaction.

"It's worth the price! More than the price!"

To say this would show his upbringing; for once he must play up to a girl, a little.

He began to eat and drink, absent-mindedly. It tasted good, but he mustn't seem to be paying too much attention to what he ate.

"Do you like sweet rolls? Or would you rather have a sandwich?"

She thought that, above all, he was interested in food, that the contents of her basket meant everything to him. Apparently she did not grasp that his thoughts were on greater things. He had already shown her what good manners he had; now he must also let her know what high ideals he harbored.

"I'm not a materialist," he said.

The girl stopped chewing for a moment and glanced at him. Perhaps she didn't know the meaning of the word. But her father was acting-stationmaster, and even though the local station was very small, his daughter ought to know what a materialist was.

She offered him a second helping of the sugar cake. He replied, inclining his head: "No, thank you!" She asked if he must be prodded and rested her big, open eyes on him. In the now bright light they seemed golden-brown.

She must not have understood that the sugar cake was of slight interest to him.

"I'm a utilitarian," he said.

The girl lowered the glass from her mouth, a few bubbles of the fizzing lemonade bursting on her lips.

"What is a utilitarian?"

He was holding his own—she didn't know what a utilitarian was. But other girls would not have asked, they would have pretended that they understood; some might even have pretended not to hear the word. This girl was awake. It looked as though he might have some exchange of thoughts with Karin.

He explained: A utilitarian was a person who aimed to make all people blessed in this world, as happy and blessed as it was possible to be. In a way he was the same as a socialist, since universal happiness could exist only in a classless society and socialism aimed at a classless world. A utilitarian was a denier, but not a materialist; his ideals were the highest in the world.

The president's explanation was not pompous, it was comradely and sincere. They were comrades in the lodge, and according to the Bylaws she had a right to make sisterly demands on any member, however high his position.

She listened, and her eyes did not leave him; now they glittered light-brown; she had the most disconcerting eyes, gilded eyes. She followed his reasoning, and it seemed that she wanted to keep the utilitarian view in mind. Other girls would have interrupted him and begun talking nonsense; he had had experience with such shallowness. But Karin was different; he even began to suspect that she was a truly soulful girl.

They had drunk the lemonade and eaten the cakes, and now she picked up one of the oranges and held it playfully to his mouth. He had seen oranges in the store, but had never bought one; now he would taste one for the first time. In a powerful bite he pressed his teeth into the fruit. The orange was tougher than he had expected, and it tasted so bitter that he made a quick grimace. The next moment he controlled himself—if he wanted to show his good breeding, he must tell her that the orange had a good taste.

"Delicious!" He pretended to enjoy it.

Karin doubled up with laughter. "You're funny!" He continued to chew the orange rind and could not understand what caused her merriment—until he saw her take out a knife and peel her own orange.

He turned his head away; his cheeks were burning. He had already swallowed some of the orange rind, but one piece still in his mouth he spat out.

He had not known that oranges must be peeled before one ate them. But she had not known what a utilitarian meant. That made them even, they could begin as equals again. What luck that she had thought he was being funny when he ate the orange peel; he had not made himself ridiculous. He must carry the joke further— he said that he had read in a medical adviser that unpeeled oranges were good against disillusion in love; he was taking the medicine as a prophylactic, to be on the safe side.

"You're awfully funny, Valter!"

She laughed so much that she got a piece of orange stuck in her throat, which he helped remove by hitting her on the back. This gave him a chance to feel her loose, soft hair, which hung conveniently between his hand and her back. They sat close together, and he noticed that she exuded an odor of earth and growth, the odor of a woman's hair. This consciousness affected him solemnly; he was approaching a great mystery that he must penetrate cautiously.

But she thought he was funny, and suddenly he was in a whimsical mood again, he didn't know how it happened. She laughed, and her laughter egged him on. Whatever subject they touched, his words took a funny turn. What caused this? Never before had he been like this when alone with a girl. He didn't recognize himself.

"I'd never thought of you as being funny," said the girl.

He guessed that the other lodge sisters with their limited intelligence had reported him as being a bore.

"Oh, I can be whatever I choose. Fundamentally, I'm seriously inclined."

He meant this seriously, but she laughed harder than ever. In view of his previous statements, this declaration sounded even more devastating. At last he was forced to laugh with her at his own words. He couldn't do anything else.

His exchange of thoughts with Karin was not turning out quite the way he had expected. Perhaps she didn't give him the understanding he had sought in a girl, but he had found something that filled his heart with happiness, and there was no need for further thought on the matter.

The semblance of night had passed and could now be called day. Across the lake, where the sun would rise, the sky had taken on a gilded sheen that reflected itself on the grass around them as if a fire had been lit. Yellow-red flames shot through blades and blossoms and glittered in dew and raindrops on the delicate stems. The carp played in the now illuminated surface of Lake Löften, which purled and bubbled like a caldron ready to boil. The reflected fire in the grass grew in intensity as the sun lighted its morning torch over the rested, rain-watered earth.

The sun was rising; the fish played in the water, the birds came to life in the bushes. The Lodestar members had waited the whole night for this moment; they had come to the shores of Lake Löften, there to enrich the membership fund.

Someone took up a song about "the meadow with its lone blossom, the forest with its spring, and the heart with its story to tell."

Valter thought that this song was a lie from beginning to end. No meadow had only one flower, some forest must exist without a spring, and who could swear that every heart had a story? He was just ready to tell Karin that the whole ditty was humbug through and through, when at the end of the song she sighed deeply and let her head fall against his shoulder, her hair touching his cheek. Perplexed, he sat in silence, without saying a word about the lies of the song.

Her lips were close to his and they were open. They opened still more as his met hers. He didn't know when it happened, but he knew it had happened. Her lips were moist and pleasantly warm.

"You have nice eyebrows," she said.

He remembered his freckles, which must seem immense to her now that she saw them so close. But she didn't mention them. She saw only the nice things in the world.

The reason he had never kissed a girl before was that he had never had the desire to do so. This needn't be anything unusual. Nor did he feel dizzying delight this first time, as he had imagined he might. But after a few tries he realized that he didn't do it right. He was afraid that he might show how inexperienced he was, and therefore he was more clumsy than he need be. He learned from her, though, and then it was different. She sucked his lips to her, harder and harder, and he responded. At last he reached a stage of delight—his head swam.

Moist and hot were the girl's lips, and they felt hotter each time. And her eyes were golden-yellow when the sun had risen above Lake Löften.

He no longer asked if anything were missing in the understanding between them—their exchange of thoughts could be postponed till later. And he said not a word about the song's lie concerning the heart's story. And perhaps some poor meadow existed where only one lone blossom grew, perhaps a spring opened in every forest. He no longer wished to deny this. He no longer wished to deny anything for sure, with Karin's head against his chest, her head with the loose hair. Only a little bit ago he had explained to her that he was a hardened denier, but now he sat here and almost wished that God had created the meadow with its lilies of the valley and its cuckoo's breeches, that He had created the playing fish, the chirruping birds, the clear light over Lake Löften, the grass in flames, and the girl's body he held in his arms. God ought to have created all this around him; then He would have been a good God.

No, he couldn't deny anything at this moment.

A thin coil of blue smoke rose from the low chimney as he reached his Trångadal home. Mother had put on the coffeepot. The sun was already warming the cottage wall, and it would be a hot day. He might as well sleep outside.

He lay down in the tall grass under the gable, where it would be shady for a few hours. If he now could get any sleep, in spite of the way the birds chirruped round the cottage until his eardrums were near bursting . . . If he now could sleep on this bed of grass, in spite of the way the grass exuded a fragrance like a girl's loose hair . . .

Now morning had come, with realization of the night's discoveries.

His opinions concerning woman's importance had not been thoroughly thought through. It was not definitely necessary that a man with his aims must live alone, denied women. Perhaps just the opposite was true: that the one destined for great things in the world needed even more than others a woman's understanding and support. A class-fighter might be just the one unable to get along without the gifts of a good woman.

Yes, he had felt the smart of his loneliness during long, dragging hours, but he had refused to admit it to himself, he had thought of it as a useful hardening, and that only a lone and denying life would give a fighter his strength and endurance. But perhaps he had been wrong. Perhaps he hadn't thought the problem through in believing a woman would be in the way. And it wouldn't be the first time he had been forced to change his opinions and drop old convictions that seemed childish after later discoveries.

Perhaps. A woman to share his successes, to stimulate and strengthen him in adversity. With woman, one could rest after the fight and gain renewed strength to carry on. Well—

After the sunrise picnic Valter had come to new understanding: A woman must participate. Man was a comrade with men, but woman, too, had her place at the side of her fighting man. He would like to lay his head on a tender woman's breast where he could find understanding. There would be something truly great in that partnership, in that idea. Perhaps it was a great idea.

During the following summer Valter did a number of things which indicated that a great change had taken place in his life.

He bought a new, light summer suit on easy payments. He bought a flat straw hat with a string to attach it to his buttonhole. He discarded the celluloid collar with its three-year guarantee against need of washing. Instead he bought a linen collar. He bought a bicycle of the trusted make "Jupiter," to be paid for in monthly installments during the coming year. Instead of parting his hair at one side he now brushed it back, which made his forehead look higher. In turn he sent for a great many ointments to eliminate freckles, each one with an unfailing guarantee.

And with the help of Karin he learned to dance passably well.

The purchase of the bicycle was the most important of these innovations. Karin owned a bicycle, and if they were to keep company, she could not ride while he walked. Valter's new bicycle practically filled the entrance hall of his mother's cottage, but he didn't have the heart to put it in the woodshed. Its wheels and mudguards were red with narrow silvery lines, it had a "New Departure" freewheeling and Dunlop's decks. On the handlebars was the name of the make: JUPITER; above it burned a large red star, the planet of the same name which rolled about among the heavenly bodies in space. Thus the wheels would roll; the bicycle would change his old life, which had been static, tied to the home neighborhood. Jupiter was a star, a planet, a whole world; it entered Valter's world and extended it.

Karin and he would drive to festivals on Sundays and dance together. The president of the Lodestar had joined the pro-dancing faction, which now got the upper hand; dancing took place after every meeting. And Valter realized that the games had been too narrow and insufficient. Dancing was an innocent enjoyment, never tempting the participants to mistreat their wives or kill anyone. And no one got an enlarged liver or fat heart from dancing. No idealist need lose sight of the higher aims in life because of dancing. The only thing against it might be the wear and tear on one's shoes.

Jupiter's wheels rolled. Another pair of wheels, belonging to a lady's bike of the make "Ceres," kept company. No one could count the number of gates these two pairs of wheels rolled through. Of late evenings, on the return trip, Jupiter and Ceres would be leaning against each other behind some bush along the road. So the two bikes might stand, hour after hour, resting their wheels.

Soldier-Hulda thought that her son had changed entirely this summer. He was out running around all the time, seldom spending a weekend night at home. On Monday morning he would go to the peat factory after an hour or two of sleep. He plagued his body, threw away his money, and ruined his health. Since joining the gang, he earned twice as much as before, and he had money to spend as he wanted; she doubted that, after giving her what she had coming for room and board, he had anything left. She blamed the bicycle, which—he told her—he had bought to get to work. That contraption could have been a great help if he had used it rightly. If she hadn't been so old, she would have liked to learn to ride it herself; then she could have got to church more often. But any woman who rode a bicycle must wear a hat; for that she was far too old; and people would have laughed at a woman on a bicycle in a kerchief.

Jupiter's wheels rolled the summer through. It was a warm and beautiful summer that year, 1914.

Yes, Jupiter's and Ceres' wheels rolled through the summer. During light, balmy nights they could be found leaning against each other behind the trees along the road. Their owners would then be close by—kissing and kissing through the hours, without satiety.

The change in Valter's life was great. He now considered Karin his fiancée. They had not yet announced their engagement, but it was obvious to all who knew them that they were "going steady." He had asked her what her parents thought about her keeping company with him; she had replied evasively. As yet he had not gone to Karin's home. He would escort her to the station-house, where her family occupied the second story, but she had never asked him in. He was too proud to mention this; if her parents had anything against him, he would not be one to force himself on them. They couldn't know much about him, except that he worked in the peat factory. They could know nothing of the plans he had made for his future. Karin's father, however, was in the opposite camp politically.

Valter was still too young to marry; he must wait a few years more, and during this time Karin's parents were sure to discover what type of man he was. He was in no hurry, but he planned for the future.

Karin and he would have two children. During their first years of marriage they would have no children; they would then wish to be free of parental duties in order to be together as much as possible and do what they pleased. The old workers, in their blind ignorance, had very early started large families, which were a burden to support and which held them down. And when the children grew up, perhaps they emigrated to America, with little joy to the parents. But the young workers of today seldom had more than one or two children. In his gang, only Mandus Karlsson was loaded down with children; he had six before he was thirty years of age. But, then, Mandus was a sort of simpleton, never learning by reading books. Most of the organized workers would read Bergegren's *Love Without Children*, or learn from the advertisements in the union papers: "French Protectives. Directly from Abroad. Full Discretion. 18 doz. for two crowns." Only a simpleton like Mandus failed to appreciate the advance of science; he lived in marital wantonness and got himself a flock of children. When his boys grew up, they would be examined by the Army to see if they were fit for slaughter, unless they had previously emigrated. Militarism fed on large families.

Valter would procreate with caution while the present unreformed society still existed.

Already, as a member of Elmer Sandin's club, Valter had gained understanding of these matters; he had been thinking of sending for a "discreet trial." But there was no hurry as yet. He had also thought that he would lend Karin *Love Without Children*. It was filled with important knowledge that must not be denied a grown girl. But so far he had found it difficult to bring up the subject; he must do it in a refined, experienced way, otherwise he might appear vulgar. But their marriage was not imminent—he would have plenty of time. When they decided on the date he would hand her the book; then she could not misunderstand. As yet, while just "going together," it was a sensitive subject; she might question his intentions.

He had never even dreamed that he might have her until after they were married. He had some notions about "free love," and according to these it would be all right to make her his woman now. But for some reason he could not approach her in this way. Perhaps he was unable to free himself from old, inherited customs. It must be an upper-class superstition that a bride should be a virgin. But it was a nice thought, a nice superstition. After all, some beautiful, worth-while notion might once in a while emanate from the upper-class.

A few years earlier Valter Sträng had written down some opinions about Woman in his notebook called *Contains Truths*. He had been rather childish and shortsighted in those days. Now he tore out the old page and wrote instead:

"A man might easily deteriorate and wither away in loneliness and denial. A leader or fighter needs a woman to stimulate him to great deeds."

This was the sum total of his discoveries that summer.

CHAPTER XV

It was a summer of retrogression: some of the workers in the peat factory thought that a war might break out among the Great Powers; even organized workers feared the possibility of war. Valter reminded his comrades that at the 1907 Stuttgart Congress all the European workers belonging to the Second Internationale had pledged themselves to use whatever means were necessary to prevent war. And if every worker on the Continent refused to participate in the "Bloody Insanity," where would the militarists find soldiers?

The work at the peat bog was at its height during the hot, quick-drying summer days. At lunchtime the members of his gang would find shade behind some wall where a cool breeze might dry their sweaty shirts. There they lounged and talked about the war rumors, even though Valter had proved to them that no danger of war existed; there might be a war in the Balkans, but not in countries where there were organized workers. Valter had a copy of the Stuttgart Resolution, and he would bring it to the factory; perhaps his comrades would believe him when they saw it in print. He was glad to have this copy now that the warmongers were at it again.

The last week in July ended, and on Saturday they received their pay. On Sunday Valter took his bike and rode down to the station, where he had a date to meet Karin. The afternoon train was coming in, and an unusually large crowd of people had gathered to buy the late papers from the train newsboy. But the boy came out on the platform and showed his empty bag. All his papers were gone! Not a single copy left!

What had happened? The explanation was now spread: Germany had declared war on Russia. In Paris a general mobilization order had been issued.

Jaurès, the Branting of France, had been murdered in a café.

Valter and Karin rode down the forest road to Lake Löften, where they sat down in a birch grove near the shore. They could hear the cowbells in the distance, and the wild ducklings swam in the reeds; it was a quiet summer evening. The month of August had commenced. Valter sat chewing on blades of grass; he neither spoke nor answered as usual, and Karin wondered if he had taken to brooding. But he heard her when she said that perhaps she would move away in the fall; her father might be transferred to Atorp, some forty miles up the line. Had she said this yesterday he would excitedly have told her that he could not let her go so far away. But now his head was filled with thoughts of an impending catastrophe that must somehow be averted.

Germany had declared war and was mobilizing, and France was mobilizing. The militarists had sprung a trap. But there were also things called railroad strikes and general strikes. The workers surely had not yet had time to act, their leaders had not yet given the signal—that was all. Tomorrow the papers would carry headlines about a general strike in Germany and France.

Karin was affectionate, and he felt a little better when they parted later in the evening.

Monday morning he picked up his copy of the Stuttgart Resolution and took it with him to the factory. But he had no opportunity to read it to his comrades. Instead, they read the late papers to him.

War had begun. No general strike, no railroad strike. Not a single locomotive engineer had refused to run the troop trains, not a single switchman had refused to turn the switches, not a single pebble on the rails hindered the trains in transporting the armies. The human slaughter had begun.

Valter threw the Stuttgart Resolution into a ditch and tramped it down in the mud, deep down.

The men talked about the war. They carried peat into the barns, their knees bent under the heavy burdens on the swaying planks, and they talked of the war. Of the militarists' war. Of other comrades failing one another. Of the great, great, incomprehensible betrayal. Of the betrayal of a high ideal—the ideal of comradeship.

For this was a betrayal by the leaders. They had pledged to prevent a war. But the soldiers of peace, the workers, had not been mobilized. No general strike had been called. Nothing could be expected from the Russian workers, ignorant and in bondage as they were. But the enlightened and free socialists of France and Germany? What had their leaders done? Apparently they had been talking nonsense at the international congress.

To hell with the Resolution! To hell with the Second Internationale! They meant nothing.

The workers should have made good their pledge. They should have broken the guns. No sane person could hope for peace from the bourgeois. Kings and emperors reaped honor from human slaughter. The officers of the army had slaughter as their profession. The army chaplains, those slaughter-dressed followers of the Prince of Peace, blessed the guns instead of breaking them, and prayed fervently to God for a successful blood bath. And the capitalists made money from manufacturing the guns. There was hope only from the workers. Their world-comradeship could have saved the world.

There were some who said that the war might even last three months.

Stationmaster Lund and his family moved to Atorp in October. Karin and Valter agreed that he would come to visit her shortly.

The first letter he received from her—the first love letter of his life—began: "King of My Dreams!" The word *king* did not especially appeal to him, as he was a convinced socialist. To abolish the monarchy and establish a republic was on his party's program. "President of My Dreams!" would have fitted better. Nevertheless, he liked the sentiment expressed in "King of My Dreams!" After he had read it a few times, it no longer bothered him. He ruled Karin's dreams. What more could he wish? This love of theirs was serious, nothing in the world could come between them, even though they might have to wait a few years before marrying. And he began a passionate letter in reply: "Queen of My Dreams!" Then it struck him that their correspondence was carried on in an old-fashioned, royalistic spirit, hardly suitable for young, emancipated people of 1914. And the word *queen* was wrong, for queens nowadays seldom had any power. He took a new sheet and began: "Thou Ruler of My Dreams!" He wrote passionate, tender, long letters, four or five double sheets, which nearly always required double postage. Sometimes he would mail two letters at the same time, to give her a pleasant surprise; sometimes he would register his letter to make her appreciate it more and make her realize that the cost of postage for a letter to her meant nothing.

Her second letter, too, began: "King of My Dreams!" and was signed: "Your own Karin." The salutation was so beautiful that she could well use it a second time. He himself tried to change expressions with each letter: "My own girl!"—"My big maiden!"—

"My little maiden!"—"My dear fiancée!"—"My wife-to-be!"—"My beloved little woman!" But in almost every letter she would come back with "King of My Dreams!" and at last he feared that she was unable to think of anything else. And her letters were, in a way, a disappointment to him; they were not quite like her. She herself was so warm and intimate and tender, but there was not much of this in the letters. She spelled and punctuated correctly, but used very few words, and these were mostly common words. She did send "hugs and kisses" at the end of her letters, but it didn't suit Karin to put this on paper; it seemed too cold and formal in some way. For hugs and kisses she must be close and participate.

To begin with, he received two letters a week—he wrote three or four himself—but after the first month only one letter a week arrived from her. Her letters had always been short; now they were even shorter. And she changed her expressions of address and the closing lines. "King of My Dreams!" had become "Dear Valter"; "Your own Karin" became "Karin" only. He thought that it might be just an oversight, but he would much rather be called her Dream King than Dear Valter.

He waited in vain for the promised invitation to come and see her in her home in Atorp, but he was not concerned until one letter arrived which began "Friend Valter." "Friend"—was that what she called the one she was to live with her whole life through? Something must be wrong. What could have happened? There was too much of a gap between the supreme ruler of her dreams and "Friend Valter." Now he must find out. He wrote and asked how he was to interpret her change of expressions—"Your eternally loving Valter."

He waited a week for an answer. He wrote her again. No reply. He wrote a third time and insured the letter for one hundred crowns. Now it must reach her, at least. No answer. He wrote a fourth time and insured the letter for five hundred crowns. She must realize that he spared no expense. No answer.

Four letters without an answer. Could she be sick? But not so sick that she was unable to write a line on a postcard. Could she have died? He began reading death notices in the paper; he located all the copies for the last weeks and read all the death notices they contained. But he found her name nowhere in the many black-bordered death announcements.

But one day he found her name in another family notice, without a black frame:

engaged:
Folke E. Lovsson
and
Karin Lund
Atorp

The north wind wailed over the old peat bog. Valter kept his job in the gang and pushed his car while the norther filled his eyes with snow. The wind of retrogression was blowing, too—the war still went on.

The rails over the bog rested on ties, and he took long steps—one step between each tie. In a hundred steps a hundred ties, or "sleepers," as the men called them. He counted the sleepers—his mind must do something. He had tramped these ties so many times now that he knew each one by heart: this one was crooked at both ends, that one looked like the figure 3, the pine sleeper with the bark on it was next, then that spindly, narrow one that was smaller than any of its two thousand brethren along the road. One must know the ground one walked on. He tramped equally heavy on all these sleepers, as heavily on the spindly ones as on the thick ones. What did it matter?—it was only dead wood. It was not like tramping purposely on a living heart.

She was alive, in good health. But no answer to four letters, two of which had been registered. Then had come the announcement, the death announcement. It had no black frame, but he had cut out a frame from another death notice and pasted it on; then he hid it among his belongings, now that it was framed in its true color.

She had a right to become engaged, he had nothing to say against that, she was old enough. But why had she for months pretended to be his sweetheart? Why? This was the blackest deceit. The same kind of betrayal committed by the labor leaders of the warring countries.

Something was wrong with humanity.

This autumn he grew pale and wretched-looking and began to cough. He had attacks of coughing in the mornings and late in the evenings. "You kill yourself in that bog," said his mother. "If you don't quit, I fear you'll get consumption."

She had promised. That time, and that, and that. When they cycled to this place, and to that. When they sat together in the forest: "You know it. I promise you. I am yours. I will always be yours. You need not worry. You can rely on my word."

There must be something radically wrong with humanity.

Her mouth never tired of kissing. He had to catch his breath at times, never she. Her lips were never satisfied. They kissed, they penetrated, they demanded, ever hot, ever eager, and his own were stimulated by hers. They might kiss hundreds of times on a Saturday evening, and as many times the following Sunday evening. Now she kissed another man equally passionately. And perhaps they went further than kissing, perhaps the other man already owned her fully.

Three times in two days Valter's car turned over, stopping the whole gang; he had not loaded properly, and the car lost its balance

on the curves. His comrades overlooked it: he had a cold, and an
ominous cough.

He had read *Woman as Sex-Being* and *Woman as Virgin, Wife
and Mother*, truly good books, advisable reading for both married
and unmarried people. In these books he had learned about "all the
spiritual and physical peculiarities in Woman." But she must have
still more peculiarities than those divulged in the books; perhaps a
woman possessed qualities that were not mentioned in any book.

Many years were to pass before the full truth about Karin became
apparent to him: she had not failed him. That girl could not fail
him. Because she could not love anyone else without his permission. She could not do anything unless he participated; she was
one of those beings he himself decided for. She was a creation of
the same kind as the man with the cart who one evening at dusk,
during his childhood, had come to the cottage with a sack full of
children's heads. In the same way that that man had been his own
creation whom no one else had seen, so Karin for the time being had
remained his own girl whom no one except himself had known,
whom no one else could know. That Karin could not fail him. But
his bitter sorrow stemmed from the fact that he had confused her
with another girl who had become engaged to another man. About
this girl he knew almost nothing.

And so it came about that he destroyed an old notebook where he
had written down a great many "truths" and given each one a number. Although a few remained, indestructible in his mind, others
were shattered, a few were pure childishness. The notebook only
pointed out how very childish he once had been. What nonsense
he had inscribed in that book about Man and Woman, as late as
last summer! Where had his brain been at that time?

Now he burned the book called *Contains Truths,* and in a new book he wrote:

"A man destined for great deeds needs peace and harmony. He must not tie himself to a woman. A woman only causes confusion and disintegration."

And so Valter's life went on, with discoveries of false discoveries. Existence, it seemed, was one continuous discovery.

CHAPTER XVI

Returning from the factory one day, Valter stopped at the post office to pick up the week's mail. There was an America-letter addressed to him personally. This was unusual, for his sister and brothers always addressed their letters to his mother. Not that it mattered much who the addressee was, as he read the letters to his mother anyway. But he was surprised to recognize Anton's hand-writing on a letter to himself.

> Dear Brother, I hope these lines reach you in good health. Sad things have happened to your brother Gunnar, he was buried two weeks ago, I was at the funeral, he lived near us . . .

As Valter read the letter, his head began to swim; the whole post office seemed upside down. He began at the beginning again: Gunnar was dead. He tried the middle of the letter, he looked at the last lines: Gunnar was dead. He had been killed in the railroad yard in Duluth by accident; while switching cars he had been crushed between two buffers. Anton had been the only one of the family to attend the funeral; the others lived long distances from Duluth.

The mail from America was slow now during the war—Gunnar had been in his grave for almost four months. This was December, and on August 15, in the evening, two buffers in the Duluth rail-road yard had crushed his chest. Valter remembered the 15th of August: it had been a Saturday, he had been out dancing with Karin.

He pushed the letter into his hip pocket and remained standing in the post office.

Gunnar was dead.

> You see, Valter, we over here think it best not to say anything
> to Mother about Gunnar. None of us here will ever write her
> about it. I have kept all the papers and taken care of all things in
> connection with his death, as they do in this country. You must
> promise not to tell Mother, Valter . . .

Gunnar was dead but he must not disturb Mother with this knowledge.

> I still live in Minnesota, but intend to move to California.
> I guess many things have changed in the old country, I aim to
> come home for a visit some summer. Don't tell Mother . . .

He had been out dancing that evening, been out for amusement, while some workingman had picked up Gunnar's body and put it on a stretcher, his brother with the crushed chest, crushed by the car buffers.

Many thousands of workers had fallen in the war that day. But none of them had been his brother. There was a difference when it concerned one's brother. And Gunnar had been the only brother he had been close to. They had stood outside on the station platform, he still knew the very spot; Gunnar had stood there, decked with flowers. They had shaken hands, he had said that he would return as he had promised, they would see each other again—good-by, then! Good-by, Gunnar!

Then the locomotive had spouted steam, and the departing whistle had blown. Then nothing more, not a single word, between two brothers in the only life that existed. *Gunnar is dead, yes, Valter . . .*

And there was no meaning to anything.

On that day, when Gunnar had left, Valter had escorted him to his grave. Mother had gone only a part of the way, but he had followed his brother all the way to the station platform. And Gunnar's chest had been decked with flowers, and Gunnar had traveled directly to Duluth, Minnesota, to get his chest crushed in, to get buried in a Duluth cemetery.

There hung in the station waiting-room a poster, it had hung there for years: "Opportunity for Youth! Join the Army!" He had asked Anton for a ticket for Gunnar to save him from militarism. To be on the safe side, Gunnar had gone to America; he had escaped the Army.

There was no meaning to anything.

Not yet twenty. Not half as old as Father when he died. He had emigrated to earn money so that he could return and buy back their home. But he had traveled to Duluth, only to be buried there. He had reached the railroad yard at exactly the right moment, had found exactly the right place between the buffers, because the cars must have his young chest between their buffers; they couldn't continue their rolling otherwise. So Gunnar had left. Good-by, then, Gunnar! Then nothing more, nothing more in the world, in time.

Swedish Youth! The World's Fastest Steamer!

What was the purpose? Twenty years, and then two iron buffers. There were other powers besides militarism. There was no meaning to anything.

He started homeward, slowly.

Anton and the others were right: Mother mustn't know. No other son was so dear to her as Gunnar. As long as they could keep it from her, then. She couldn't read the letters; sometimes she would sit and hold them in her fingers, look at them, feel them, feel the paper that her children had written on, that their fingers had touched. But he had better burn this letter from Anton; Mother might happen to show it to some visitor. If Gunnar's name was mentioned in any other letter, he could easily skip it while reading to Mother.

Valter reached home sooner than he wished that evening. He didn't speak to his mother at first; he went to the kitchen, picked up the enameled washbowl, and went outside to clean the peat from his face. He kept washing for a long time today, as if it were Saturday. And he thought to himself: I must put on a new clean shirt tonight, the old one is sticking to my body, cold with perspiration.

He put on a clean shirt before he sat down to eat. Mother had boiled jacket-potatoes, and fried pork. He liked fried pork. But he had no appetite tonight. He thought of a sugar cake with a black cross on it. That time also his appetite had failed him.

Hulda said: "Eat, now! You need to, with your work." He felt the long America-envelope in his pocket; when she was looking another way, he pushed it deeper. He mustn't forget to burn it.

"Are you going out tonight?"

"No."

"But you've changed."

"Only wanted to clean up."

They should both have dressed for a funeral tonight. He should have worn his black gloves, his white tie, his stiff collar that chafed his neck. Mother should have put on her black skirt, her silk kerchief. Six of Gunnar's school chums should have carried the coffin—in gloves and silk hats—as they had done when Miller's Ernst died; they had held their heads awkwardly, wearing tall hats for the first time, but they couldn't very well carry a coffin in sport caps. But he and Mother had already followed Gunnar to the grave; it had been a fine spring evening, the cuckoo singing goodby; and Gunnar had said: I'll buy some peppermints when I get to Gothenburg. Well, good-by, then, said Mother. Good-by, then. Then there had been nothing more between Mother and Gunnar in the only life that existed.

"Did you ask for the mail?"

"Yes. Nothing."

"Well, nothing."

Nothing. Nothing had any meaning.

He remembered now that Gunnar had not written for a long time. But it often happened that America-relatives were silent for long periods; some gave up writing altogether.

"Do you suppose someone in the store has picked up our mail?"

He said that he would ask next time he went in there.

Mother had lately suffered from abscessed roots that remained after she lost her teeth, and she had slept badly; she would have no peace until the roots ached themselves loose and fell out, and this took time with old people. She had had no teeth for as long as he could remember; she must have been quite young when she had begun soaking bread crusts. It was the lot of the poor to lose their teeth early. The rich had not only good teeth, they had good food to chew with them—another injustice. The rich could also buy store teeth, should they need them.

The mother went to bed after having washed the dishes and put things in order, this evening as all evenings. Valter sat for a while and read the paper. Trouble was brewing, perhaps they would have to go on strike at the peat factory. Their local was demanding three öre an hour, but the owners refused the raise.

He wondered if Mother's teeth ached tonight or if she had gone to sleep. Many nights he heard her groan. But she lay silent tonight; perhaps she had no ache. Perhaps she was already asleep. But he must go outside, whether she slept or not. The first evening after Father's death—he had been twelve then—he had wept bitterly. It was different now, but he wasn't quite sure what would happen, and Mother might hear. Anyway, it was stuffy in here, he felt choked. He blew out the lamp and stepped outside the little cottage.

It was a starry evening with early frost; the old withered grass crunched stiff and dry underfoot. A great, wide hazel bush behind the cottage stretched its gnarled, nude branches toward the stars, like arms reaching for help from above. A few stars glowed reddish, boding bad weather; perhaps there would be a blizzard over the peat bog tomorrow.

Gunnar had had such a good head. His own gifts were nothing in comparison. Gunnar could have passed the highest schools. But he had had to go to Duluth, Minnesota, to be put in the cemetery there with a crushed chest. Who would make up for the injustice now, that he had been allowed to live only twenty years before his breast was crushed?

Horrible to think of oneself as not existing, Gunnar had said. There was no meaning to anything.

Who indemnified him now? What did God do, if He existed? Nothing.

His throat felt thick. Valter was standing in the yard, looking at the starlit heavens, clearing his throat, spitting. That damned peat!

It blew right down one's lungs. But it was not known to cause consumption. He coughed, but otherwise he was well in body. He would find out next spring, at budding-time, the trying season for the chest-sick. Anyway, what did it matter when there was no meaning to anything?

The glittering stars up there were many, but all one could see were accounted for. Perhaps two thousand were visible tonight. A hell of a lot of illumination for the wretched earth creatures. Each star shone clear and innocent as a Christmas-tree decoration. The sky was a Christmas tree tonight. But if the earth was a star, then it must shine blood-red now during the war. It must appear like an oozing liver, dripping with innocent blood. Inhabitants of other planets must snort in disgust when seeing it: Look at that pitiful earth-star! Revolting devil! That is the earth!

He spat on the earth under his feet, he spat where he stood, and looked up at the stars again. Gunnar had said: Nothing cannot exist, there must be a world, and therefore someone or something must exist who has created it. Perhaps there must be a God . . . That was the time they had caught the big pike, it had got out of the net and almost back into the water as they pulled it in, but Gunnar had thrown himself upon it and caught it with his hands. He had yelled with pride, both of them had been pleased, the pike had weighed six pounds. Afterward they had stretched out in a wild-strawberry patch and talked about eternity. Gunnar had said: No world and no life? I'm unable to imagine nothing. Horrible to think of oneself being no more.

Those had been Gunnar's thoughts. If there was anything to learn about God and a life hereafter, then he must know it now. He must know everything. If there was anything.

But if he still could think, then he must suffer and regret the poor twenty years he had lived on earth. What recompense was there for his short life?

Valter had wished to save him from militarism: You mustn't sign up, Gunnar. Better to go to America. Better to emigrate to Duluth, Minnesota. Death to the Sword! But there were other powers he hadn't been able to cope with. If there was a God, then He must be laughing at him now. Valter had helped obtain the America-ticket for Gunnar, who must hurry to get between the two railroad cars when they met.

Who was to blame for the injustice done his brother? The two cars he was coupling might have been loaded with luxuries for some millionaire. Yet, the capitalist society was not to blame for his death. The truth must be acknowledged: an accident in a railroad yard could happen even in a socialistic society. In a socialistic society Gunnar would not have been killed at car-switching—his keen mind would have given him different work—but some other man would have stood between the cars and got his chest crushed in Gunnar's place. And what was the difference whether he mourned his brother Gunnar or another young man mourned a brother with another name?

Injustices existed which could never be recompensed. Social justice on earth was not enough. Things happened like this accident to Gunnar. And if injustices as such could not be abolished or recompensed, then there was no sense to anything. And if there was no sense to anything, what meaning was there in the class-fight?

And why did he demand a meaning? Why must something exist?

It was almost a midwinter sky, with the sun in Sagittarius. The Milky Way flung its light banner through the heavens from east to west, the Big Dipper hung over the dark forests to the north. He looked for the constellation Cetus, the Whale, which at this time of evening was supposed to be visible in the south below Aries and Pisces. Like Branting, he studied astronomy in his spare time. He was not sure of the stars in Cetus, but he easily found Orion, and the two Dogs, Orion's companions. Why was Sirius called the Dog Star—Sirius, the most brilliant star in the heavens? That simple name would have been more fitting for some inconspicuous star.

He spat again on the earth on which he stood. He had been given a dark planet to live on. He had tried to think thoughts that might lighten it, sought ideas to believe in. But suddenly the light had gone out: Gunnar had been denied life above twenty years, and there was no one to give compensation for the years lost. Millions died innocently, suffered agonies, without compensation.

But when the stars grew old and worn-out and burned-out like the wick in a lamp's oil chamber, then they too went out and disappeared. Even the stars died. Yet he demanded life for his brother, life for himself. He insisted on it because he must find a meaning. He wished to make the earth a bright planet.

"Impossible to imagine nothing!" Gunnar had been a keen thinker: to strive for something beyond the short, insufficient physical life—that was the only thing, and perhaps that was the meaning. For one couldn't think of oneself as nonexistent.

Now Gunnar knew everything. The meaning, if there was one. He knew all. If there was anything to know. The blackest, most awful thought was: if there was nothing to know.

Valter must find a meaning. This physical life was insufficient. The word God would have been the greatest word if God had existed. Perhaps he wasn't yet rid of God, if he still could question His existence. Religion was a personal thing, he had read in the party program; they did not insist on a denial. In the final analysis, perhaps everything important was personal, death and all.

One could wish for a God. He did wish for one now, as he spat on the earth and scanned the distant light of the stars. But a just God, a God Who would allow no spilling of innocent blood, Who couldn't endure the wailing of suffering children, Who didn't keep

His silence in His heaven in the face of all earthly Injustice, Who wouldn't let the priests condemn the workers who strove for their rights. He wished for a God Who made good for the evil that took place on this dark planet.

A God Who would recompense Gunnar.

Valter cried a little, at last, before he went inside to bed.

It was a few weeks later; Valter was coming home from the peat factory and had barely stepped over the threshold.

"An America-letter has arrived," said his mother.

He looked at the long envelope on the table and wondered who had written this time.

"It's from Gunnar," said his mother. "He's written at last."

Valter was pulling off his jacket, but his arm froze in its motion: Gunnar had written at last; Mother had been waiting for months.

Valter stood with one arm in his jacket, and it remained frozen in its position. On the table lay a long white envelope, addressed to him, and he recognized the handwriting—it was Gunnar's. Gunnar wrote with finished penmanship; even Mother had recognized the elegant turns of the letters.

She said she had picked up the letter in the store when she went shopping.

Valter took a step closer to the table, his hand trembling as he picked up the letter. His brother had written, his brother who knew all. He held the letter in his hand. He closed his eyes for a moment, and when he opened them the letter still rested in his hand.

It was from Gunnar—there was no mistaking that handwriting.

Why was he waiting? Why didn't he open the letter? What was he afraid of? Didn't he want to read a letter from Gunnar? Now that his brother knew all? If there was anything to know?

A piece of paper had been plastered over one end of the envelope:"Opened by censor."The letter had been delayed and had been opened. The slow mail now during the war: perhaps—perhaps that explained it. The thought gave him strength to open the envelope. He pulled out the letter: Duluth, August 7, 1914. There was the simple explanation: it had been written eight days before—

Valter sat down on a chair, his legs wobbly, his mind in a turmoil. What had he expected? There was nothing strange about this letter—it had been written eight days before it had happened.

His mother grew concerned over his silence. "Gunnar is well, isn't he?"

He had forgotten her presence. He began to read the letter to her.

Dear Mother and Brother,

I must write you a few lines to let you know that all is well with me and wishing you the same. I have a good job with the railroad. Everything is fine in this country, you can buy anything if you have money. There are many automobiles here. I read about the war in Europe and hope you escape it. I long to be back in Sweden at times, I enjoyed our fishing on Sundays. As soon as I have earned what I need, I shall come home again. And then I'll buy back our old place. It is depressing to think of how much people at home had to suffer in the old days. How is Mother's health?

I have had the rest of my decayed teeth pulled and have had new ones put in. You wouldn't recognize my mouth now, Valter. You wrote me you had a fine new bicycle. Best wishes to Mother and tell her all is well with me and nothing is wanting. I close these lines with greetings to my dear ones. Write soon.

Your brother Gunnar

Gunnar wrote well and spelled correctly and had not been in America long enough to mix English words into his letters.

Valter had been reading slowly so that his mother could follow. She sat silently on her chair and listened, and lived with the letter long after he had finished; she asked now and again about this and that.

Well, Gunnar was in good health. And he liked his work.

"You think he'll come home next summer?"

"He doesn't write when."

She went on: She hoped the old place was for sale so Gunnar could buy it. How much did Valter think Johannes of Kvarn would ask for it? He had paid eleven hundred crowns, but she guessed he would want a good profit, he was such a miser. They must both see to it that Gunnar didn't pay too much when he came back.

Valter had no reply for this. He walked over to the fireplace corner and began washing the eternal peat from his face.

Mother continued: The old soldier-place was dear to Gunnar, he wanted to live there, so he could fish and hunt. She hoped it was for sale, she hoped he brought enough money; there would be other expenses as well. And he had spent some money already, or didn't he write he had had new teeth put in?

"I wonder how much they cost him," said Soldier-Hulda.

"Yes, I wonder," replied Valter.

He had written eight days before the accident. He had had his old teeth pulled. He wore his new teeth on the evening of August 15. They were completed when he stood in his place between the railroad cars. "You wouldn't recognize my mouth, Valter."

If there could be any meaning to anything.

Gunnar wrote that all was well with him now, nothing was wanting.

"You must answer him soon," said Mother.

"As soon as I get to it."

"It takes so long before he gets the letter. The boats go so slow now during the war."

Valter had left the letter on the table; she picked it up and felt the paper.

"Write that he is welcome home!"

"Yes."

"Why don't you write tonight? After I have gone to bed? Then there's nothing to disturb you."

Yes, Valter agreed. It was much easier to write when no one disturbed him. Sitting alone with his thoughts in the silence of the night, then it would be easier for him to write to Gunnar.

CHAPTER XVII

A strike broke out in the peat factory and lasted almost through the summer. Its end brought humiliation to Valter and his comrades: they must return to their work on the same conditions as before.

But Valter did not return to the peat bog—he took a job as farm-hand with Aldo Samuel. He had *made his decision.* And he saved, pinched pennies, was stingy, and hid his savings. He had already saved some; all winter he had denied himself things that he needed, refusing to spend one unnecessary penny: he was saving money for a ticket on a ship. He had written the agent of the White Star Line to inquire about sailings; he thought that September would be about right.

He was fed up with the factory and the peat, he was tired of tramping the ground of his fatherland. Here in Sweden one was born and grew up. When of age, one emigrated to America.

The good food at Aldo Samuel's made him put on weight; his muscles grew firmer, and he felt stronger than ever before. His worries about his cough—and possible consumption—quickly left him. Perhaps he hadn't taken the loss of Karin so deeply as he had feared. It was said that disillusion in love might cause consumption, but Valter thought that most likely it was caused by poor food, lack of cleanliness, and crowded conditions in the small cottages with their many brats. Drafty floors, un-chinked walls, and poverty in general also brought on this dreaded disease. It was an upper-class lie that consumption was caused by grief. A girl's deceit, however great, would not beget a single consumption germ.

He liked to be around Anny, Aldo's maid, and this, too, he took as a sign of his returning health.

Valter would soon be eighteen, but as yet he had not "possessed" a woman. The novels used the expression "to possess," but there were other words also. "To possess" was not a good expression; as if the woman were a personal knickknack that one put in one's pocket, in the same way one handled a watch or a wallet. And it was only the man who "possessed," never the woman. She only "gave herself," she never possessed anything. Here a word was missing. After reading a few hundred love novels, he realized that a verb was missing from his mother tongue. "Sleep with" was not good either. It said nothing except that one slept in the same bed as the woman, and sleep was hardly the main occupation on such occasions. It mattered little where one slept, as long as one rested well. "Lie with" came a little closer, but was not clear enough. People's common name for the act—constantly used among boys—was too vulgar in some way; it caused offense and could only be used among men. He would have liked to invent a word, a new word for the union of man and woman, a beautiful word, soft, lyrical, and at the same time clearly expressing the act, a word that one could use in conversation with girls without earning the epithet "vulgar."

He had occupied himself greatly with the word, but never with the act.

Aldo Samuel's Anny was a buxom girl with full breasts. She had flaming-red hair and gray-green eyes, listless, lazy eyes. Her complexion was transparently clear, like a ripe apple skin, except for a few freckles on her cheeks; indeed, it was the presence of her freckles which first had made Valter feel friendly toward her—his own many freckles established a bond, as it were. They got along well at their work in the fields. And he had heard so much gossip about Anny that he was curious. One could with Anny. She permitted it if one wanted to.

Sometimes she would bring his meals to him out in the field, and then she usually added some delicacy. But this did not necessarily prove that she was as generous with her body as rumor had it. But she was redheaded and had big breasts, and the heels of her shoes wore on the inside—all signs of a willing and wanton girl. And her languishing eyes caused a vague stimulation, perhaps a promise, or perhaps a disappointment.

He was most anxious to learn if the rumor about her was true; nor was it because of curiosity alone that he wanted to discover it. Anny had such warm hands, warmer than any other girl he had shaken hands with, and it was not the usual warmth. And whenever he touched her body he felt a reaction in his own: of strength, of weakness, of immense strength, of infinite weakness. Such a reaction no girl had ever caused in him before. This quality of Anny's must be what people called wantonness.

One could have a mistress. It needn't be serious. It needn't wreck or diffuse one's work in life.

One balmy evening in July he and Anny walked homeward together after a day of haying. Threatening thunderclouds towered above them. She carried her rake, and she exuded an odor of sweet, flower-spiced hay—cummin, clover, sedge, and sun-bloom. The balmy air, the evening hour created a desire to give in, to stretch out on the ground, to enjoy a wonderful fatigue. They sat down to rest, and he pulled her over onto his knee. He kissed her, and he could kiss with conviction now. She was not unwilling and let him go on, though expressing no great response in her kisses. Even now she showed a strange disinterest that egged him on. He grew bolder and touched her with unquestionable intention.

Without reproach or fluster but with a nonchalant yawning she asked quietly: "What do you want?" He mumbled that she must know.

Of course she understood. She said: "The same as you want with all girls."

He denied this accusation firmly and with clear conscience. He didn't go with girls for that purpose only; he wanted understanding first and foremost; he insisted on harmony between a boy and a girl. But he might have been allowed—sometimes—if he had insisted.

Her lips were hot after his many kisses, and he felt her warm breath; he was communicating something to her, too, and it made him proud.

Like a warm breath of wind, the girl's lips were suddenly at his ear:

"Have you got any of those with you?"

He was not prepared for this question, and he delayed answering for a moment. There was no misunderstanding her question, but for a few seconds perplexity seized him, almost culminating in disinterest. Her question embodied everything, but he was not so satisfied with his success as he should have been. He would get his will, but it came too suddenly, too directly. She ought at least to have indicated that she liked him and got his assurance of his feelings for her. Now he must keep his balance, show her he was experienced and able to meet any situation.

He said that he didn't have any. That he would get some next time. That of course he was responsible for any consequences. That he had always been—it was the man's duty. He, as the man, took all the responsibility.

She said, without reproach: "You must have had many before?"

"A few. Not many."

He refrained from asking her a similar question. He could not believe that she would be willing with anyone, he wanted to feel that the men before him had at least been decent, sober men, at least as good as he.

Now he knew: next time. All he need do was send for a "discreet sample." This was the man's business, if he was conscientious.

A week later the opportunity came. At Anny's suggestion he returned to the farm late, after bedtime, when the household slept. Anny's bed was in the kitchen. He knocked lightly on her window and was let in.

Before anything took place between them, she said:

"Promise me one thing: don't ever tell anyone!"

He felt ashamed. How could she believe that he would tell other people about his experience with her? Did she really think he was that low? Had she known his real self ever so little, she would never have asked for this promise.

Before he had time to assure her fully, she added: "I mean to other boys. They talk so silly about the girls."

He promised, with a feeling that the promise degraded him, and her as well.

Valter lay in Aldo Samuel's kitchen, in a large, old-fashioned, homy farm kitchen, one evening after his day's work, and there he possessed the first woman in his life.

It was a disappointment. He felt a peculiar letdown afterward. Was there nothing else, nothing more? This was hardly a discovery of something mysterious and great. Perhaps it was the fault of the prophylactic; it could never have been meant originally that one must use them. But the suspicion that his own inexperience and clumsiness were to blame humiliated him. Nothing corresponded to his expectations. If this was all, how could men and women make such great sacrifices in order to participate? It was not what his longing and dreams had promised. Therefore, there must be something else, something greater. And the memory of Karin and her passionate kisses returned and tortured him; with her it would have been different.

And his conscience bothered him inexplicably afterward, as if he had done something wrong to the girl at his side and owed her a great debt. He spoke endearing words to Anny which he didn't mean at heart.

But the thought remained with him that it could be different. Another time it must be different; he resolved that it would be.

And the next time he was with her he felt a little more satisfaction, though he felt sure that this was only a foretaste of something entirely different, still far away, something he was unable to reach. He sensed that he was outside the great mystery, denied admittance. He approached it, but was repelled each time. And again this bad conscience, caused by—what? He could not understand what wrong he had done, for he didn't believe in sin. Yet he had a feeling of having sinned against Anny. Their bodies had communicated, but she was more closed and more of a stranger to him than before. Afterward she would lie silent, her eyes closed, with not the least sign of emotion. He alone was excited and disturbed.

But another time it would be different. Next time it must be different—it was a resolution with him. He must—yes, perhaps it was all his own fault.

And he yearned for her heavy, lustful-soft body, more each time.

The following evening he returned to the farm after bedtime, even though he had failed to tell Anny he would be coming. The kitchen lamp was blown out. He knocked cautiously on the window. He heard her turn in her bed. She wasn't expecting him tonight, but there was no reason why he shouldn't come. He whispered, with his mouth close to the pane: "It's only me, no one else. All alone."

He waited. And then he heard whispering in the kitchen. In fact, there were two voices, whispering to each other in the bed, and one was a man's voice.

He stepped back from the window. Then he noticed a bicycle leaning against the corner of the house. He examined it and found that it was a "Nordstjernan," a rare make in this village. He recognized it at once: it belonged to Harry, the good-for-nothing son of the section boss, Harry who had been expelled from the lodge six or seven times for drinking.

Valter walked homeward, whistling to himself as if he were just out walking for the fun of it. It was a nice evening, just right for an evening stroll.

It had not been agreed that he should come. Harry, that spineless fool! She was not very choosy. He had a strong desire to do something; shouldn't he let the air out of Harry's tires? Next moment he felt ashamed of the thought; he was no longer a school-age brat.

It was all over, then. He wouldn't let on that he knew, he wouldn't say a word to her. Twice—that was all. That next time, when he had resolved that it would be different—it wouldn't ever take place. Well, it was over. He was suddenly furious, damn mad, but felt that this, too, would quickly pass. He did not hate Harry—it didn't matter. He had not been in love with redheaded, freckly Anny; if he hadn't known it before, he knew now.

And now he understood why she had asked him to keep quiet—she didn't want all the boys who shared her to discuss her among themselves. She had not deceived him, for they had never agreed

that he should come tonight. She had never promised to be faith-
ful. But what if he had arrived before Harry? Which one of them
would have been permitted to stay? Perhaps it would have been all
the same to her.

His feeling of guilt was gone. He must have liked her, at least a
little, or he wouldn't have wanted her. And perhaps he had wronged
her. But if he had used her as a sex-being only—an expression he
had seen in print and highly applicable—then she, too, had used
him the same way. It wasn't *him* she wanted, it was a man, any man.
This was a vulgar thought, but a true one. Thus, they were even.

He was not proud of what had happened, as it had come to such
a disgraceful end for him. But the sum total was a new discovery:
he had found new qualities in womankind, and he had gained
experience. From now on he must be even more careful. New discoveries were always useful, and his new experience might be useful to him, now that he intended to move to another continent. It
didn't hurt an emigrant to be tested and hardened before he left;
now he need not enter America lacking in manhood experience.

CHAPTER XVIII

There were only three weeks left before his ship would sail. A ticket had been ordered from the White Star Line agent. Valter had not written his brothers or his sister to ask for help; as they hadn't offered, he wouldn't ask. He wanted to show them that he could emigrate with his own money. The America-journey would be entirely his own doing.

To his mother he had said nothing as yet.

There was always the possibility that he would never return. The *Lusitania* had been sunk—who knew what might happen to his ship? Perhaps he would never again tramp the hills round Trângadal. And he began to view things with a perhaps-the-last-time look. The thickets where the birds built their nests, the clear springs under the spruces, the meadows with their ancient oaks, the groves with their ever trembling aspens, the black pools of the moor where he and Gunnar had thrown out their net for pike. Perhaps he would miss all this in the New World.

On Sundays he visited with neighbors in the cottages—some of the old people, intimately connected with his childhood, whom he wished to see once more. He did not tell them that he had come to say good-by; he would not mention his America-plans until the ticket had arrived and he had fetched his papers from the minister.

Carpenter-Elof had been closely associated with his father's death; he it was who had heard Father's last words: "I'm not sad any longer." Ever since that day Valter had held the old man in shy reverence. Now Elof suffered with rheumatism and could not leave his chair by himself. There he sat with the closed-in smell of his poverty-cottage, patient, gentle, sustaining his life on milk and potatoes and a big herring for holidays; he was beyond all desires for more tasty things—all else was worldly. The daughter attending him was nasty, ill-tempered, nagging, but nothing touched him: he did not hear evil words. He had a persistent ache in his back and limbs, but he did not complain: that was all worldly. He could see far beyond the ephemeral, transient life on this earth. In his silent patience he sat there and waited for God to take him to His heaven.

The old man was worthy of respect. He had never hurt a single creature in this world. And perhaps he was right in believing that a Higher Being existed, someone who could be called God as well as by any other name. But Elof was not aware of his own poverty, or of the wretchedness of his neighbor cotters. If all workers were like old Elof, then the poor would always remain poor—forever they would live in poverty and wretchedness. Carpenter-Elof furthered the interests of the clergy and the upper-class: their theme was to dissuade the workers from seeking the good of this world and instead accumulate riches for the world hereafter; the riches of this world they wanted to keep for themselves.

Shoemaker-Janne was still busy at his calling. He stood by his cottage wall and whittled his wooden shoes from alder logs, week days and holidays. Janne had never become entirely insensible to worldly success, and he refused to view his existence only as a preparation for eternity. He loved the snuff in his box, and hated the new wooden shoes from Skåne which had begun to appear in the neighborhood and threatened competition with his own. He spoke degradingly about these "foreign" shoes that caused blisters on the instep and generally ruined people's feet. He wondered if Valter's local could do anything to help him fight the "Skånings." Janne was remarkably healthy, except for a bladder ailment that attacked him in spring and fall when he wore old torn pants that allowed the cold wind free access to his groin.

For fifty years Janne had taken care of the cotters' feet. In his wooden shoes they had tramped at their daily labor, in his shoes they had trudged to and from their heavy work. Many thousands of pairs of wooden shoes, carved by his hands, these people had worn out—on the roads, in the fields, in the forest, on the dunghill, in the barn, and in the byre. They had worn his shoes as long as their feet had been able to move, until they had turned their tired, ache-swollen feet upward for the last time. Janne's wooden shoes had been their inseparable companions as long as they could walk, as long as health permitted them another day's work. His calling was interwoven with the cotters' thralldom.

Janne was famous for his well-made, comfortable shoes. But as far as Valter himself was concerned, these shoes would now come to an end: in the New World a worker did not wear wooden shoes.

He continued his childhood path through the forest. He stopped outside Kalle-Miller's cottage and listened. As a little boy, he had used to stop like that and listen to hear if anyone inside was coughing. Today it was silent, no one in sight. Only two children of Kalle-Miller's large flock had survived consumption.

He came to Balk-Emma, who had been ill in bed this last year. The cracks in her cottage walls were so wide that daylight shone in through them. To protect herself against the draft, she had gathered together all her pieces of clothing and piled them on herself in the bed: old skirts, vests, kerchiefs. Her coffee-brown face had paled since he had last seen her; it was now almost yellow, transparent. She did not keep to her bed for pleasure.

"Is it the soldier's little one?"

The old woman raised herself on her elbow, panting; no, she wasn't mistaken, it was Soldier-Valter who had come to see her. Soldier-Hulda had been mighty sick that time when he came into the world, and she, Emma, had been there to give a hand. It had been so bad that they had talked about sending for the midwife. How he had grown, the soldier's little one! He had been a sizable brat already at birth, and what a yeller! He would yell until he lost his breath and was forced to quit; if he hadn't lost his breath now and again, his mother would never have had any peace. And she, poor woman, she had closed up after his birth, been barren ever since. It looked as if Hulda had overdone herself with him; she had never managed to get thick with child again.

Emma herself had been thick with child thirteen times, and ten of the brats she had borne were still in life.

"Now you must have some coffee, little one!"

"Don't bother, Emma, now that you're sick—"

Balk-Emma tore into her pile of clothing, found her coffeepot among the pillows at her back, still tied up in the gray shawl: she was not so ill as to forget honor and duty. As yet no such disgrace could be credited to her as allowing a guest to leave her house without a treat. Such dishonor would not cling to her while she still could lift her eyelids.

She handed Valter his childhood fear—the cat-owl with its long shawl-ears—and he was forced to accept it. A clean cup he would find on the mantle. He sat down at the table and drank the coffee under Emma's supervision. The coffee was lukewarm, thick, and evil-tasting, but it wouldn't kill him. If he had wanted to, he could have poured the coffee into the fireplace when she turned her back to him for a moment, but he couldn't cheat Balk-Emma on his last visit to her. She had lent a hand in pulling him into the world, she had done him a service. Had she been careless and butterfingered that time, his mother might have lost her life. Or he himself might have receded into the darkness of lifelessness. It might well be that he had her yellow, dried-up old hands to thank for his life.

"You must have a second cup, little one!"

But he declined after one cup and handed the cat-owl back to the bedded woman, who buried it carefully in her stack of circumfused clothing, where it would remain hidden and keep lukewarm until the next guest stepped across her threshold.

But perhaps no other caller came, perhaps Valter was her last visitor. Eight days later Balk-Emma was found dead in her bed. No evil could be said over Emma's dead bones; she was laid in her grave with her hospitality honor intact. The pauper's honor.

Valter had got his new emigration suit and tried it on one Sunday. It fitted well and he was pleased with it, but one thing still worried him: autumn was close, and it might be cold and windy at sea; after paying for his ticket, he would not have enough money left for an overcoat. Gunnar had left without an overcoat, but it had been spring, with summer warmth imminent and balmy days on the Atlantic. How his older brothers had been dressed when leaving he could not remember for sure, but he doubted that either Anton or Fredrik had worn an overcoat. He wondered what percentage of the Swedish emigrants had been without overcoats when they left their homeland and started out for the New World. Probably no inquiry in this matter had been undertaken.

He wouldn't take anything superfluous to America, he wouldn't take along from his poor homeland any more than he absolutely needed. But a few books he must pack; he couldn't leave all of them behind, he now had no less than sixty-five. And plenty of underwear. He had heard that an emigrant must wear warm underwear; probably he had better take an extra pair or two of long underdrawers.

He bought a pair of long underdrawers of the best quality the store offered; they seemed to him excellent emigrant drawers. When he came home with the parcel under his arm, his mother noticed it, and he must open it and show her what he had acquired.

"But you have underdrawers. Why have you bought new ones?"

She had seen him buy a new suit, new shoes, a starched shirt, and she wondered if he now intended to hoard underdrawers. After this, he could no longer hide it from her. And why should he be such a coward? He had been acting as if he were trying to sneak away to America without her noticing.

The journey concerned only one person besides himself, and it was because of this that he had delayed telling her.

"I'm getting ready. I'll leave soon."

Soldier-Hulda stood at the table and felt the underdrawers, pinching the woolen cloth between her fingers. She glanced quickly at her son, but said nothing.

"Yes, I'm leaving. It's my turn at last."

It didn't enter his mind that he had omitted saying where he intended to go, and he would have been surprised had his mother asked him; it could mean only one journey.

The mother looked at the floor, wiped the tip of her nose, slowly, still silent.

The ticket hadn't come yet, he continued, and that was why he hadn't told her before; nor had he been to the minister for his papers.

"Two other boys are leaving; we'll be three to make the voyage."

His mother didn't reply to this either, and her silence began to worry him.

Perhaps he had better tell her what he long had been prepared to say: All his brothers and his sister were there, all his uncles and aunts, all his cousins, many of his school chums. Why should he remain here? He had nothing to thank this country for. He had worked and slaved to earn his living since he was big enough to lift a tool. This was a good country for children with rich parents; it was not a country for cotter children. Here, if he stayed, he would have to tramp the peat bog until he died.

His mother did not gainsay him. But at last she spoke.

"Who is sending your ticket?"

"No one. I've saved for it myself."

And he was proud to add that during the last year he had managed to put aside three hundred crowns, which he thought would cover the cost of the ticket.

She nodded. Something had been cleared up in her mind. He had been very cautious with money this last year, and she had wondered what he did with the part of his earnings he didn't give her.

"Yes, now it's my turn."

"Then you must get yourself ready."

Soldier-Hulda turned her eyes toward the bureau in the farthest corner of the cottage. There stood pictures of all those who had left; some were stuck away in the drawer—there wasn't enough room for all on top of the bureau.

"The other six I helped make ready. This last one must do it for himself."

And Valter looked at the bureau, which had room for no more America-pictures.

His mother's hand brushed her nose's tip again, this time in the opposite direction, and she said a few words so low that he barely could catch them:

"Had hoped one would stay."

Then she felt once more the new underdrawers from the store: "Thick and soft; not bad."

These words she said loudly and clearly, but they passed her son by. He was caught by the others, the ones she had whispered just before. Perhaps she had meant that no one should hear them: "Had hoped one would stay."

Nothing more was said about America that day, nor the following day, nor on the third day. Day after day passed in Trångadal, and about America not a word was said. His mother prepared Valter's food and he ate, she made his bed and he slept. He asked her for no other help, and she offered no other help. He did not ask her advice, and she gave none. She had only implied that the seventh and last of Soldier-Sträng's children must make his own preparations for the New World.

She might have said something more at least, only a few words more. A few words besides the ones he perhaps was not supposed to hear: "Had hoped one would stay." It concerned, after all, a long and important journey.

There is quite a lot to get in order if one intends to move from one continent to another.

He brought home socks he had bought and showed them to his mother. Not bad, she would say. But she didn't offer to knit him any; he remembered she had knitted socks for his brothers when they left, thick, warm socks from the wool she had earned through day labor on the farms.

She had readied six. He was the seventh and last.

His mother had been the only one of her brothers and sisters to remain in Sweden. She had stayed for the sake of her mother, who must have someone. She had told him so herself, many years ago, when he was quite little.

It wasn't that he needed help to get ready, but she might at least have said something. So closed and silent she had never been before.

They sat across from each other at table and he noticed her eyes were red. Perhaps it was the toothache at night that kept her from sleeping. But the ache she had had a long time and he had never before noticed that her eyes were red. Again, red eyes might have many different causes, perhaps quite natural.

It was his bad luck that he was the seventh and last, but he couldn't help that. His brothers and sister, of course, took it for granted that he would stay at home, or why had no one offered him a ticket? But neither had any one of them asked him to stay home. Not even his mother. She had only said to herself: "Had hoped one would stay." And after that she had said nothing more.

Earlier she had sometimes mentioned Gunnar: Why hadn't he written? It was almost a year since they had got his last letter. Well, some wrote at intervals of a year or more, some stopped writing altogether after a few years in America. But she wondered about Gunnar, her favorite son. He must have moved, and she had asked Valter to write one of the others to get his address. Or perhaps he had stopped writing because he intended to come home. It would be like Gunnar to surprise them, to step gently across the threshold one quiet evening, as if returning from some errand to the store.

Her eyes were red; he noticed it particularly in the mornings. He couldn't remember having noticed it before. Perhaps he would find out if he asked her directly. While eating, he said casually:

"Your eyes are red."

"My eyes? No."

"Look in the mirror."

"Well, maybe."

"The whites are red."

"Some dust I must have got—"

But she did not look in the mirror. Perhaps some dust had got into her eyes; that could happen. He had got his reply.

The days rolled by, and soon it would be his turn. But he couldn't help it. He couldn't help it that he was the seventh instead of the first or the second. Why should his conscience bother him for something that wasn't his fault?

There was one place he had not been to say good-by. He had saved this place for the last because it meant the most. But one evening at twilight he walked with thoughtful steps to the old home.

The deserted cottage still stood, badly bruised and mistreated, every pane of glass broken. Against these windows he had pressed his nose during long twilight evenings and searched the road and waited for someone to come. Now he stood outside and looked in: the cottage's poked-in window-eyes stared blackly at him from the depth of desolation and emptiness inside, a few as yet unbroken window frames rising patiently like crosses to further emphasize the gloom of approaching night. The old home lay deserted, decaying in its helplessness. From a distance in the wastelands a lone cowbell rang like a soft Angelus. It was autumn, with the ground yellowing, but in the yard the dark-green grass was turning still darker with the falling dusk.

He sat down on the half-rotten bench under the pear tree; Father had nailed up that board on a Midsummer Eve after having decorated the stoop with fresh birches.

Here a home had stood, a place where children had been born, crawled out into the yard, grown up, and gone. As yet people might say in passing: This was the soldier-cottage. But soon no one would know anything about Father, the last village soldier, and nothing about his seven children who had emigrated to America. Soon one would remember nothing of those who had lived here; one would only observe, perhaps, the stones that once had formed the foundation, kick them a little and gradually dislodge them from their rectangle, while commenting: There must have been a house here once.

A bell-cow, strayed from her byre, wandered this evening through the wastelands, her bell tolling sadly: Nevermore! From all around him came the same echo: Nevermore! From the broken windows, the fallen chimney, from the depth of the well, from the overgrown path, from the very ground that no longer was tramped by feet: Nevermore! All has come to an end here! And perhaps in the not too distant future someone might walk by and touch the stones and say: There must have been a house here. Once.

In early spring cowslips grew on the hill below the cellarhouse, small, delicate flowers. In May, the usual emigration month, the departing one would pick a bunch to take along on the voyage. The simple blooms of the yard gladdened those who picked them for their journey to the other continent. Impoverished emigrants— it was almost as if they had had a root-hold here in the yard, as if they had had a homeland to leave. One could think what one wanted, but it was strange about those slender little cowslips at emigration time—they were never left unpicked.

A near-simpleton of a corporal in Father's company had once written touching verses, rhyming on "the home brink—the tender link." Some people were like that; they became attached to a place. Some place like this one, with its little-yielding ground, the poorest ground, which the villagers set aside for their soldier. People would pick flowers from such a place and act as if it had been their "good homeland."

Here under the pear tree—now withered and wizened—he had sat with Father one evening, a little earlier in the fall than now, before the swallows had left. A few days before the 29th of August.

But the cowbell had rung that evening as tonight, and the grass had felt cool under his bare feet. Then Father had said something that only later he had remembered and thought about: "One of you must stay. She'll need someone."

Father had sat with his back to the tree, exactly as he now sat here himself, and his voice had suddenly vibrated with unusual clearness and strength. Valter could still hear the words of his father: "One of you must stay. She'll need someone."

The swallows had been shooting by in all directions, and just then Mother had called him to help her get the cow home. But he had not gone at once, he hadn't wanted to leave his father in that moment when Father's voice was so strangely clear: "One of you must stay."

It had been a mild evening, like tonight, with a cowbell in the distance, but his father had been alive then, sitting beside him on the bench, leaning his back against the pear tree: "She'll need someone."

Father had been the one to manage and decide while he was still alive and had his eyesight. Mother could work and slave as well as Father, but she couldn't manage so well, as was soon apparent. And she was gullible and easily cheated by the farmers, who paid her too little for her labor. It was the truth, he had thought about it many times, he was thinking of it now—Father had been right that time when he had said: "She'll need someone."

The words had stayed with him, though he had suppressed them in his memory until now.

"One of you, Gunnar or you."

They could mean no one but him, now.

"Had hoped one would stay." Those had been Mother's words when he told her he was emigrating. Since then she had said nothing. Otherwise, she was the same. Only, she had got something in her eyes. In both of them. Dust perhaps. Some specks of dirt might have lodged under the eyelids, and when she rubbed them her eyes got red. Red eyes one could get from many causes. That one could.

Had hoped one of you would stay—well—

Now she would have to go to outsiders to get her letters read or written. And perhaps she wouldn't wish to tell how things were with her when outsiders wrote for her. It might well happen that no letter would be written when most needed. It might happen that he one day would receive a letter from the minister or the Alderman, notifying him that an auction had been held at Trångadal after the recent demise of Soldier-Sträng's widow—whose relatives all lived in North America. That could happen. Then one might feel that perhaps—well, yes, if only one had—

One can make a decision, but a decision can be changed. Plans can be altered, delayed. Sometimes one sees things from another angle, from a new angle, or from an old. As one saw them before. One might remember a word, an old word, uttered as long ago as 1909, for example, and one might remember it as clearly as if it were spoken this very moment. The past can return and speak in one's ears and give advice for the future.

"She'll need someone, one of you two." Hearing these words now, as he sat on the old bench alone, he knew that they could mean no one except him.

He had come here to have a last look at his old home. It happened to be evening, with a tinkling cowbell in the yellowing fields. It was a good-by evening.

And it had been a good-by evening when he had sat here with Father shortly before the 29th of August, with the swallows still remaining, ever crisscrossing the sky. Mother had been calling that he must help her.

Yes, the years would be long and lonely for her in the cottage. Cottage! It was only a shack that soon would fall in a heap if not looked after. And as the years gathered, old age would be upon her, and then it might happen—well, who could tell what might happen? But she might need someone.

Decisions could be changed if new thoughts, old thoughts, interfered, thoughts six years old. It wasn't impossible, and perhaps it was right to follow an old thought, long forgotten.

Only to a few intimates had he mentioned his emigration, but he hadn't said anything so definite that it mattered. He wasn't one to spread news about events still unsure; he knew how one might have to eat one's words. Everything was changeable. He could return the ticket, he hadn't paid for it yet; that was a small matter. And his two companions-to-be could travel without him; they would understand if he changed his mind.

What would Father have thought and said, had he been sitting here this moment?

One of you two—one of you should stay—

He knew. He felt his father's meaning. What Father had wished, he had known ever since that evening under the pear tree when Father's voice grew so clear and strong. It was then that the words had been spoken, those words that came back so potently tonight, those old words that could mean no one except him—Soldier-Valter.

Evening fell over the forest, over the deserted cottage, over the dark grass in the yard, over the yellowing fields, over the wizened old pear tree, and over the hill behind the cellarhouse where the cowslips would shoot up in spring—during the emigration season.

He would remain.